RAISING DAWN

RAISING DAWN

Diana Richmond

RAISING DAWN

iUniverse books may be ordered through booksellers or by contacting:

iUniverse
1663 Liberty Drive
Bloomington, IN 47403
www.iuniverse.com
1-800-Authors (1-800-288-4677)

ISBN: 978-1-5320-2502-0 (sc)
ISBN: 978-1-5320-2321-7 (e)

Library of Congress Control Number: 2017910345

Print information available on the last page.

iUniverse rev. date: 07/13/2017

under the arm, sky-blue eyes, and flaming red hair. This donor (number Y6478) is six-foot-three, weighs 187 pounds, with blue eyes and Welsh ancestry (like many of the early miners in Nevada City), Protestant, 42 years old (I like that he is one year older than I), a history professor who plays flute and reads poetry as his avocations.

That's as much as I ever learned about Dawn's father. I'm starting to think I know even less about Patty, or myself for that matter.

Patty had it all put together, I thought, a husband who loves her and two healthy children. Though I could never lead her conventional life, I admire her practicality. She'd been practical about getting a husband, and I never was, never would be. My time with Abe, my last boyfriend, is the perfect example.

Abe and I met when he came to a little book party that Harmony Books gave for me when I published *Cleo and the Leopard*. Parents had brought their children, and the back part of the store had more little people's chairs than ones for adults. It was a dank February evening, with mist sulking low over the roads, and the children's jackets smelled like wet puppies. He hadn't known there was a book party until he got there; he was just in town to stock up on some new reading. He stood in line where I was signing books, fingering his full brown beard, as curly as a spaniel's ear. It softened his narrow face. When I asked to whom I should sign it, he just asked me to sign my name, and add my phone number at the bottom. I glanced up at him, but his dark eyes just looked thoughtful, not flirtatious, and I assumed he wanted the phone number in case he wanted to buy more books. I did notice he had no children with him.

He called me the next day and asked if he could cook me a good dinner, at his house. He did mention he lived in Washington, one of many old gold mining towns in this part of the Sierra foothills. It lay at the bottom of a deep gorge, next to the South Fork of the Yuba River. To get there, I'd have to drive six miles down a steep, winding road that terrified me in any wet weather and I refused to drive at all in the winter except on a dry warm day. If you slipped on ice on that road, your car would probably take off in a spectacular arc like a dying firework and drop right to the bottom of that cold canyon. Even to get to the turnoff to his town, I had to drive half an hour on a woodsy, winding road that sometimes closed in the winter before the snowplows could get in. On a perfect day, it took forty-five minutes to drive those twenty miles.

I told him I'd meet him for dinner somewhere in Nevada City. After grumbling a little bit about how you can't get a good meal in Nevada City (which isn't true), he agreed to meet me for dinner at the Corner House Café. It was my first clue as to how little he liked leaving the canyon. People should pay more attention to the first issue they have to negotiate with another person; it could save a lot of time and trouble.

In the beginning I was sort of enchanted by where he lived. The town itself had most of its original buildings, all six of them – a hotel with a false front and saloon at the bottom, a general store, a stone jail with metal doors, the remains of a lumber mill, and two clapboard houses. No school. Abe lived in a trailer outside the town, just enough above the river that his home wouldn't flood in the spring. The Yuba never froze; its burbling in late summer changed to a surging roar in a wet winter. He had built a detached screen porch, where we slept on hot summer nights, and sometimes we saw deer or coyotes just outside. Sex with Abe was untamed, ragged and surprising. After the baby arguments began, it went extinct, or nearly so. And then we began to argue about whether he'd drive to my house or I to his.

His trailer sat among fifteen or twenty others and a few shambling houses, set far enough apart from each other to give almost total privacy. Some of the trailer owners – Abe was one of them – had active mining claims on the river, though I never saw anyone actually working his mine.

In the summer, we followed winding trails from where he lived to the most secluded, idyllic swimming holes on the river. We took camp chairs and books and perched on huge boulders overlooking the river, where we'd read for hours. Sometimes he fished, and we grilled trout on an open fire. He was an incredibly good cook, even with the tiny amenities of his trailer kitchen. He grew most of his own vegetables and stir-fried them in a huge wok.

Summers were easier than winters. After it started to rain in November and the days went dank and cold, I wanted us to stay in my little house in Nevada City, where we could light a fire in the fireplace and I, at least, would not have to drive down that winding road. We argued many times about where we'd meet. In the winter, I won most of the arguments, and between late April and October, he did. We never actually spent more than two or three nights a week together.

It wasn't until the third year we were together that we started to argue about having a child. He told me a hundred times it wasn't practical, and of course he had the better side of that argument, but practicality was the least of my concerns. Our relationship wasn't the least bit practical. That he didn't want to become a parent at all was a larger issue. He'd hinted at his own parents being neglectful and derisive. One of them - I can't remember now which one – was a drinker. Abe learned to grow up on his own and he liked living alone. He didn't drink at all, not even a beer, which made him something of a social outcast in his town, but I liked that about him.

Toward the end, I practically begged him just to let me have a child with him. He would have no responsibility, I promised.

"I couldn't have a child that way," he told me.

I thought I was making the same deal with Patty, that she'd have no responsibility for my child.

The night with the popcorn was six years ago. Patty agreed to drive down to Berkeley with me for whatever number of inseminations required. I told her I could drive perfectly well myself, but she insisted.

"You might need to lie down afterward."

"Huh?"

"And the stress might distract you from driving safely."

I thought of asking her whether she thought it necessary to lie down and refrain from driving after she had sex, but I appreciated her generosity and didn't say anything. Usually she had to bring her kids along, which I loved and they didn't seem to mind. Sandra was four then and had just started preschool in the mornings. Ian was just over a year when we began these journeys. I'd read them books like *The Runaway Bunny* or *Where the Wild Things Are* or sometimes a book I was writing. Illustrations came later in the process, and it was difficult to hook them on the text alone.

Sandra was unnaturally serious, like her namesake Sandra Day O'Connor, one of Patty's heroes when she was in law school. That's where she met Doug, who joined an insurance defense firm after graduation.

That Patty chose to become an attorney is a curious story all its own. In the summer when she was fifteen and I was about to start my senior year in high school, she went off to a cheerleading camp in Sacramento for a month. Our parents must have worried that I would miss her or be jealous of her becoming a cheerleader – or both. She, the pert, limber one with the bright smile, cast a light in any group. I, though slim, receded into any available background. Patty was athletic; I couldn't do a split without injuring myself. However jealous I might have been, cheerleading was out of the question for me. At dinner one evening before Patty left for camp, our dad suggested, a bit too casually, that I should get a job that summer and that he could use me in his law office. I wasn't angling to become a lawyer, then or now, but the idea of working with Dad beat out all other likely summer jobs. I glanced over at Patty, who had stopped chewing, and, fork in hand, gave me a look that wanted me dead, and a really quick glance at Dad that was naked with its longing. Both her looks vanished in a second, and I don't think either of our parents noticed them. In the next moment, before I could say anything, Patty smiled her cheerleader smile and announced what a good job that would be.

Although I told Dad I would really like to work for him, I wondered whether there would be anything useful for me to do. He started me filing papers, showing me himself what papers belonged where in a client file, how to keep the pleadings separate and how to label them. That's where I learned to read legal documents. When his secretary went on vacation, I answered the phone for two weeks. I liked the work, and I loved being close to Dad, who was spare with his criticism and generous with his time, but there was never any question that the law held no interest for me. It was too negative. He worked every day with people arguing with each other. And the rules: every step he took was bounded by some code section or local rule. I couldn't be that bounded.

Later, when Patty announced she wanted to go to law school, I wasn't entirely surprised. I didn't think she'd like it, but that was beside the point. The next two summers, before her senior year and before she went off to college, Patty worked in Dad's office. She'd spend an hour pouffing her hair and putting on makeup before joining him at the office, strutting out the door as if she ruled the world.

By the time Patty started law school, Dad had left Mom, telling us almost nothing about why. 'We had irreconcilable differences,' was all he told us. Which I knew from my summer with him was the legal ground for divorce in California.

By the time Patty finished law school three years later, Dad's practice was already in shambles. But by then, Patty had found Doug, a fellow law student at Davis. They married the summer after their graduation. Patty became pregnant right away, giving her the perfect excuse for not having to practice law.

My niece Sandra (Patty doesn't use any diminutives for children's names) listened very intently to *The Runaway Bunny*, then told me, very seriously, "I don't think the little bunny really wanted to run away." Ian was easier: he had a ready sense of humor and I could make him laugh just by rhyming his name. Ian be-an, string be-an;

Ian amphibi-an, a painted turtle; Ian crayon, an orange crayon. "Crayon doesn't rhyme with Ian," Sandra corrected me.

By the time I gave up on my being inseminated, Patty and I had driven to Berkeley nine times, and Ian had celebrated his second birthday. My Nevada City gynecologist wondered whether I had any viable eggs left, but I didn't believe her until I saw a gynecologist at the fertility center at UCSF. I learned from her that each month at menstruation a woman loses one of the eggs she was born with, and over time the quality of those eggs diminishes. Mine were worthless. She suggested I consider an ovum donor. I could pick an anonymous donor, or — as she recommended — I could ask a friend or relative to donate her eggs. Of course I thought of Patty.

When I told Patty my news — I had made this trip myself and driven home in blinding rain, sobbing much of the way, wishing I'd had windshield wipers for my eyes, stopping at her house on the way home — she immediately offered to donate her eggs. After all, she said, pointing at Sandra and Ian, "you know I have good eggs." "You're a good egg yourself," I told her, managing a half-laugh in my misery. She'd said it spontaneously; it struck me as incredibly generous. Even more so when we learned what she would have to do in order to donate her eggs: take hormones to synchronize her periods with mine and then undergo mini-surgery to 'harvest' her eggs. It was no small feat. Doug, to his credit, tried to talk her out of it. He didn't know why, he said, but it seemed like a dicey thing to do.

Patty really did have good eggs. She went through the whole process of injecting herself with hormones and having her eggs surgically extracted, without any help from me. I conceived on the first try. I remember whooping on the phone to her as soon as I tested positive: "It worked! It worked!" She told me to come right over, and I sailed down the hill to her home. She cooked me what was then my favorite dinner — curried shrimp — and announced to Sandra and Ian that they were going to have a cousin. After seeing their blank looks – they didn't know what a cousin was – she explained that I was going to have a baby.

"Where is it?" Sandra looked skeptical. "Your belly looks too tiny." How could a child of five be so dour?

"It takes a while. Just watch," I told her proudly.

I must have had the world's easiest pregnancy. I wasn't nauseated once – unlike Patty, who used to constantly nibble furtively on crackers tucked into her handbag and then disappear into the nearest bathroom to barf. As I rounded out (for the first time in my life, I actually had round cheeks on my face and butt and spare flesh on my frame), I began to feel infused with some magical hormone that made me feel in harmony with the universe and constantly optimistic. I wrote a new children's book, about a joey, a young kangaroo that loved to go places in his mom's pouch, and I finished some of the illustrations.

"You're way too bouncy," my friends Megan and Jenny told me.

My energy started to flag in the eighth month. Carrying what seemed like a boulder between my thin hips sapped much of my drive. I'd spend what seemed like most of a morning setting up my easel and readjusting my frame into a chair, painting very little and tossing out most of what I managed to put on paper. My work was uninspired. I was too ungainly to hike to the river, since I could no longer trust my balance and the paths were too steep for me to take any risks. When I slept at all, which only happened after what seemed like hours of shifting and re-adjusting the pillows I massed around me so that some part of me wouldn't ache, I dreamed of being thin again, of climbing a tree like an agile ten-year old, of playing dodge-ball, or swinging on a rope swing one of my parents' friends had installed on a huge limb on the bank of the Yuba.

My friend Jenny rescued me from this despondency two days after I was due. I was so weary of carrying the extra weight, its own premonition of aging in my low back. Jenny took me to a swimming hole we didn't have to hike to. I eased myself into the river at a tiny sand bar and discovered to my huge relief that in the water I could take the burden off my back, floating on my stomach in the slack current, kicking every few minutes to keep myself in place, and laughing when I tried to float on my back and the sheer gravity of my belly rolled me over each time. I was so happy that day, tired and happy and eager for the profound change coming.

I remember resting against a huge, smooth boulder, warmed by the sun, and closing my eyes. On the bank a small bird called, a single prolonged, descending note. The stream burbled around me. I opened my eyes. Not two feet from me, a single thistle whorl rolled across the surface of the water like a beach ball on sand, propelled by nothing more than its own lightness on an intangible breeze. The hairs radiating from its seed barely touched the water's surface, each one grazing the surface only long enough to allow the next its turn. As if traveling with a goal, not once submerging into the river, it rolled across my line of vision. I blew a puff of air at it, and it accelerated, bound for the earth on the far side. I watched as it neared the faster stream, waiting for it to be caught and drowned. Instead, as if tripping, it lofted itself and floated away.

Dawn. That's what I named her on the morning of her birth. Dawn was on my list of names, along with Ondine and Zoe and Iris, which I had obsessed over for months without being able to decide. I had a list of boy's names too, since I had refused to be told what sex child I would have. "Surprise me," I'd told the amnio staff, when they told me the fetus was healthy and asked if I wanted to know its sex.

Dawn. This is all about her, after all, not me or Abe or Patty. She has curly hair the color of persimmons. Most people would say carrots, but if you walk down a country lane in late fall, when the trees are barren and their leaves rustle underfoot, the air is gray and frosty, and all color is drained from most growing things - if you come upon a persimmon tree, you will know what I mean. On those dark brown limbs, against a gray horizon, hang the brightest balls of orange you can imagine. That's what it's like to come upon

Dawn. She's a bob of curly hair encircling a cheerful face on the worst of days, and she's always in motion, the most curious child I've ever met.

I spent months of her first year just watching her discover herself, finding her fingers and her toes, tasting them, finding ways to make her fingers work to pick up cheerios and toys and pull my ears. It was like watching evolution in fast motion. While she napped, I sketched and painted. I quickly completed the illustrations for my kangaroo book, and my editor got me a publishing contract. I had an idea of writing a new children's book about hands, and I compiled maybe forty different sketches of her baby hands, though I still haven't been able to put it together.

I've always liked being around children. When I sit in a group of children reading to them, I watch for their reactions. I love the ones who interrupt to ask why the caterpillar has so many hairs or what baboon poop looks like. I worry about the ones who just sit there with no expression whatever. Dawn is full of questions. Like what made me so sad that she had to go live with Aunt Patty, and when could she come back home.

2

A few weeks after Dawn was born, I took her to see my mother. Patty offered to come with me, knowing this would somehow be fraught, and Doug stayed home with Sandra and Ian. Each time I walked up the path to Greenwood, a Memory Care Facility, while making some cruel play on the words of its title, I reminded myself not to expect too much ("Myrtle no longer remembers you are her daughter"), but each time was so variable, so treacherous, that I almost always began by draping my invisible gauze of hope around her head and shoulders, tucking in wisps of her fine hairs, searching for my mother in the recesses of her eyes (as always, the color of early morning), and that lovely gauze was almost always shredded, unraveled, tattered, or burnt to an ashy crisp by the end of the visit.

As each of us bent to kiss her (she still, somehow, smelled of lavender), she remembered us, by name. "Karen," she said, with no question mark in her tone. She reached out for the baby with confident hands. I placed Dawn in the cradle of her elbow. I could see Dawn relax into the security of that nest and close her eyes. Mother stroked the tiny red curls that already marked her as different from the rest of us. She hummed a little, unrecognizably, and I heard Patty filling in behind me the lullaby Mother used to sing to us when we were little. Dawn lay contentedly sleeping in Mother's arms for the remainder of our visit, while I told her about my labor starting as soon as I'd come home from a swim, how I thought it would never end, how grateful I was to sit in a hot bath for part of it. "Her name is Dawn, Mother. Can you say her name?" And she did; I could tell she was proud of herself as she said it. Patty told her how excited Sandra and Ian were with their new cousin. I didn't correct her, but Ian had literally jumped with excitement when I brought Dawn to their home, while Sandra hung back frowning.

Patty stood up, as a signal that we should go. It had been such a perfect visit; I was reluctant to break the spell. I too got up and reached over to take Dawn from her arms, but Mother looked at me with a frown and, urgency overcoming the difficulty of speech, said "No." I recoiled, then tried to regroup and explain that it was time for me to take Dawn back home -- soon she would be hungry -- whatever excuse I could muster. Mother turned to Patty and handed Dawn to her.

Patty's eyes sought mine, seeking permission and apology, but I couldn't even look at her. I slumped back into my chair and closed my eyes. I wanted to strangle Mother with that gauze mantle. She had always preferred Patty, didn't know what to make of me. By the time I could get up again, Patty was outside with Dawn. She handed her back as soon as I closed the door.

"She has Alzheimer's," she began. I shot her a look.

"Don't even try. Don't go there. Don't make any excuses for her. Even before Alzheimer's, she could never imagine me as a mother." I sat in the back next to Dawn in her car seat on the way home, my hand never letting go of hers. I said nothing. I couldn't even cry. Patty didn't know what to say to me. She knew the enormity of the sting; she knew what I said was true; she knew there were no words to comfort me.

I had managed to forget this whole episode, a temporary grace, until it flooded back at my deposition five years later.

"Cultivate being self-reliant," Dad blurted. "You have what it takes." It was the summer in high school that I worked in his office. We had just eaten a simple lunch on Broad Street and he had taken a different direction as we walked back to the office. I don't remember saying anything at the time. His advice came with no preface and no context. I wondered then why he had said it, but he never explained. We were walking uphill, huffing slightly from the pace he maintained, and I can see now the fronds of the willow tree that I had to sweep out of my way as we passed underneath. The scene, complete with the sound of his penetrating voice, is like a video clip that keeps interjecting itself into the scene of my life, at unpredictable times.

I took his advice to heart, quite literally and proudly, until I became a mother. I had interpreted self-reliance as taking care of myself exclusively. The territory of being solely responsible for another -- tiny and completely dependent -- human almost undid me. Almost from the start, at unpredictable intervals, I felt overwhelmed. I'd wake up with fear in my gut, a steady clenching in the part of my body that had so recently been hard and swollen with its enclosed new life. Now she was outside and frail. The only predictable relief was when she was nursing. I could feel my milk respond to her suckling, its flow a miracle of nature, and her tiny hand would open and clasp the soft flesh around her busy mouth. My own contentment matched hers, and often we both dozed afterward.

But when she cried and I could find no way to soothe her, often in the early evening, I felt ignorant and sad and inept. I was an unnatural creature, lacking in the instinct of care. This doubt expanded within me like a cancer, and as she began to eat solid food, she nursed less and my source of comfort abated. When I visited with Patty, I asked her if she'd felt this way. She told me that Sandra had refused to nurse and had been cranky in her first six months, but that her doctor had told her some babies could not easily be comforted. She had 'just got through it' somehow. I asked her how long it had lasted but she couldn't remember. 'A few months,' was all she said, and I was then in my eighth or ninth month of this dark cavern of self-doubt. It didn't help that when she picked up

Dawn to comfort her, Dawn would quiet almost instantly. It was my inadequacy after all.

I admit I was not a naturally gifted mother, but who is? During the first few months I was full of energy and resolve. I'd wake at dawn with the roosters (some neighbor raised chickens) and glance over at my sleeping daughter. I'd shoved my queen bed into the corner and let her sleep on the inside, with me on the outside. It gave us both plenty of room and allowed me to just turn over to nurse her at night, without having to get up. I was careful, of course, to put her back far to the inside, so that I could not roll over onto her.

Someone had given me a big, soft sling to carry her, and I took walks with her every day. Having her snuggled up to me was delicious, but by the time she was six months old, she became too heavy, so I reverted to the stroller Jenny had passed down to me.

I'd managed to complete the illustrations for the kangaroo book, all eighteen watercolors, by painting while Dawn napped in the afternoon. But soon I needed naps too, and the afternoon painting lapsed. I became dull-headed, and my book ideas about baby's hands became too ambitious even to begin.

Megan and Jenny offered to stay with her, so that I could go to the gym or hike to the river, but I always said no. I wanted to be with Dawn all the time, didn't want to have to pump milk and save it for her, didn't even want to be out of sight of her.

Once when Patty came over and drove us down to Roseville to have dinner with her and Doug and their children, I fell asleep in the car on the ride down, and then again at dinner. I must have just dozed off in my seat. I didn't drop my food or anything obviously embarrassing, but when I looked up, they were all staring at me. I apologized several times but Patty insisted that I spend the night. Since she had driven me down, I couldn't refuse. She put me into the guest room, and Dawn into Ian's old crib in his room. That was the first night we slept apart. I slept nine uninterrupted hours. When Patty woke me, she held a squirming Dawn in her arms and just handed her to me to nurse.

"It's time to start weaning her," she told me at breakfast. "You need the rest, and she will sleep through the night better." Dawn was ten months old then. I nodded to Patty but didn't take her advice. I was in the hospital when Dawn was finally weaned, at twenty months.

I think that night at Patty's marked my recognition of how tired I was getting, how dull-headed my days were becoming. Being tired became being sad also. I mourned what I could no longer do: paint, hike, read, visit with friends.... I changed diapers, fed and dressed Dawn, shopped for groceries and made us simple meals, read to Dawn and played with her, following her around as she crawled and tried to pull open drawers and cabinet doors.

Megan and Jenny offered to take me out to dinner for my birthday in May, offering a babysitter, but I wouldn't even consider it. I would have no babysitter, not even Megan's daughter Sam, who had known Dawn since birth and liked being with her.

I didn't know I was steadily sinking into the very dark hole that caused my hospitalization, but I remember that last, pivotal day.

collecting snacks, books, diapers and a jacket for Dawn, as well as one for me. We all piled into Patty's car, already outfitted with an extra kid-seat for Dawn and headed to the Grass Valley Memorial Hospital.

"You rest here," Patty told me in the waiting room, while she took Dawn in to be examined and x-rayed. Sandra followed them into the room rather than be stranded with me.

I have no concept of how long they were in there, and I must have closed my eyes, but the next thing I remember was a doctor sitting down next to me. Owlish eyes behind round glasses, and unruly eyebrows, a face in ordinary life I would love to have sketched. He looked at me kindly for a few seconds, then held out his arm to help me up.

"Follow me," he said in a soft voice. I would have willingly followed him anywhere.

I found myself in an examining room, where he identified himself as Dr. Reuther. He asked if he could ask me some questions and of course I said yes. What surprised me initially was that all of the questions were about me, not Dawn. At first it seemed plausible, a family history, and that seemed relevant enough, but when he began to ask what medications I took, whether I used drugs, whether I had any history of depression, I became suspicious. When I asked why, he told me Patty had told him I'd been extremely tired and down lately, which was true enough, and I let him continue. He ultimately examined me physically, probing my throat and neck, taking my blood pressure, and ordering an EKG. Someone came in to draw blood. When he left the room, he told me to rest, that it would be a little while before he came back. I felt an odd sense of relief.

By late afternoon, I'd been checked into the psychiatric ward. My admission records, which I have since read, reflect that I asked for the daffodils. I stopped talking altogether for the first few days, when I realized I'd been deposited someplace from which I could neither escape nor be with Dawn. For the first week or so, whether the product of drugs they gave me or the state in which they'd admitted me, I was like a bear in hibernation. Un-bearlike, I was wakened to eat, but I had no appetite. Trays were brought to my room but removed after being almost untouched for hours.

I dreamt. I don't know if bears dream during the winter, but I dreamt of Dawn, always that I was losing her to some peril. She stood on a boulder overhanging the river and lost her balance and I couldn't get to her in time. The walls of our little house started to crumble in an earthquake, and I couldn't reach her on her bed. I must have cried out during one of these dreams because I have a vague memory of a nurse bringing me up to a sitting position, stroking my hand, her other arm around my shoulder, telling me in soothing tones that it was only a dream. I remember the physical comfort of easing into her arm, as if I were small again and she were my mother. But the next day, I could not even tell which nurse had rescued me.

After a time they induced me to get up for meals and join the other inmates in the cafeteria. A custodian held my elbow as I shuffled into the dining area. I could feel in the muscles of his arm and in the cadence of his steps that he was impatient with me, but I didn't care. From all my time asleep, I felt dizzy when I first got up, and my own muscles must have atrophied. The cafeteria was a not unpleasant yellow hue, I remember that, and I was not the only slow one. There were many shufflers among us, and the food line moved at a torpid pace. It didn't matter; I wasn't impatient. I was the farthest thing from impatient. I noticed that there were other inmates, but I couldn't describe even one of them. We didn't look at one another's faces, and we didn't talk. Each of us served his or her own sentence.

At some point I became aware of the pill bearers, a retinue of ever-changing attendants who brought me some medication, one or more pills of varying colors and shapes in a tiny paper cup. With one hand the pill bearer handed me the paper cup and then the water cup from the other hand once I took the pills. I made the acquaintance of only one of them, a black woman with the lilting accent of Jamaica who, after giving me my pills, exclaimed that it had been over a week with no shower. She promised to return and give me one. To get clean, I needed to leave my room and go next door, where there was a shared shower, always locked. This remarkable woman – Radiance was her name – returned with a large towel. Supporting me by holding me under both shoulders, since my leg muscles had become useless in my prolonged idleness, she walked me to the shower room, unlocked it, and explained to me that a shower might help me to feel better (her common sense itself refreshing). She seated me on a bench while she turned on the shower and waited for it to reach a good temperature. Then she seated me on a plastic stool inside the shower stall after unstringing my hospital gown. She even asked if I'd like her to wash my hair, and as she massaged my itchy scalp I felt more human than I had since my arrival. Her touch was at the same time vigorous and gentle, and my nakedness meant nothing to her, or so it seemed, because I was indifferent to it. She came back often after that, taking me to the shower and telling me about her own children as she walked, washed and dried me. She is the only attendant I remember with any clarity.

Radiance embodied her name -- she had a broad, dark face with a huge smile of extraordinarily white teeth, and bulging eyes that emanated humanity. She was the only pill bearer who told me what she was giving me. I vaguely knew at the time that they tried me on different medications. Some made me sleepier; others made me nauseous. One day the color or shape of the pill would change, but no one except Radiance told me what she or he was giving me. Here's your Abilify, she said.

"Abilify?" I asked. Even in my debilitated condition, I thought 'Abilify' signaled improvement. I wanted to be abilified. It made me expect instant improvement on swallowing it. Radiance must have discerned that, for my review of my records reveals that they tried Abilify only in the beginning, and that afterward I received Paxil. So she must have intentionally given me the wrong information, just to encourage me. I hope her supervisor never finds out.

23

I know now that it was some weeks before they even noticed that I had a severely hypothyroid condition; had they picked this up in the initial blood tests, I might have been spared the menu of heavy antidepressants they imposed on me.

Once I began a course of thyroid medication, each new day brought some tiny measure of improvement. I became an expert on reading these small signs. I could appreciate the leafing out of the maple trees outside my room, from buds to furls of tiny leaves, to full, new-green leaves. I developed the energy to dress myself rather than survive each day in the tie-on hospital gowns. I began to want to walk, to venture outside, even though this required advance arrangement for an attendant to accompany me. At first, I was surprisingly weak and didn't mind the attendant's hand on the back waistband of my jeans. Best of all, I developed an appetite. Meals created a pleasant rhythm to my day and sufficient diversion. I was in the fourth week before I'd recovered energy to feel the need for more activity. An attendant would take me to morning and afternoon crafts classes, where we cut and pasted illustrations from magazines onto cardboard and wove colored yarn and popsicle sticks into star-shaped ornaments for room decorations.

I was well into the second week before Patty and Doug brought Dawn to see me. Then the pattern of my days wove around Wednesdays at two and Sundays at one, when Dawn came to spend an hour with me. I would count the days until the next visit; I would wash my hair in the morning of a visit, create a drawing for her and center my day around her as my highlight. It was almost enough to know that the pattern would repeat. Mondays were tolerable knowing that Wednesday ensued. On the days I did not see her, I needed some variation on the slow pattern of the place; even the hour with the psychiatrist on alternate days created some structure to relieve the tedium. Patty brought me two books: *The Power of Positive Thinking* (which I managed to misplace within hours since it epitomized Patty's admonitory nature) and *The Color Purple* (which – she said this herself – she bought because she knew purple was my favorite color). I consumed it in a day and a half, as if I had never read it before. In the library I found a Scrabble game and began to play both sides of it, trading seats with each move. I tried to train myself to remember the 'other' player's tray of letters, but that required more memory than I possessed. The games tended to be low-scoring on both sides, a product of my drugged and underused mind.

In that rehab center I developed a passivity I didn't recognize before as part of me, as well as a habit of silence, speaking only when it was necessary, in my psychiatric sessions. My speech became slower too, and after I returned to normal life, it remained slower than it had been before – so slow that I perceived some people regarded me as subnormal.

It's no wonder that even today it is difficult for me to imagine myself as an authority on anything, however trivial or commonplace. Patty only intensified my doubts.

4

I used to be grateful to Patty every single day. When Dawn was first born, I lay in the hospital terrified that I wouldn't even know how to hold or feed her. Dr. Lockhart came in and showed me how to swathe her, to wrap her so tightly that she looked like a little mummy. It made a newborn feel secure, he told me. When I did it, the blanket unwound in a minute. Patty told me it didn't matter. All that mattered was to keep her close. Which is what I wanted most of all. Dawn lay next to me every single night that first year.

Patty and Doug took good care of her while I was in the hospital and then the rehab center. But when I wanted to take Dawn back home with me, the trouble began.

"When you're ready, she'll come back home to you," Patty reassured me, when I signed the papers giving her what I thought was temporary legal guardianship, while I was hospitalized.

I don't know how many times she told me that since then. For the first year after I'd been out, I think I heard it almost every week. Patty allowed me to visit her home whenever I wanted, and to pick up Dawn every Friday for the weekend, returning her on Sunday after an early supper.

Four months into that routine, when I brought Dawn back to her home after my weekend with her, Dawn clung to my leg as I was about to walk out the door. "No," she whined. I caught the wince on

Patty's face just before I knelt down to reassure Dawn that I would be back soon.

It was that small clutch on my leg that gave me my first ounce of courage.

"Patty, I think it's time." I looked up at her while I knelt in front of Dawn, caressing her back and running my fingers through her curls.

Patty's face had NO all over it. "We'll talk during the week."

I stood up. I'm taller than Patty by almost two inches, and this time it felt good. But I didn't want to have this conversation in front of Dawn. "Let me put her to bed." I carried Dawn down the hall to the bedroom she shared with Ian and turned on the light. Patty followed.

"Where are your PJs, honey?" Dawn pointed to the dresser behind me. Patty opened the drawer and flung them onto the bed before withdrawing to the doorway, where she took up a stance with her arms crossed in front of her.

As I undressed my girl, she rested her head on my shoulder. "Toes," she insisted when I pulled off her socks. I lifted her onto the bed and nibbled her big toes, while she giggled, and then I tucked them under the cover. "Bridge book," she wheedled as she nestled onto her side, facing me.

"Do you have…?" I started to ask Patty, but she was already moving to get my book.

Patty handed it to me abruptly and left the room. "I am a bridge," I began. "Every day I feel lots of little feet on my back, like a massage. I help the children walk to school in the morning and back home in the afternoon." Dawn fell asleep before I had finished the story, but I kept reading until the end. I sat there for a while afterward, wondering if Dawn had created this little performance. She isn't usually easy to put to bed, or quick to fall asleep.

I found Patty in the kitchen, taking dinner dishes out of the dishwasher and putting them away.

"I think it's time for her to come back," I said as gently as I could. "You've been so generous...."

"Karen, I did what needed to be done. You don't have to butter me up. But are you sure you're ready for taking this on full-time? I don't want to have to do this all over again if ..."

"It won't happen again." She threw me a skeptical look. "I'm stronger and healthy and I know what mothering takes now. I didn't before."

"It was more than that."

"You want a letter from my doctor? I thought you knew me better than that."

"I do, Karen; that's part of why I'm..." A glass slipped from her hand and broke on the floor. She pushed me aside to get to the broom closet.

"Let me help."

"No! Don't touch anything," she yelled at me.

"What's..."

"Just leave. Now. I can't talk to you now."

On the way home, I marveled at Dawn's complicity in my effort to bring her home. She was definitely ready. I began to wonder if Patty needed her too, that she wasn't just protecting her from my supposed frailty. For what did Patty need her? She already had two children she loved. Why did she need mine too?

I called Patty early the next afternoon, when I thought Ian would be napping and Sandra still at school. She answered on the fourth ring, with a wary hello, seeing my number on her cell.

"Patty, can we talk about this? I think it's time for Dawn to come home and you apparently don't. Why don't you tell me what you're worried about? I want to put your mind at rest. You and Doug have been so wonderful – you rescued Dawn when I couldn't take care of her. I'll never forget that. But now I can and want to take care of her myself."

I heard a stifled sigh, and dishes clinking in the background, but no words for a long time.

"Karen, how do I know you're not going to go off the deep end again? I worry for her."

I waited to answer until I could speak really calmly. "You don't know, and I don't either. But are we going to live the rest of our lives as if I'm going to 'go off the deep end' the next day? I don't live that way and I hope you don't either." I almost added that she'd raise a fearful child if she did, but I bit my tongue. "Would it make you feel better to talk to my therapist?"

"Let me think about it. I want to talk to Doug."

"Okay; talk to Doug." I trusted him. After I hung up, I wanted to call him myself. But that would only aggravate Patty.

I called her again on Thursday, the day before I was to pick up Dawn again. "What did Doug say?"

"Karen, is that all you can think about? You don't even know what's going on around here. My whole family is down with the flu."

"I'm sorry. Is there anything I can do? Should I take Dawn and Ian for the weekend? Would that help? Can I bring you anything from the store?"

"No. Dawn has a fever and shouldn't go out. I went out this morning for groceries."

"How high is her fever? Why didn't you tell me?" As soon as the words were out, I knew I had violated our dad's rule of asking one too many questions.

"A little over a hundred." Her words turned cold. "Why didn't you call?"

"Is she awake now? Can I talk to her?"

"She's resting."

"Why don't you check and see if she wants to talk to me?"

"Karen, she's sick. I want to let her rest."

"Okay, Patty, you let her rest. I'll come by in a couple of hours to pick her up."

"I don't think you should."

"Patty, she's my daughter. Unless she's at death's door, I can take care of her at my house this weekend. It'll give you a break."

"I don't need a break!" she shrieked and hung up the phone.

When I arrived at four as usual (though on a Thursday instead of Friday), Doug appeared at the door in his sweats and showed me in. "I'm sorry you are all sick. How bad is it?"

"Not so bad medically, but I feel achy all over and the kids are whimpering and we all have runny noses. I feel like shit, actually." He smiled ruefully. That he could feel so sick and still smile at me made me grateful all over again that he was my brother-in-law.

"How long have you all been down?"

"Dawn came down first, on Tuesday, then Ian and Patty, and Sandra and I just today. Dawn's actually getting better, doesn't have a fever any more."

He led me down the hall to her room. She was sitting at the foot end of her bed, dressed, her jacket next to her. "Mommy," she said weakly. "Up." Ian lay in the bed next to her.

"Hi, Aunty Karen."

"Hi back; I'm sorry you're all sick."

"I'll pick you up, sweetie." As I bent down to kiss her, I could hear her stuffy breathing. I put her limp arms into the jacket sleeves, zipped the jacket and lifted her.

"Ian, I hope you get all better real soon." He waved at me weakly.

I turned to say goodbye to Doug, but he had left the room. Patty was nowhere to be seen. I walked down the hall toward the front door, thinking I would see him or Patty in the living room or kitchen, but no one appeared.

I called out goodbye into the empty spaces. Maybe it was just because everyone was sick, but I had never left their home before without someone saying goodbye.

Dawn fell asleep in the car within a few minutes, her head drooped to the side in her car seat and snot bubbling out her nose. At least it was loose and clear. She slept, snoring, all the way home. As I started to unstrap her from the car seat, she awoke and reached up for me to carry her. She laid her head on my shoulder, her body limp. I nuzzled her, told her I'd try to help her feel better soon.

"Bafroom," she whispered, as soon as we got inside.

"Let's use the one inside," I told her. "I'll carry you."

"No. I want the outhouse. Look for bats." Sometimes we watched for bats swooping around outside. I carried her out and opened the door. As soon as she sat down, she started to pee. Usually, she giggled at the sound of her pee spilling so far down, unlike the toilets at Patty's house. Tonight she had no energy for giggling. I even had to wipe her.

"I'm cold," she complained as soon as we got inside. I felt her forehead. "You have a fever, honey. Let me take your temperature while I make you dinner." I put the thermometer under her tongue and counted out loud to one hundred while she sat still and waited. Meanwhile, I heated macaroni and cheese on the stove; it was what she wanted the first night she was with me, every week.

The mercury line stuck at one hundred and two. I put a blanket around her and set her at the table. One little arm emerged from the blanket, picked up a few macaroni and put them into her mouth.

"Fork," I reminded her. She picked it up listlessly and started halfheartedly eating.

"Can't," she said after a few mouthfuls. "It hurts my throat."

"How 'bout if I heat some milk and honey?"

When it was warm, I tasted it to make sure it wouldn't burn her. When I put it in front of her, she looked at me balefully, her eyes like dull marbles. When I lifted the glass and put it to her lips, she smiled. She wanted me to feed her. She took little audible gulps and winced at each swallow. I felt the sides of her throat under her ears and sensed they might be swelling.

I wondered whether I should take her to the doctor, but it was six twenty and the office would be closed. If I took her to the ER, it would be at least an hour in the car that she could be resting in bed. I called her pediatrician and left word for the on-call doctor. I managed to get her to down the whole glass of warm milk, but she wouldn't eat anything, so I carried her to bed, took off her clothes and put on her warmest pajamas.

"We're going to cook that fever out of you," I told her with a smile. "I'll give you an extra blanket to keep you warm. By the time you wake up, you'll be toasty warm and the fever will be gone – poof into the night." I promised, waving my arm as if to banish it.

"Poof," she rasped, trying to smile.

I sat with her for a while, brushing her wet curls from her forehead and wondering just how sick she was. In all the time she had been with me, she'd never had an ear infection or anything worse than a cold. I had to think back to my own childhood to try to resurrect what to do. I remember my mother smearing Vicks on my chest when I had a cold. Once I had strep throat and had to take antibiotics and stay home for a week. She helped me cut out paper dolls and played kids' board games with me, and gave me as much ice cream as I wanted.

I went back to the kitchen and microwaved the rest of the macaroni and cheese for myself, thinking idly that what Dawn had was contagious and it probably wasn't a good idea, but feeling too lazy to make anything else for myself. When the doctor called back at eight, I was still at the kitchen table, staring into space. She told me that she'd want to culture Dawn's throat for strep, but that it could wait until the morning. She told me to call her in the morning and report on her fever an hour after she awoke. I wondered if I had any ice cream in the house.

I was in the shower at ten that night when Dawn woke up the first time. Rather than use her throat to call me, she got up and banged on the shower door. Her hand was at her throat. "Hurts," she whispered. I asked if she wanted more warm milk. She shook her head and started to cry. I put my towel around her and carried her back to her bed. "Gotta keep you warm," I said as I tucked her back in. "And I need to get dry." I dried myself in front of her, wondering what I could do to lessen her pain. I had no sore throat medicine. I couldn't drive to a pharmacy and leave her here alone.

"I've got just the thing," I touted, "a very special thing for sore throats." I ground up an aspirin in a glass, mixed in lemon juice and drowned it in honey until I had a gooey sweet mixture, all the while feeling a bit frantic. What did I know about taking care of a sick child? But I remembered my mother having made this for me when I'd had a sore throat as a child.

She was both crying and trying not to at the same time when I returned to her room with the gooey stuff. "Hurts too much to cry?" I asked. She nodded. "I know what you mean." I held out a spoonful of my concoction. "Magic honey goo for a sore throat," I told her. She opened her mouth willingly and I slipped in the first spoonful.

"Try to swallow it slowly; let it just melt down that throat." She winced but swallowed and opened her mouth again, like a baby bird. It felt like an hour passed before I could get the whole cup into her, but she took every spoonful, lay down again and fell asleep almost immediately.

It was eleven before I dragged myself into bed. All my insecure voices clammered. I need to be vigilant for her; I need to sleep; I need to fill my house with the usual childhood medicines so I don't find myself alone and in need like this again. No wonder people pair up before having children – someone has to stay home with the child while the other goes to the pharmacy. For the first time since we got home, I thought of Patty. Were they all sick too? I'd call her in the morning.

I picked up a book of Mary Oliver's poetry, comforting myself with her images. I'd always wanted to illustrate one of her books. I awoke by Dawn pulling on my arm. "Do you need some more magic goo?" She just shook her head and crawled into bed with me. Good, I thought, now I'll know how she is. And we both fell asleep.

When I next awoke, the sky was gray with early morning and Dawn was still asleep, curled against my left side like a large cat. Without moving my body, I felt her forehead, which seemed normal, and then my own, which felt a little cooler than hers. Don't kid yourself, I reminded myself; temperature is always lowest early in the morning.

We lay in place like that for another hour or so, while I dozed and let my mind wander. When I was Dawn's age and Patty was a year younger, she sometimes crept into bed with me, often after I'd gone to sleep. I'd wake up with a warm weight in my bed, breathing on my shoulder. I knew our mother thought it was important for each of us to be in our own beds, but I liked how it felt to wake up with her. I loved having a sister.

I watched the sky turn gradually blue, and the field behind our house turn yellow with the rising sun. I wanted to get up but I wanted also to preserve this moment with Dawn at my side.

By the time Dawn awoke, I had already in my mind called the doctor and planned what to get for the house on our way back from the office. As I'd predicted, her fever reawakened soon after she did, and we went to the doctor's office for her to swab a culture. "It's so likely to be strep that I'm going to give you the prescription now," she told me. "Keep her away from other children until we know on Monday." I felt a new confidence with the prescription in hand; help was on the way, and I swooped up a variety of children's cold and sore throat medications on my way out of the pharmacy.

Dawn was an easy patient. She slept much of that Friday, woke long enough to take more medication and drink warm milk with honey or honey-goo, as she had taken to calling it. I read to her. While she slept, I sketched for the book I was working on. I decided to wait until Sunday before calling Patty. By then, Dawn still had a fever, though it was lower and her throat still hurt; but we had a treatment plan in place and we were both pretty relaxed. She was in bed but looking at books when I went into the other room to call Patty.

This time she answered on the second ring with a civil hello.

"How are you all? I hope better."

"Ian is better, but Sandra and Doug both have a bad sore throat and a fever." She sounded reluctant to tell me.

"I'm sorry to hear it. Dawn has the same thing, and her doctor thinks it's strep. She told me to keep her away from other children until we know for sure."

"Yuck. I was hoping it wouldn't be that."

I told Patty I thought it would be best for everyone if I kept Dawn with me until she recovered. I kept my voice down because sound carries throughout my little house.

"You're probably right. Let's check in with each other midweek." I felt a huge relief.

"How are you feeling?"

"Awful," she confessed and then hung up.

Dawn looked up expectantly when I came back into her room. She has a sense for what goes on.

"You don't have to go back to Aunt Patty's today," I told her. "Not 'til you get better." I could have sworn I saw a sly smile on her face as she looked back down at her book.

5

About six years ago, when I was still visiting my dad in Sacramento on Sundays, he recommended a family lawyer to me. We were in the midst of brunch, and I was just forking a piece of eggs benedict into my mouth when he made that statement, totally out of any context. I remember the eggs because I paused at what a bizarre, random comment he had just made, and some eggy hollandaise dribbled onto my shirt. It must have been when I was still pregnant; I was eating heartily and I stopped making those visits soon after Dawn was born. *Why did you say that, Dad?* He must have seen the question on my face.

"Just in case," he'd said elliptically, refusing to elaborate.

That was some time after he'd closed his office in Nevada City and retreated to a condo in Sacramento with his girlfriend, whom he later married. His established practice in town had dried up after word got out that he'd taken up with a local waitress twenty years his junior soon after Mom was diagnosed with Alzheimer's. I can't remember whether he was still on contract then with the nine-man firm that did personal injury, estate planning and family law or whether he had retired. He hadn't exactly thrived in Sacramento, but at one time his was the go-to solo practice in Nevada City for everyone's legal problems. When I worked for him that summer in high school, it was obvious from the phone calls and the clients I greeted that he was in demand and respected.

If he were still alive, I would have asked him how to end Patty's guardianship. The irony is that he died of a stroke while I was still in the hospital and Mom remains alive to this day. Patty didn't even tell me at the time because it could have added to my depression, and on this point I can't disagree. I missed his memorial service and the wake at Patty's home. If he were here, I think he'd still give me advice, even though Patty is my opponent.

I comfort myself to think that he lived long enough to meet Dawn, while she was still a swaddled infant. His face cracked wide open and his gray eyes welled. *Can I hold her?* He asked, and then expertly laid his large left hand under her head, kissed her gently on her forehead and cradled her. *Red hair -- did you expect that? People will ask you who the father is.* I'd told him I could handle that.

His meeting Dawn was such a contrast to Mom's, but I need to stop thinking of her as having intention.

It's so odd that I still remember the name of the lawyer Dad gave me: Herb Well (a better name for a doctor than a lawyer, but not a bad name to announce in court).

Some people take pleasure in the wellbeing of others, and encourage others when they need it. Patty was not among them – even though she had been in my early days with Dawn. When I called her on Wednesday to report that Dawn was well, the first thing she told me was that both her children were down with strep throat. When I asked how she and Doug were feeling, all she said was 'weary'. I suggested that I keep Dawn with me through the following weekend, and she agreed. I tried to wish her children a speedy recovery, but she just hung up.

On Sunday, I watched Dawn pick out the clothes to wear when she returned to Patty's house. She chose a blue skirt and matching sweater, not her usual jeans or bright colors. She objected when I tousled her hair. "Mama, don't mess it. Aunt Patty likes it combed neatly." Combing Dawn's fine, curly, tangled hair is a tortuous process, painful for her and me both. I keep her hair short, and usually brush it straight when it is wet and then fluff it with my fingers and let it dry that way. It worked for us but apparently not for Aunt Patty. I asked if she wanted me to wet her hair, but she said no, just comb it through. I did it carefully, wondering about this preparation ritual, but she winced at each stroke. When I finished, she looked at herself in the mirror and patted down her errant fluffs.

When I returned Dawn to Roseville at the usual time, everyone in the family had recovered. Doug gave me a hug when he answered the door, and Ian came running out to greet Dawn. He had a new game he wanted to show her, and they ran hand in hand to his room. Patty emerged with her arm over Sandra's shoulder. As usual these days, Sandra gave me a skeptical look, and just mumbled when I told her I was glad she was feeling well again. As if on cue, Doug told Sandra he needed her help with something in the other room, leaving me to face Patty alone.

"You've had her a week and two weekends in a row now," she announced as if she were an accountant.

"Yes, and it felt good, even though she was sick part of the time. I..."

"Don't come next weekend."

I found myself stammering. I always had Dawn on weekends.

"Not the next one," and she moved to hustle me out the door.

I called her back from the road; I couldn't quite believe what she had told me, and I felt my anger rising. Patty answered on the first ring, obviously not surprised by my call, and in her calm voice explained that they were having a birthday party for Ian the next weekend and wanted Dawn to be part of it.

"When is the party? I'll bring her back for it."

"No. Dawn is part of this family and hasn't been here for a while. We all miss her."

"And I'm not part of *this* family?"

"Yes, of course you are, but it would be difficult the way you've been lately." All this she said in the voice of an old schoolteacher talking to a delinquent student.

"When can I pick her up?"

"You had her for the equivalent of two weekends, so you can skip this one and pick her up the following Friday."

"Patty, I don't play games with your children, so —"

"This is not a game, Karen."

The name Herb Well came back to me before I even got back home. I felt I owed it to Dad to contact him if he was still in practice. When I looked him up on my computer, the state bar website showed him as having his own office on York Street, near the courthouse, on the same block where my Dad had had his office years ago. Herb Well had a low bar number, under 50,000. He must be old. Dad's was 47,973. Odd, the random details I picked up while working for him so many years ago.

I called Herb Well's office the next day and was unsettled that he answered the phone himself, "Well here." An invitation to a joke, but I wasn't up to it. He explained, too self-consciously, that his secretary had just stepped out for an errand. He gave me an appointment the next day.

His office was cozy and old-fashioned, like Dad's had been, with his name painted in black gothic letters on the glass of the door to the old house facing the courthouse. He even had an old oak secretary desk behind his chair, like Dad's, and an oak table facing the client chairs. He did in fact have a secretary, and she opened the door to his office for me. Herb Well himself did not fill the image I had been creating. He looked maybe seventy, with bushy gray hair pulled back into a loose ponytail at the nape of his neck. He had attempted to tuck it into the collar of his shirt, but it escaped like hay stuffed into a shirt.

"Hello, Karen," he said as he shook my hand. I didn't want him to call me by my first name. "What brings you to see a lawyer?" It came out as 'law-yer'. I found myself wanting to see someone who called himself an attorney.

We spent more than an hour together, with his taking my

family history, my rendition of my hospitalization and recovery, the frequency of my visits with Dawn, her health, her sperm donor, my occupation and income. He told me his granddaughter had one of my books and when he told me the title, I believed him. After I regurgitated all this information, he described the procedure for terminating a guardianship. He would file a petition based on my narrative as to why Dawn no longer needs a guardian other than me, deliver it to Patty so that she could respond, and the court would hold a hearing. They may also do an evaluation and report to the court, he told me.

I asked what it would cost. Fifteen hundred dollars, if it's not complicated. I blanched at what was a big chunk of one of my book illustration fees. To have to pay legal fees to get my daughter back was beyond my reckoning. I had eighty-two thousand dollars in the bank, all of my inheritance from my Dad and some interest on it, but I had never touched it. It was my reserve for Dawn's future education.

"I've actually given you a discount," he explained, "since you are Neville Haskins' daughter. Legal fees are expensive." He seemed to read my face. "I can do you one better. I remember from years ago that you know how to fill out legal forms, and you certainly know how to write. I could show you what you need to file and help you with the papers, and you could handle it yourself. That would only cost you the filing fees, a few hundred dollars."

I found myself thanking him profusely and insincerely. I insisted on writing him a check for his time. I told him I would call him back if I couldn't talk Patty into consenting.

After getting into my car, I sagged into the seat. Meeting with an attorney was something I never thought I'd need to do. As I heard the slight grind in the starter I realized I'd rather spend the money to get my car repaired than to have to file a lawsuit against my own sister. And there was no way on this earth that I would do it myself.

Only after I was nearly home did I realize that in his thorough questioning he had failed to discover that Dawn has Patty's genes, not mine. To be fair, I had not volunteered this far-from-obvious detail. Far more important, as I learned later, he neglected to tell me of an important deadline I nearly missed.

It was many weeks later before I finally brought myself to the point of hiring an attorney to get my daughter back. I skipped the weekend as Patty had demanded, brought Ian a birthday present the following weekend, and then we fell back into our usual weekly pattern until the beginning of that summer.

My birthday fell on the Tuesday after Memorial Day weekend, so Patty 'allowed' me the long weekend and extra day with Dawn. I suspected this 'gift' was the result of her realizing she had blown it by cutting me out of Ian's birthday.

6

I wake up early on Friday, the day I pick up Dawn for my weekend with her. The birds wake me while the sky is still bone-gray, singing at each other rather than the call and response they do later in the day. This is a contest for who has the biggest bird lungs. This is the tuning up for the day, no harmony intended, like an orchestra warming up before the concert begins. They fall silent as the sky takes on a hint of pale yellow, before it turns blue. I get up around six, still in the birds' silent interval.

Today begins my birthday weekend. The refrigerator is full of berries, Dawn's favorite fruit. I shopped yesterday and bought blueberries, raspberries and strawberries, which I mixed together with bits of mint from our garden. She and I can eat berry salad until we are bloated. I have a little for breakfast on my oat flakes and then drive down the hill to Roseville.

Patty has said I can arrive any time after nine, and it is 9:09 when I pull into their driveway. Sandra stands vigil at the front door. How can an eight-year-old look so dour?

"Good morning, Sandra," I say as cheerily as I can. "Where's your mom?"

"In the shower." She wastes no words on me. But Dawn has heard my voice and comes bounding down the hall calling 'Mommy!'

"My girl, my darling girl." I hoist her up so that her legs and arms surround me. She kisses my cheeks and ear and I know that nothing can spoil this weekend.

"Ian and I made you a surprise." At this point Ian appears in the hall, running and then slowing down as he catches Sandra's sour look. He wishes me happy birthday and hands me a plastic baggie. I put Dawn down to give Ian a hug and look at the little package. Dawn takes it from me and carefully lifts out a necklace of clover flowers and a card that she and Ian have signed. "You treasures," I tell them in a damp voice. I didn't know children still made clover chains; this is a remnant from my own childhood. Their card is filled with hand-drawn hearts. Dawn has made hers in green because, she explains, it's summer.

I ask Dawn if she has her water shoes. Sandra answers for her: "You still have them from last weekend." She is probably correct, the shoe-counter. She will be a security guard when she grows up. For a Swiss bank.

Ian and Dawn walk with me to the car, each holding one of my hands. As soon as I open the car door, I remember the car seat and go back for it.

"You forgot the car seat," Sandra admonishes.

"I was just coming back for it," I tell her, trying not to sound snotty.

As I am latching the car seat into the back seat, I hear footsteps behind me.

"Happy birthday," Patty says drily to my backside.

I back out of the car and turn to face her. This will be the first of my birthdays since she was born that we will not spend together. We used to camp out together in the back yard in a tent on my birthday, just us two. Each year we took our first swim from the rope swing on my birthday. Even when we were in high school and she was the busy, popular one, she saved my birthday for being with me.

Her face, flushed from the hot shower, is unguarded. Without makeup, she has no mask. Still, I cannot read her expression. I hug her, but she is as unresponsive as a tree.

In the car, Dawn keeps up a constant chatter, about where Ian and she found the clover, their collecting it in a basket and Ian showing her how to tie the knots, and their racing each other in the pool. I tell her what a good swimmer she is, though I know the limits of her dog paddling. She sings to herself, a little song I do not recognize. Then we count cars together; she counts seventeen red cars, to my eleven blue cars. Will I have a birthday party with all my friends? I tell her that we are going to Megan's house this evening and that Jenny and her boys will be there too.

By the time we get home, she has to pee. Take me to the outhouse, she demands, and I do. She swings her legs while on the pot and asks, for the umpteenth time, why there is a half-moon carved into the backside. I try to give her a different answer each time. It's not a full moon because then people could look inside, is all I can muster.

On the way back to the house, she points to the miners' misery plants. "Dizzy kids," she says. That's her version of kidkidizzi, the Native American word for these plants. She asks me to say the word because she likes the sound, and she repeats it correctly several times, but I expect it will come out as dizzy kids the next time she says it. She also says 'flutterby' for butterfly.

The rest of the day passes as sweetly as this start, and she loves my birthday party at Megan's, even though the other children are teenagers. Because they are enough older, they cater to her, enjoy reading to her or cutting food for her. Megan's fourteen-year-old daughter Sam has always been protective of Dawn.

I decide to cap the joy of this weekend with a swim in the river. Megan and Sam come with us, and I carry Dawn in the aluminum frame backpack. Though she is a small four-year-old, she is still heavy and I am unused to this weight on my back. The river is low this year, from a dry winter, but there are plenty of green pools, where the water is warmer this year from the low flow. I catch the sweet scent of the buckeyes blooming profusely along the path. Megan offers to lead me to a swimming hole I don't know about. How far, I ask her, but she assures me it is not a long way. Sam leads the way on the dusty path. I worry when the trail leads us upward, where the river looks a longer way down, a rocky trough filled with shimmering green, clear mountain water. Dawn tells me not to touch the poison oak; we have trained her well and she recognizes the shiny leaves all around us. Although it is early in the day, the heat relents only when we are in the shade of the cedars. Sam turns downward onto a steep, narrow trail down the hill. I am able to keep my balance by holding onto trees along the path, but by the time we get to the river's edge, my back is wet with sweat and my calf muscles feel wobbly. Sam has found us a gem of a spot, entirely private and with a small sandy area near the water's edge. The pool itself looks mainly shallow except for a darker green area near the far bank. I lower the frame onto the sand with Dawn still in it, and lift her out. Her back is as drenched as mine, and the band of her sunhat is equally wet. She and I each take off our shoes. I lift her into my arms, with her facing me now, and pick my way across the hot sand to the water's edge.

"You smell like a dusty puppy," I tell her, and she tells me dusty puppy wants to swim. Megan and Sam are behind us taking off their clothes. With a nod toward Patty's sensibilities, Dawn and I are wearing swimsuits.

The first sense of the water is bracing, but as welcome as iced lemonade for thirst. The gravel pokes my feet. Much as I'd like to think of myself as a country girl, I have city feet. I venture one step further, onto a smooth rock. As I bend over to let Dawn stand in the river herself, my foot slides off the rock and I am suddenly crashing to my knees. Dawn goes down into the river in front of me, her eyes and mouth wide open in mute surprise. I fall on top of her, my hand hitting gravel as I try to avoid her. I roll my weight off Dawn, trying at the same time to lift her head out of the water. My left knee feels like a sledge hammer hit it, and I can't move that leg. Dawn comes up herself, snorting water, coughing, and bleeding from the back of her head. Megan is there in an instant, lifting Dawn, slapping her on the back to help her cough out water.

I drag myself up with the Sam's help and limp out to the sand.

I stare at Megan's hand on Dawn's back. It is streaking red, and I can't tell why, until I glance upward, as if in slow motion, and see blood oozing from the back of Dawn's head. As Megan turns around, I see Dawn's face with that same look of complete puzzlement.

"Mommy, why did you drop me on my head?"

I gasp and start to sob. Megan lowers her onto my lap. I tell her it was an accident and I am so sorry, but the words sound hollow and stupid and I can only clutch her tightly and sob and accuse myself. Megan now rubs her hand on my back and tells us both it was an accident and no one's fault, but I can take no comfort. Dawn has taken hold of my right earlobe with her thumb and finger and pinched it hard. From infancy, she took comfort by stroking one of my earlobes. "Ouch," I whisper into her ear. She eases into a tiny smile and lightens her touch on my ear. "Don't cry, Mommy," she whispers into my ear. She has brought me back into myself.

Together, Megan and I examine the wound at the back of Dawn's head. Sam has wet her teeshirt and I dab it on the wound. It looks shallow, Megan tries to reassure me, but I can see a bump rising and we look at each other, knowing we need to go to the ER to make sure she has not concussed. I press the teeshirt onto her head and soothe her as best I can.

"Your knee looks worse," Megan tells me but I cannot yet feel it. I tell Dawn that she is going to wear a special bandana to cool her head on the hike out. After Sam rinses it in the river, I tie it around the top of Dawn's head. Sam tells Dawn she looks like a tennis player, with that headband.

Megan offers to carry Dawn on the way out, and we each take a long swig of water from our packs before Megan lifts a reluctant Dawn out of my arms and puts her back into the carrier.

When I try to get up, I fall down again from the pain in my left knee. It too is scraped, but there is not much blood. No protruding bones, I joke -- badly, but I cannot get up without help. Once on my feet, I can barely put any weight on my left leg. The wizard Megan has brought a collapsible walking stick in her own backpack and hands it to me. With it, I can make my way, but I moan with each step.

"Go ahead of me," I tell Megan. I don't want Dawn to hear me. Sam walks behind me and grabs my arm when it looks like I am about to slip.

Once in the car, I start to shake uncontrollably. Until now, I have only thought about how to get us safely out of there. Now I see what I have done. I sit in the back next to Dawn in her car seat, my left leg extended as much as I can muster and my right hand on the side of Dawn's head, stroking her cheek.

Fortunately, it takes us only forty minutes to get to the Grass Valley Memorial Hospital. Dawn has fallen asleep in her car seat, her head leaning heavily on my hand. The makeshift bandana is barely damp now; the air is so dry. While I unlatch the car seat she wakes up and looks around, asking where we are. I remove the bandana and see that her wound has swollen to the size of a plum and is taking on a rich purple hue. I explain that we are taking her to the doctor to look at her head. As I try to get myself out of the car, I see a big swelling on my own knee and quickly realize that I can barely walk, let alone carry her. Megan lifts Dawn out of her car seat and offers to carry her, but Dawn insists on walking next to me, holding my right hand. I try as hard as I can to walk as if each step does not burn, but I groan anyway.

"Mommy needs a doctor," Dawn explains to Megan.

"You're right, honey," Megan tells her.

Of course there are others waiting in the emergency room, but luckily not many. A young man with a bare chest and tattoos lacing both arms has road rash on his elbow, shoulder and head, and a flapping tear in his leather motorcycle pants. They will take him before us. A young woman with stringy hair holds a whimpering infant wrapped in a blanket. I can't tell if their issues are urgent. At the moment we enter, two attendants support an elderly man under each of his shoulders as they walk him to an examining room.

I am given two forms at the desk, one each for Dawn and me. I start mine first and complete the basic stats easily. On the second page are fifty questions about medical history. I pause at previous hospitalizations. My bout for depression has no bearing on my knee injury, but I check the box and truthfully identify the hospital and the reason. My history is otherwise uncomplicated. When I get to Dawn's form, I clutch at the second line, her address. Megan sees me pause and points to my own, silently telling me to use it. At the line for primary physician, I pause again. I had a pediatrician for her in Nevada City while she was living with me, but Patty has found another in Roseville since, and I don't even know that doctor's name. I use the one I had before. At the line for signature of parent/guardian, it comes home to me that Patty is the one with legal authority. She is the legal guardian. I feel tears coming. I want to throw the pen. Will they even let me get treatment for Dawn? I glance up at Megan, whose intense look tells me to just sign the form. I press so hard that the page underneath is indented.

As we wait, Dawn wanders around the room, searching the magazine racks for something of interest. Megan, who can read me well, tells me this could happen to anyone and it is not my fault. Later, she will tell me about the time she dropped Sam, but Sam does not remember and now is not the time for her to be reminded.

Dawn has found a children's book called *Masie Saw an Elephant* and tries to climb onto my lap for me to read it to her, but my left leg is hoisted onto the seat to my left and I can read to her only by her standing in front of my chair. I hold the book by circling my arms around her. It is an inane, poorly illustrated story of a girl who sees her first circus elephant, but it keeps Dawn occupied.

When it is our turn, the tech asks who the patient is. Dawn and I each point to the other, and the tech laughs. "Let's take you first," she tells Dawn, asking her what happened. The tech wears those earrings inside her earlobes that create dime-sized holes.

"Mommy fell on me in the river."

At least she does not say that I dropped her on her head.

The tech glances up at me for details, which I provide. She asks Dawn if anything hurts, and Dawn points to the back of her head. I find myself liking this no-nonsense woman with her butch haircut, strong arms and ready laugh, as she gently probes Dawn's neck, shoulders, and arms for tenderness. "I'm going to touch the sore part of your head now," she warns, and Dawn winces but does not struggle. She asks Dawn to walk from where we stand to the end of the room and back, and she does so, with her little skipping step.

When the tech stands up to question me, I read the nametag on her blue scrubs – Ellen Manck, M.D. She asks if Dawn lost consciousness, and I explain that she fell asleep in her car seat but woke up as soon as the car stopped. She asks whether Dawn has seemed dazed or confused or nauseous.

"What's nauseous?" Dawn asks her.

"Did you feel like barfing?" Dr. Manck asks her directly.

"No. I'm hungry."

"That's a good sign," Dr. Manck tells us both.

Dr. Manck asks if we have any questions.

"Can I touch your ear?" Dawn asks, and the doctor leans down to allow Dawn to insert her finger into the hole. Her first finger fits all the way through the hole.

"Why do you have a hole there?"

The doctor and I both laugh, but she seems to struggle for a reply, glancing at me as if wondering whether this is a bad example. Abruptly she asks if we have any food with us. She takes Dawn back out to Megan and Sam to have one of the oat-nut bars and oranges we were going to snack on at the river.

When she returns, she probes the bones in my calf gently, then the front of my knee, which makes me jerk my leg in pain. "This may also hurt," she warns, and with one hand on my thigh just above my knee and the other on my calf, she pushes my calf strongly toward my knee. "That's good," she reports, when I don't react to that maneuver. "I was worried about your ACL." She sends me in for an x-ray, which is done promptly, and then explains that, while nothing appears to be broken, I will need to wear a brace over my knee for at least a week. A tech produces a huge black contraption that, once fitted, makes me look like a cartoon bionic woman. It is about three times the girth of my knee and has a large joint with metal struts radiating like calipers from my knee.

"No long pants for a while, I guess."

"No tight short ones either," she jokes, and I wonder if this is an oblique flirtation. "Keep weight off it as much as you can and ice it when you get home." No driving with this contraption, she directs. And come back if it doesn't get better.

"What about Dawn?"

She produces a sheet listing signs of concussion and directs me to bring her back if she exhibits any of them.

"If in doubt, bring her in; a concussion can be subtle. And keep her quiet for the next few days." I start to say I don't have the next few days, but hold my tongue. I am already worrying about what to tell Patty on Tuesday when Dawn has to go back.

Megan stops at the grocery store for me on our way back home. I've only brought a twenty with me, but she won't take it. At my house, she unpacks the groceries.

"I'm afraid you're stuck with frozen dinners for the next few nights. I've got rehearsals. Stay home, and keep this on your knee." Megan tosses me a package of frozen peas.

I limp to the door with her as she leaves and ask what to tell Patty. She pauses, as if the answer is obvious, but she does not give me one.

"You're not driving anywhere; that's for sure."

As soon as Megan and Sam leave, Dawn and I devour the bowl of berries and two microwaved pasta dinners that Megan left with us. I realize how lost we would have been without her and that I didn't even thank her.

"I'm wasted; what about you?" Dawn nods. We both collapse onto my bed, she on her stomach and I on my back. I curve the package of frozen peas around the lump on her head and lean back into my own pillow. The rhythm of her breathing puts me to sleep.

When I wake, the angle of light on the pine trees outside is low but I can't tell if it is late afternoon or early evening. A raucous jay rips into some complaint, and a few smaller birds twitter, but the frenetic bird chorus of day's end has not yet begun. A squirrel clatters across our roof. Dawn is on her back next to me, her mouth a small o. Whorls of hair are flattened on her forehead. The peas are wedged between us, far from frozen. There is no reason to move, none at all, and I lapse into a doze of absolute contentment.

My second waking is at the frantic bird sound of day's end, a competition of solo calls, broadcasting anxiety at the coming of night. Dawn is as peacefully still as she was earlier, but I have caught the birds' tension. I need to call Patty. I can almost hear her question me about how I managed to drop my child into the river. But something has shifted inside me. I know, at least this once, that while I had this accident, much as I wish it hadn't happened, I had taken good care of my daughter. I should be the one to watch over her for the next few days, to make sure she does not have a concussion. I believe I can do that. Even with my bum knee, I will find a way to take care of us.

I can do this. This sensation is so new; I almost don't recognize it. I can take care of my own child, and I know what to do. The thought forms into a mantra, my birthday gift to myself.

On Tuesday morning the phone rings early, before I can muster myself to call Patty. I pick up the phone from beside the bed, though I wince even turning my left leg.

"I need to run some errands today and want to know when you'll bring Dawn back." Her voice is studiously friendly.

"I can't bring her back today. We had an accident at the river." *Bad start.* I rush into the silence and explain in excruciating detail what happened, ending with the doctor's instruction not to drive for a week.

"I'll pick her up then."

"No – don't. I can take care of her, and I want to do this. You need to start trusting that I can and will take care of my own child." *Karen, you fool, never ever tell your sister what she must do.*

She reminds me I am not mobile, I can't even cook for Dawn, or bathe her or dress her. I tell her confidently that I can do all those things and will. What if you need to go back to the hospital? I tell her I will find a ride if that happens. I go too far and tell her that Dawn wants to stay here, which is probably a dare to her. Although we go back and forth, asserting why she should stay or go ("she has day camp this week with Ian"), neither of us declares war. She tells me she will talk to Doug and call me back in a day or so. That's a good outcome; Doug has always been the more reasonable of the two of them and he has nothing to prove to me.

I install my "rig" as I will call it, tightening the Velcro strips at my thigh and calf. Hoisting myself upright and putting weight on my legs, I realize almost immediately that I cannot walk on this leg without a shooting pain. I can bend it with the rig, but walking is an agony. Dawn watches me intently and offers to get me breakfast, but she cannot reach the cereal shelf. I limp into our kitchen and watch in admiration as Dawn brings berries and milk to the table for us. I realize that tomorrow is my volunteer day at Rock Creek Farm and call to explain why I cannot come in this week. As I wonder how to fill our day Dawn tells me she wants to paint together. She clears the breakfast table and brings her own watercolor set to the table. She even brings two bowls of water to the table, one for her and one for me. "Paint here with me," she asks, knowing I usually paint at my easel, and I agree to use the table with her.

She goes to work immediately, mixing red and brown together in a small puddle that morphs into a dragonfly on the paper. I find myself watching her rather than painting myself. Children don't stare at blank paper as adults do, waiting for inspiration. Whatever it is that edits, restrains, inhibits, or judges our impressions has not yet formed, and expression blooms.

I decide to paint a portrait of Patty. I begin with a full face, but it forces me in too close, so I lay that aside and begin with a full body portrait of her seated in a chair; she should be in one of the white upholstered chairs in her living room, with each arm perched regally on the arms of the chair. In a navy blue dress, with a draped neckline and pearls, she looks direct and sincere, but not too severe. Her legs are crossed at the ankles, and her delicate sandals reveal colored nails. I am sketching these details with speed, putting a wash on the sides of the chair. From which direction comes the light? I decide that it comes from a hidden window on her right, at the left side of the portrait. It bisects her face at only a slight angle, her nose creating a slanted shadow down her left cheek. The side of her face in the light is bright yellow, a cheerful but unnatural yellow. The left side presents a far more complicated question, to which the answer becomes green, gray-green in the nose-shadow, brighter green below where the blue of her dress melds with the yellow of the sunlight, and a bruised purple-green in an arc below her left eye, a paler flesh/purple blend on her left forehead. I like that purplish arc and replicate it under her right eye, where it becomes rosier in the yellow wash already in place. I have pulled her hair back, as if in a ponytail. Her right eyebrow is raised, a skeptical curve; the left is furrowed, a darker slash. Her right eye is fully revealed, a cheerful blue, but the left is shadowy, enigmatic.

In the time that I have become absorbed in my own painting, Dawn has painted a portrait of the two of us, me with a grotesquely outsized left leg, which makes me laugh. She glances at my portrait of Patty but makes no comment.

Our Tuesday passes as companionably as Monday did. Jenny calls to wish me happy birthday and offers to bring us dinner, which I gladly accept. We laugh together at my outsized leg. She inspects Dawn's bump and proclaims it a first-class bruise, full purple. Dawn wants to see it but we can't arrange a mirror at the right angle to do it. Dawn is as giddy as we are and clearly not suffering, though the spot is tender. It has been a good birthday.

On Wednesday morning we both sleep in, and are resting in bed together when there is a loud knock on the front door. I get up, but it takes me extra time to put on my leg apparatus and throw on my robe. I glance at the clock and out the front window. Patty's car is parked outside, and it's 9:10. Patty has never been to this little house before. My eyes dart around; I know she will hate it.

I open the door, and she marches in like an inspector, asking me first why it took me so long to answer the door. I confess that we had been sleeping in and that it takes me a few moments to put on my leg brace.

"You're worse than I thought," she comments as she glances down at my leg. "How's Dawn?"

"Much better. She has a big bruise on the back of her head but no concussion or other problems."

Patty makes no comment but marches uninvited into Dawn's bedroom, where Dawn is getting dressed.

"Hi sweetheart, how's your head?" Dawn murmurs okay and keeps pulling up her pants. Patty hovers over Dawn, turning her around by her shoulders so that she can see the back of Dawn's head. Patty says nothing but shoots me an accusing look.

"I've come to take you home," she says to Dawn. "Since your mom can't drive you." Dawn glances up at me with the obvious question.

"Patty, let's talk outside." I open the front door. She walks through it and sits down on one of the two rocking chairs on the porch. I tell her it's time for her to let me manage my own daughter, that I can do this and she didn't need to just show up on our doorstep. Though she manages to keep her voice down, she practically hisses her reply: "You get one four-day span and manage to injure both of you. No way can you be trusted to take her back." She gets up and tells Dawn to gather her things to go back home.

"Aunt Patty wants you back," I say as I hug her as best I can without being able to bend my left leg. She hugs me hard and follows Patty out the door.

I did not see this coming. Maybe I should have. I walk around the little house in a kind of daze. I make my bed. I make myself some coffee and a piece of toast. I have worked myself into a fury by the time the cup is drained, but I am no longer accusing myself.

I throw open my computer and google best Sacramento family law attorneys. Herb Well is not up to dealing with Patty. I find half a dozen different resources, including Super Lawyers (which sounds like blow-up toys), Best Lawyers, Yelp and other sites that remind me of looking for restaurants rather than for a professional. Sore loser stories abound. But I locate someone I find promising.

Analee Meriwether has less than ten years in the practice but is already listed as one of the Best Lawyers in Sacramento. She's served as president of the young lawyers group in the county bar. She handled many child custody matters and her Yelp comments praise her dedication in these cases. Her photo reveals a plain face, direct gaze and stocky build; I don't know why but I find that reassuring. And the woman who answers the telephone – Gerta Dobner -- takes some real information from me, including Patty's name (for "conflict of interest" check, she said). She sounds like a wise old teacher, and I tell her more than I intend. Gerta calls me back within an hour to report no conflict and offers me an appointment for the following week.

7

Analee Meriwether's office is quite modern, with upholstered, comfortable chairs in the waiting room. The Teutonic woman who presides over the space is obviously Gerta, whose warm smile belies her severe mien. She stands to greet me, an imposing woman of about sixty-five, her gray hair in a bun curled around the side of her face as if pasted at night into that shape. She could easily have been a German frau in a film from the forties. She asks me to fill out a form with my name, age, address and information about Dawn, as well as the name and age of my spouse, which I leave blank.

After I hand the form back to her, she begins to ask me questions, all with a smile, but I can't help thinking she is there to gather intelligence. I feel pegged when she asks if I am related to Neville Haskins, and I admit he was my father.

"He was an able lawyer," is all she says about him. She takes the form into the attorney's office after knocking on the door peremptorily, closes the door behind her, and remains in there for about five minutes before returning to her desk and bowing her head over her computer.

The door opens again, this time by the attorney herself, and I am surprised how short she is, a tree stump of a woman. Her face is as plain as her photo, with eyebrows that are two straight lines above her eyes, but her eyes animate her with their intensity. She introduces herself and shakes my hand in a firm but friendly manner, and gestures me to one of the chairs facing her desk.

"What brings you here?" she asks, although I am fairly certain she already knows why I have come. I tell her about Dawn and wanting to end the guardianship.

After what seems like a lot of preliminary history, she asks to see a photo of Dawn, which I show her.

"She doesn't look much like you; how did she get those gorgeous red curls?"

And so I tell her about Dawn's origins, relieved that she has asked a vital question. She asks if Patty's husband was the sperm donor, and I tell her I had chosen a complete stranger from a sperm bank, which seems to reassure her. I shudder inside to think of how much worse this would be if all Dawn's genes belonged to Patty and Doug. I tell her all about the hospitalization, what led up to it, and the time since.

When she asks me what happened to my leg, I tell her about my birthday accident on the river and the precipitating event that led to my being here. I tell her I think Patty regards my fall into the river with Dawn as proof of my incompetence as a mother. After asking how Dawn had fared in the river incident, she tells me she thinks there is hardly a parent alive who has not had some mishap with her child. She even tells me she had once slipped into the Sacramento River while carrying one of her children on her back; they'd both come home slathered in mud and wet from sliding into the river. We laughed, both of us. She made me feel human.

She explains that seeking to end the guardianship might or might not be simple, depending on whether the court wants an evaluation. If not, it could be a simple court appearance, such as Herb Well had described to me; but if an evaluation were ordered, it would take longer and entail interviews and home inspections for Patty and me. I tell her Patty would come out on top on the home inspection front, with her faux mansion in Roseville. As soon as I say those words, I wince; for all I know this attorney may live in a similar place.

"I know just what you are describing," she says, "Roseville seems to have more than its share of them."

"What are my chances? On the surface, Patty and Doug look so much more put together than I do."

"But you are indisputably Dawn's mother, and you seem to have recovered the ability to care for her again. Barring something I don't know about your caretaking, the guardianship should be terminated."

She looks at me fixedly. "Is there anything else I should know?"

She has been so thorough; I assure her I have told her everything.

"Would you represent me to terminate the guardianship?"

"Of course."

"What will it cost?"

She explains that it will depend on whether the court orders an investigation, that she charges $350 an hour and will need a $2,500 deposit, which she will apply monthly to her bill. If there is no investigation, the deposit will probably cover her charges, but the overall charge will be unpredictable if an investigation is done.

Twenty-five hundred dollars. I have not had to spend that much money on anything since I rented my house, and needed first and last months' rent and a deposit. I do have the money, from what I inherited from Dad, but I have intentionally not touched this money. It still feels tainted.

When Mom was first diagnosed with Alzheimer's, he divorced her and placed her into a residential home – probably well before she needed it – and he took all their assets, their home, his practice, and whatever savings they had. He'd explained to Patty at the time, but not to me, that he needed to own all their money in order for Mom to receive Medicaid for her residential care. Without the divorce, they would have been wiped out. Patty was the only one to whom that made sense. Mom resented him from then forward, refused to see him in her residential care facility, and the Nevada

City community seemed to reject him also, which is apparently why he relocated to Sacramento.

"Do you want to retain me?" The lawyer looked at me as if I had spaced out.

"Yes. I can write you a check now, but I ask that you hold it until tomorrow. I need to move some money." Whatever the source of the money, I really want this lawyer.

"Of course." She picks up her phone and instructs Gerta to prepare a retainer agreement for terminating a guardianship, gives her the details, and hangs up.

"One more thing," she adds, "and I won't charge you for this. I want to make a home visit, not with Dawn there, but to see where and how you live, so that I can inform the court if there are any questions."

I must have sat there, gap-mouthed, for a second. She adds, "It may feel intrusive, but if the court has questions, I want to be able to answer them."

I don't know what I was thinking. I am definitely stunned by her thoroughness, but also I cringe a bit at how my home may look to her. Judging by the modern, clean feel of her office, and her business suit and pearls, I wonder if my environment will put her off.

"You mean you'll drive to Rough and Ready on your own nickel, just to see how I live?"

"Yup."

"If you come this Saturday, I can take you on a hike along the river. It's beautiful." I already know Patty won't give me Dawn this coming weekend, having only recovered her eight days earlier. She will like the river more than she likes my little house. I make the invitation without thinking of my knee.

"You're on, but will you be able to walk with your knee? I'll definitely come, and we can see how your knee is on Saturday."

I sign her retainer agreement, and we agree to meet at my house the following Saturday morning.

Driving home, I feel shaky and overwhelmed. It has nothing to do with my knee, which is clumsy but painless while I drive. I have hired a lawyer to sue my sister to get my daughter back. On top of that, I have mixed feelings about the lawyer's coming to see my house. My first reaction is to admire her thoroughness and my own good judgment in choosing her, but somewhere down the road the thought turns into her not trusting me and wanting to check up on whether I am worthy to be her client. The doubt makes me look at my little house much more defensively.

After I get home, and before I transfer the money, I call Patty to check if she will relent about this coming weekend. As expected, she tells me no, but she is civil. She tells me Ian and Sandra have missed Dawn. I tell her to say hi to Ian and Sandra for me, hang up the phone, and transfer the money.

8

ANALEE

She darts about in her narrative, this one, like a squirrel switching back and forth before dashing across a road. Of course, new clients all ramble a bit in their first session, and I let them go on for a while, so I can see better what they reveal when unfettered by my questions. But this one is taking no cues when I shift in my chair, as if to call an end to a paragraph, and I can see it will be difficult to insert a question. So I keep watching and listening. I find myself curious about her, and her story is certainly unusual. What a way to conceive a child!

She has a forlorn, waif-like affect, looking out at me from under the floppy brim of a dark blue hat. She is so thin, concave in her middle, where I bulge. I want to feed her. She helps herself to the bowl of jelly bellies I keep on my desk, eating them one at a time between thoughts. Her wide-spaced, round eyes, blue as cornflowers, framed by sliver-moon eyebrows, fool me into thinking she is much younger than her forty-six years. The only lines on her face are deep ones, at the corners of her mouth, unseen counterweights to any attempt at a smile. Certainly she is quirky, which appeals to me, and she seems to have a sense of humor, although self-deprecating. She has a colorful way of expressing herself. At the same time, I am professionally cautious; I may be seeing only the nicest part of her in this initial interview.

"Tell me a little about Dawn. What's she like?"

"She's my life. She's a little ball of energy with impossibly curly hair the color of persimmons. You know how it is to come on a persimmon tree on a gray November day, when everything else is dying and then suddenly there are these balls of bright orange? That's what it's like to meet her. She's cheerful, bright, curious - and very affectionate."

"Do you have a photo of her?"

"Of course." Karen opens her phone and lets me scroll through many shots of a carrot-headed little girl. I must have looked up at her quizzically. The child whose photo I see looks nothing like her mother. In one of my least tactful moments, I ask if Dawn is Karen's natural child.

"Good question; most people are too polite to ask." She explains that she had borne and birthed this child, whose embryo consisted of her sister's egg and a donor's sperm. I like her all the more for not taking umbrage at my blunt question.

"How did it come about that your sister became her guardian?"

"I fell into a deep depression." Karen shakes her head slowly. "I'd never been a depressed person, and I didn't recognize it at first, but I slipped slowly into such a funk that I barely got out of bed. Dawn would be running around the house, and I could barely get up to feed her, not to mention playing with her or making sure she didn't get into trouble. My sister noticed it too; she knew I wasn't feeling well and she'd come a couple times a week. Finally, she had me hospitalized for depression. When I got out, she asked whether it wouldn't make more sense for Dawn to stay with her and her family for a time, while I sorted out my life. She and I had always been close. She was a great mother to her two kids, and even I had to admit I couldn't handle her." Karen shrugs, a trace of a smile on her face.

"It was a good idea at the time."

"What about your depression? What sort of treatment did you get?"

"I was actually hospitalized, for a little less than a week, and then spent several months in a rehab center. They did a number of tests and found out it was partly hormonal; my thyroid was underperforming and they put me on a regimen of thyroid pills. They started me on antidepressants too. The first round didn't agree with me at all: they made me anxious and nauseous. But then I was put on something gentler – and it helped. I gradually came out of it."

"Was there anything else going on in your life that you think caused this depression?"

"You sound like my therapist – who, by the way, I really like. Well, breaking up with my last boyfriend may have had something to do with it, and getting used to being a mother. But I've thought about this a lot, and I still think it was changes in my own body – the thyroid and beginnings of menopause – that triggered it."

"Are you still seeing this therapist?"

"Yes, once a week now. She and I have begun to talk about terminating therapy, but this trouble over ending the guardianship makes her think we should continue."

"What happened when you asked Patty to terminate the guardianship?"

"I didn't use those words; I just spoke of Dawn coming back to live with me. She told me I wasn't ready to take full responsibility for Dawn. 'What if it happens again?' she throws back at me. And now, with my fall in the river, she acts as if her fears are well founded."

"What do you think?"

"I'm well now, and it's time for my daughter to come back home." Karen looks at me pointedly.

"What's your home like?"

"Well, it's not the same home that she left." Karen looks down for a moment. "I had a really nice house in Nevada City but lost it during my depression. I'm renting a house now in Rough and Ready. It's kind of old, but Dawn's bedroom is really nice."

I ask if she has a copy of the guardianship papers, and she hauls out of her handbag a rumpled copy of the letters of guardianship, a good sign that she has come prepared. I note the date and ask Gerta to come in to photocopy it.

"This was almost two full years ago. Why did you wait so long?"

This time I am being intentionally blunt, testing her.

"I didn't trust myself at first and then I couldn't get Patty to agree. It's still hard for me to think of taking my sister to court."

I explain to her that if she is ready to do it now, she should act promptly because, once the guardianship lasts at least two years, Patty could ask the court to terminate her parental rights. The guardianship has been in effect for nineteen months. I catch a glance of panic in Karen's eyes an instant before she says she wants to hire me.

I make a note to myself to get her permission to obtain her hospitalization records. I sense she has glossed over her depression and put too much emphasis on her thyroid and menopausal factors. Also, I will seek her permission next time to contact her therapist. But first I want to see for myself where she lives. I don't want to dig a hole for myself professionally by my fascination with this unusual person. And a hike to the river will be a sort of bonus for me for the day; I love to hike and don't get up to the Sierra foothill rivers enough.

I try to be thorough, especially if I have to go to some hick county. I have Siri talking to me from my car, but I also have a California map on the car seat next to me. Maps are my friends, sets of clues for any journey to a new place. Rough and Ready is a tiny dot on the map only five miles west of Grass Valley on a two-lane road that makes me think not many people even pass through it. When I first hear that my new client lives in Rough and Ready, I wince mentally at how even the name might prejudice a Sacramento judge. Rough and Ready conjures up front yards littered with old washing machines and outlived trucks, an Appalachian scene from

James Dickey's "land of the three-fingered people." Competent mothers do not live in Rough and Ready. Competent mothers live in Roseville or even Nevada City, where city people take weekend outings to shop the tidy gas-lit streets of the old Gold country town.

I am a little surprised I have insisted on Karen's allowing me to come visit her. I've been blind-sided before by clients, and I want to be able to convincingly describe it to the judge without being inaccurate. I also want to know what a child custody evaluator would see. But this day is to be more; Karen has invited me to take a hike along the Yuba River, to "experience her environment" the way she does. I don't believe in socializing with my clients. I keep a professional distance to avoid misunderstandings about boundaries in the relationship. But here I am, backpack at hand, prepared for a jaunt in the country with someone I barely know but need to know better.

I already had second thoughts about giving up this day without even being able to bill for it. I could well have used this day to take my own children biking with Adam, but then again, I give up other Saturdays to give lectures or train volunteer lawyers in custody matters, so what is one more Saturday? This client can barely afford me even at the reduced rate I had quoted her. Wrong attitude, I tell myself, and decide to try to make it an adventure, by taking the back roads.

Oddly, as much as I like to know my way, I also like to meander. Often I'm less interested in the destination than in the journey. The way there, I thought, would show me the difference between where I start from and where Karen lives, especially if I take back roads. So, instead of going up 80 and 49, I take 99 North to 20 East, which winds through miles of nut tree orchards, along the edges of Yuba City with its Indian restaurants and sari shops, across a stretch of flat ranch land with horses and cattle, and finally through a few miles of homesteads with leaning weathered barns and trailers with old trucks. One has a bumper sticker that reads: 'I brake for snakes.' The town of Rough and Ready itself is little more than a clump of remnant buildings, a mining supply shop, a farm store, a ramshackle bar, and a post office. At the entrance to the town is a welcome sign to Rough and Ready, which reads on the second line, 'Seceded from Union 1850.' A faded, hand-painted billboard on the side of one building advertises Secession Day – Last Sunday in June.

The town doesn't even have a grocery store, except for a tiny general store. I stop there, to check it out and buy an orange to take on the hike; but they don't even sell bottled water (just rows of cold beer) and the only available fruits are a few blackened bananas and weeks'-old apples. I make a mental note to ask Karen where she shops for groceries (if she shops for groceries; it is a little test). Karen Haskins lives on Stagecoach Way, a mile or so past the town's old cemetery. The region is littered with road signs depicting its past: Prospector Road, Riffle Box Road, To Hell and Back Lane, Black Gold Road….

The house itself looks as if it could have been a miner's cabin a hundred years ago. The corrugated tin roof slopes down over a front porch as wide as the little house, with rocking chairs, and the four-pane windows are slightly rippled and bear the tiny bubbles of old glass. The porch creaks with reassurance of its age. I don't need to search for a nonexistent doorbell; Karen opens the door to let me in, and the screen door thwacks behind me as I step inside.

"Welcome to the country," Karen says with an ironic smile. "Lemonade?"

I accept and look around her as Karen goes to the refrigerator, which looks like one my mother had when she was a child, with feet and a handle you raise to open the door. Karen catches my look. "It works," she reassures me. The kitchen sink is a broad, deep ceramic basin, with the original pump next to it. I am relieved to see it has an ordinary faucet as well. Watching me gape at her old sink, Karen reports, "this is where Dawn takes a bath." I wonder what the bathroom will look like.

Karen offers to walk me around the house, starting with Dawn's bedroom at the back. A cheerful blue, it has been recently painted, and framed, hand-painted illustrations from children's books hang on the walls. I go closer to look at them. Three of them are signed by Karen Haskins and dated 2000, 2002 and 2008. One is a frog with a whimsical expression on its face and up-tilted eyebrows. Another features two young children, balancing on rocks as they cross a forest stream. The third depicts a cocky blue jay with an exaggerated black crest and a sack slung over its back. Each of them depicts confidence, originality and lovely color. I note quickly that the bed is a single mattress on the floor, and that there is no chest of drawers, just a row of plastic bins with a few articles of clothing folded and stacked in them. The room has no closet.

"From your books?"

Karen nods, obviously pleased by my attention to her illustrations.

"They're beautiful – and quite original. Are you working on another now?"

"Yes, I'll show you later. Here's my room." Karen backs out of Dawn's room into the one across from it. It too has been recently painted, an egg-yolk yellow. An antidote to her depression, I think. Karen's bed has an old metal frame, painted white, and a well-made wedding ring quilt laid over the top. This room has a small closet, its door open, and I can see a child's green jacket hanging alongside a few adult shirts and jackets and one or two dresses. In this room there is an unfinished pine chest of drawers with a lace runner over the top and a carved wooden box sitting on top of it. Also clean lace curtains over the windows, through which I catch a glimpse of an old outhouse in the back yard, an archetypal half moon on its door.

We walk back to the front room, which has no wall separating it from the kitchen behind it. This room has not been painted, and its planked walls are a weathered gray. Karen has arranged it such that a large brown corduroy sofa flanks one wall and a pink, child-sized upholstered chair and brown easy chair sit up against the adjacent wall. An old triangular table higher than the top of the child's chair rests in the corner, stacked with books. A lamp made from the stump of a small tree sits on top of it. In the center of the room is a square dining table with an oilskin tablecloth and two wooden chairs tucked into the sides opposite the other furniture in the room.

"Where do you write and paint?" I ask.

"At that table. That's why there's oilskin on it now. I was painting earlier this morning, before you came. When I'm writing, I put my laptop on this table."

"Where's your television?" I realize I hadn't seen one.

"I don't have one, never did." Karen shrugs. "If I want to watch movies, I watch on my computer." I don't think I've ever met anyone who didn't have a television.

"May I use your bathroom before we go?" I ask.

Karen hesitates. "Well, you have a choice. There's the one out back," and she points to the outhouse, "or you can use the one down the hall, but it doesn't have a floor right now, so you have to be really careful." Karen's look makes this a test of my character.

It takes a nanosecond for me to choose the indoor bathroom. An old toilet sits on struts, as does the sink next to it, and the under-flooring lays about three inches below. I balance on two of the floor struts and close the door behind me, shaking my head in disbelief. *Did this woman even think a child custody evaluator would allow a child to live here?* I have to do a delicate turn on the two-by-four struts before I can let myself down onto the toilet. The toilet paper roll sits atop the back of the toilet. There is no paper holder on the wall, and a towel hangs by a nail next to the sink. *How could she live like this?*

"You have to get that fixed." I tell Karen as soon as I come out of the bathroom. "No court evaluator will let a child live in a house with no working bathroom."

"It does work," she starts to say but catches my look.

"Okay, okay," she says, but I think I catch a glimpse of Karen rolling her eyes before she turns her head away. I decide I should leave it alone until we are back in the office, but I can't.

"How does Dawn manage with that toilet?"

"Usually we use the outhouse." Karen looks back to catch my shocked expression.

"What if she has to go to the bathroom in the night?" I ask in disbelief.

"She wakes me and we go out together with a flashlight. Or she uses the chamber pot."

"You're joking." I hope.

"Only partly. She hates the chamber pot and likes the adventure of the outhouse," Karen says casually as we leave the house without locking the door. She stuffs two water bottles, a floppy hat and a towel into a backpack and we leave in my white Subaru. I notice she is walking with only a slight limp, and no brace.

"How's your knee? You seem to be walking much better." She nods and holds up her walking sticks for me to see.

"This car is really clean," Karen notes, looking around it admiringly. "It's going to need a bath after our trip today."

I shrug. "That's what car washes are for."

Karen gives me helpful, unobtrusive directions to the river as we wind through fields and then down a steep narrow dirt road to the river. There are so many pot-holes, I worry about my car's suspension. But I say nothing, blaming myself for this adventure.

I park at the trailhead. Karen slides out of the passenger side, dons the floppy hat, grabs her walking sticks and flings the backpack over her shoulder before I can even fetch my own backpack from the back seat. She waits, amused, as I fit myself with my own backpack. Others arrive at nearly the same time, locals wearing shorts and dusty hiking boots, or water sandals, surrounded by their various unruly dogs. Is there anyone up here except Karen who doesn't have a dog?

A muddy black mongrel with a blunt, aggressive nose butts my backpack. Instinctively, I back away, but that only encourages the invader as he presses with more assurance at the bottom of the backpack, then sticks his head into my crotch. "Go away," I order, pushing away his wet neck. Its owner, smirking, calls his dog back to his side, and the mongrel trots instead toward a pair of border collies sitting next to the young woman with them, stirring them into a trio of sniffers, each with its nose at the other's rear end. I take out a handy-wipe and clean my hands with it, then stuff it into a pocket of the backpack. Karen suggests we wait until the other hikers have gone ahead a bit.

A cat would never act this way, I know, barging into a stranger's intimate parts and demanding a sniff. A cat would take its time to assess a stranger, approaching aslant, and maybe glide next to a leg to test whether the stranger will welcome it. You have to know a cat pretty well before it will trust you with the barest contact with its nose. I love the self-sufficiency of cats and resent the rude, bumping dependency of dogs on contact, contact, contact. Dogs need to be walked, bathed and cleaned up after, while cats can do everything themselves. I've always wondered about my neighbors who trail their dogs in the morning, plastic bags in hand, bending over to collect their steaming turds as if collecting relics of a sacred being.

A crooked, low-leaning branch obscures the trailhead, but Karen knows where the trail begins and holds the branch to one side while I pass. When she releases it, it springs back like a screen door. Karen strides ahead with the familiarity of home ground, barely a limp in her gait. "There should be a patch of wild ginger up here soon," she predicts and then kneels before some heart-shaped leaves. "Under here," she points, "is the flower."

"Can you use it for cooking?" I ask as she bends down obligingly to show me.

"I never thought of it," Karen replies.

I wonder to myself why anyone would be interested in some obscure brown bowl of a flower hidden on the ground. But I like the brisk pace that Karen sets on the trail, even limping slightly, and want to get some exercise today because I hadn't run this morning and it will be too hot by the time I get back to Sacramento.

Unfortunately for me, the woods are full of wildflowers, and Karen stops to admire them and explain something about each one to me. "See this one?" Karen points to a small pink head of blossoms. "That's twining brodiaea. It finds some other plant to cling to and twines itself around the other plant's stem."

"Uh-huh," I acknowledge, barely, and swat away the insects crowding my face.

After a while, Karen still bends to admire each new flower she sees, but no longer bothers to explain them to me. But she warns me to watch out for poison oak. That, I assure her, I recognize.

The trail winds alongside the Yuba River, at first just above it, its flow sloshing noisily; but then gradually we climb and the river becomes a ribbon of gold-flecked green below us. At times, the edge of the trail is a cliff; at others, the woods slope more gradually, hiding the river. I notice Karen cringe slightly at the cliff sides and walk on the inside edge. Heights don't bother me.

What has begun as a warm day becomes sweltering. I feel the sweat running down the front of me and my head begins to ache. I have no hat. I pull a bottle of water from my backpack and drink nearly half of the bottle. How much farther, I want to ask, but don't. Karen gives me her hat, saying she is more used to the heat. I take it gratefully and gradually feel stronger. When Karen bends down to look at yet another wildflower, I step around her and go on ahead.

The heat is unrelenting, even with Karen's hat. I keep my eyes down and focus on plodding one foot in front of the other. As I round a sharp curve in the path, I nearly trip over the black dog that had so ingratiated itself with me at the trailhead.

It barks fiercely, and I jump back. Barking repeatedly, it stands directly in front of me but facing the other way. When the barking pauses, I think I hear a dry rattling, like seeds in a husk. The dog backs toward me a little, and I back up to the edge of the curve in the path. The dog growls, its tail pointed and twitching. Finally, I can see what has caused the alarm: a large rattlesnake lies curled in the center of the trail, its tail buzzing with irritation. I might have walked right into it but for the dog, which is now backing up further.

Its owner appears from around another curve ahead of them on the trail, calling "Ranger."

"Careful!" I call to him. "There's a rattlesnake. On the path."

"I see it," the man calls back. He grabs a long stick and comes toward the snake with it. I back up further and call for Ranger to come. The dog comes to me and sits at my side. I pat its head tentatively, my heart still pounding. The dog's owner pokes at the snake from behind, forcing it to turn around. I fear it will strike at him. Instead, it slithers off the path, down the hill. The man comes back to where Ranger sits beside me. He kneels and hugs his dog, lavishing "good boy" on him repeatedly.

"He was amazing," I say gratefully.

Karen catches up with me at this point. I explain how the dog had saved me from the rattlesnake. Karen shakes her head, smiling.

"I was wondering why you were suddenly best friends with the dog."

9

KAREN

As soon as we finish stumbling down the hill to the river, Analee strips off her boots and hiking socks. She wears full wool hiking socks, and I want to ask her if she thought this would be some scene from "Wild." Next come the buttons to her pants; I hold my breath and look away. I am not prepared to see my lawyer naked. I take off my own shoes and glance again in her direction. She is wearing a swimsuit, a simple black one like swimmers who race. Blaming my own lack of planning, I have no suit. But I can feel the sweat running down the center of my chest, and there is no way I will not go into the river, so I just wade in and flop into the cool water in my clothes, which will dry before we clamber back up the hill to the trail. I kick my way toward the edge of the pool where the current runs and allow myself to drift a little downstream, before I swim back to where our shoes are. I feel good to be able to use my knee without pain. I glance back and see that Analee has found a big flat rock on the opposite shore where she lies in the full sun. I swim back to join her, pulling myself up onto a slab near her, but not without slipping back into the water first. She lends me her arm to hoist me up, but I get up on the second try without her help.

"This is heaven," she pronounces as soon as I have settled my body onto the rock.

I just lie back and smile, glad to hear the real appreciation in her voice. I hope she can just lie here and listen to the gurgle of the river and the occasional birdsong. But silence does not appear to be her style.

"Do you take Dawn here?"

"Not yet. It's too far and too steep for her to walk, and there are easier access points down river near where we parked."

"Does she like the river?"

"Loves it. Patty gave her swimming lessons about a year ago in a pool, but she likes the river better. She gets excited when she sees fish. She wants to follow them."

"My boys don't like to swim where there are fish. Spooked by them, I guess. Crazy. My husband tries to take them into the Sacramento River, but they won't go in beyond their knees. He says we should be glad we have kids who aren't likely to drown by being daredevils."

"Do you agree?"

"No. When I'm with them, I dare them to follow me, but they refuse. I drive my husband nuts that way."

I laugh with recognition. If I had her kids, I'd do the same.

"How old are they?"

"Alex is six and Andy is four, the same age as Dawn."

"I have sandwiches in my pack. Can I lure you back to the other side?"

Analee is in the water practically before I finish the question, and beats me easily back to the other shore.

"I'm starving," she announces as she hauls a miniature towel out of her pack, wipes off her face, then her legs and feet. Then she unrolls her shirt from her backpack, puts it on and buttons it. She seems to do all this before I have even removed the sandwiches and oranges from my pack.

"They're egg salad. I hope that's okay with you."

She is ahead of me again, biting greedily into hers. I notice a small clot of it fall onto the mound of her belly but say nothing.

"There's dill in here; I love that." A momentary pause while she chews. "My mother always used to add fresh dill from the garden to our egg salad." More chewing. Then her face takes on a curious look.

"Is your mother still alive? I know a little about your father, but nothing about your mom."

I bristle.

"Am I being interviewed?" As soon as I hear the barb in my question, I regret it. A glance at Analee's face reveals hurt, before she recovers. She pauses a moment, as I do too, my apology too slow in coming.

"I'm sorry," she says, "if I'm overstepping my bounds. I always ask a lot of questions, and sometimes in social conversation they're rude. No, I'm not interviewing you and you don't owe me an answer."

I still can't talk, my throat suddenly thick. I fumble my hold on my own sandwich and almost drop it into the sand.

"No, I should apologize to you. My mom has Alzheimer's and is in a residential facility, has been for over six years."

"That must be tough." She leaves it at that and I don't add anything more. I change the subject.

"What are your boys like? -- if you don't mind my asking."

Analee gives me a broad smile. "Andy -- the younger one -- is a total eccentric, eats only red and green food, and helps me in the garden. He's got his own little tomato garden, in the raised beds we have behind our home. He knows the difference between Early Girls and Genovese and favors an obscure species called Lakota Black, which we found at our local farmers' market a year ago. He and I are the family foodies. Alex is a budding scientist, always building space stations or rocket launchers." What she says makes me suddenly grateful for my own child, her predilections so compatible with my own. I want to ask her how it is like for her as a parent, but know I shouldn't, after the way I cut her off about my own mother.

From her first step on my porch this morning, I have felt she was judging me. "Welcome to the boondocks," was my way of greeting her, and her tentative step onto my front porch and look around told me that's what she was thinking. Of course, it only got worse when she saw my bathroom and heard me talk about Dawn preferring the outhouse. I had told the old man who owned my house that the bathroom needed fixing, but he has never gotten around to it and we have just adapted to the unfinished floor.

When she looked at my illustrations on the walls, she asked me if all of my stories were for girls. No one has ever asked me that before. Rather than answering the question, I rummaged into the old suitcase where I keep copies of "Cleo and the Leopard" and gave her one for her boys.

"Here's one I hope your boys might like; it's about animals." I asked Analee their names and inscribed it to Alex and Andy.

From the way Analee looked up at me when she thanked me, I had the impression she'd never received an autographed book before. Maybe she wasn't even a reader herself.

We are going to have to get used to each other.

10

ANALEE

I don't like going to court unprepared. Two weeks earlier, I had phoned two separate colleagues in Nevada County and asked them about Judge Hobson, who has been assigned to our case. Each of them told me that Judge Hobson is an experienced family law judge and that he really cares about families. They couldn't tell me whether "really cares about families" means he would favor a two-parent guardian family over a single parent. At least he knows the law, which is unhelpfully broad – whether it is in the child's best interest to terminate the guardianship.

Karen's sister has hired a lawyer in Sacramento who, I know, has never handled a guardianship before. Geraldine Hennefer - she is elegant on her feet, a master at insinuation and surprise, unreliable, and inclined toward the 'gotcha' style of lawyering. She appears on nearly every larger case I have had, and each turns nasty. Her responsive declaration, served on the last hour of the deadline day, regales how well adjusted 'little Dawn' is in Patty and Doug's home and in her preschool, voices Patty's doubts about Karen's recovery since her hospitalization, and implies that Karen is dependent on anti-depressants or other drugs. I've arranged for Karen to be available on the day after the response was due, so that we could pound out a reply debunking Patty's allegations. "I took Paxil for seven months, and I've been off it now for over a year," she reports calmly. We filed our reply on time.

The hearing is set for 8:30 on a Monday morning in mid-July, and Karen has offered to let me stay at her home the night before. The thought of trying to shower and dress in that shack of hers is too awful to imagine, so I get up early and am on the road to Nevada City before seven, arriving as the courthouse doors are being unlocked at eight o'clock.

Judge Hobson's department is still locked when I arrive, but the docket shows only two matters on the calendar, and ours is the first. Karen arrives a few minutes after me. I am relieved to see her dressed appropriately. I'd told her to dress like a successful writer and illustrator of children's books at a book reading. "Cornflower Blue," that old Kate Wolf song, comes to mind – it is the color of her short-sleeved dress, tied at the waist in the back. It masks her extreme thinness.

But she paces and darts about maddeningly, going to the bathroom twice in the twenty minutes we wait for the doors to open, twiddling her hair and swinging her leg while she tries to sit, jumping up and asking me extraneous questions. This is usually my time to calm myself, empty my own mind and prepare it for the myriad of unexpected challenges that can arise in any hearing. I would be a better lawyer if I could be sociable at this time, calming my client with patter and assurances that everything will go well.

Patty and her lawyer march in like a small armada, their high heels echoing in unison on the stone floors, Geraldine's paralegal flanking them with the file in hand. Geraldine's paralegal is well known in Sacramento courts; she sits at counsel table and takes all the notes. I glance at Karen to see how she greets Patty. Seated on the bench, she looks away.

"Good morning, Gerry," I say as she approaches, knowing she doesn't like to hear her shortened name in front of clients. She introduces me to Patty, who shakes my hand firmly and says, "Good morning, counsel," as if playing lawyer for the day.

I introduce Geraldine to Karen, who, to my relief, stands up and says 'hello' politely. She mutters 'hello' to her sister, not meeting her eye. Patty may or may not have heard her. She looks past Karen's head and turns away without greeting her sister. Patty looks like a shorter and more well fed and well dressed version of Karen, with eye makeup.

The courtroom doors are finally opened at eight forty, ten minutes after the hearing was to have begun. Country time, I think to myself, but the clerk explains apologetically that Judge Hobson is ill and we have a visiting judge from Sierra County, Judge Shottell, I thought she said. So that's why there are only two matters on calendar: all the locals knew and had already continued their matters to another day to avoid the visiting judge. This is just the kind of unknown that makes it unwise for a city lawyer like me to travel to an unfamiliar small county. How did I get myself into this?

As soon as I see the judge, I wonder if I should seek a postponement. His face hangs like a granite cliff with everything below his ponderous brow having cleaved away centuries ago. His eyes hide under the shadow of his brow, and only when he looks up is their intensity revealed. I try unsuccessfully to read the nameplate on his desk as I recite my appearance.

"Good morning, Judge...."

"Shotkill." I quail. He looks up and the granite cracks on his face. He smiles disarmingly. "It works well at sentencing hearings. Don't let it deter you."

"Thank you, your Honor." I marvel that he is trying to put me at ease.

I begin to explain my motion as a routine step, to end a guardianship begun as a temporary measure, now that my client has fully recovered from her illness. My client had responsibly asked her sister to care for her daughter when she became ill, and now it is obvious that she has fully recovered and Dawn should come back home. I have submitted with my papers a declaration from Karen's treating psychiatrist that he had overseen her since the beginning of her hospitalization and there was now no reason she could not resume care of her own daughter.

"I've read the file," the judge tells me curtly. He turns to Geraldine.

"How often has Ms. Haskins been visiting her daughter?"

"For the first six months after she was hospitalized, she came every Saturday for a few hours. After that, it was every weekend."

"How long on the weekends?"

Geraldine looks toward Patty, who interjects, "Friday afternoon to Sunday at five."

Judge Shotkill directs the clerk to swear both parties as witnesses. He begins to question Patty directly.

"And does Dawn spend the weekends at her mother's home?"

"Yes."

His questions come at rapid fire. Was Karen faithful in visiting every weekend? Did Karen handle all of the pick-ups and drop-offs? Was Dawn happy to see her mother? Did Dawn come back from the visits with any problems? If Patty was concerned about Karen's use of drugs, had she ever asked Karen what drugs she was taking? Had she ever come to inspect Karen's home? Had she ever asked Karen to consult with her doctors about her recovery?

He is doing my cross-examination for me, and draws out of Patty better, shorter, more helpful answers than I could because he is far more intimidating. I can't see Patty's face because Geraldine sits between her and me, but I can hear her faltering voice.

"Your Honor," Geraldine begins.

"I'm not finished," Judge Shotkill pronounces, and Geraldine sits down abruptly while he continues his blunt questioning and Patty continues to make my case.

"Now," he says, directing his attention to Geraldine, "do you have any direct evidence whatsoever that Ms. Haskins is not fit to resume full-time parenting of her daughter?" It comes out as a pronouncement, no inflection of a question.

"Your Honor, fitness is not the appropriate legal standard. This court's task is to determine whether it would be in Dawn's best interest to remain in my client's intact family or to disrupt that routine by returning to Ms. Haskins' custody."

"I find," he looks up so that his eyes come out of their shadow and penetrate downward at Geraldine, "that Dawn's best interests are served by her returning to her mother's full-time care. The guardianship is terminated, effective today." Turning to me, he asks if I have prepared an order.

"It's attached to my moving papers, your Honor."

He signs it, hands it to the clerk to stamp it filed, and she hands it back to me. In the half-minute it takes for him to pronounce and sign the order, Geraldine has neglected to ask for visitation rights. I hurriedly pack up my papers while the judge calls the next matter and gesture for Karen to follow me out of the courtroom.

Karen practically flies at me once we get out of the courtroom. Hugging me with those wiry arms of hers, she breathes into my ear, "You're my hero."

"It's better than I'd hoped for. I'm happy for you and Dawn. I need to go to the clerk's office and get this order filed." The judge could have put it over for an evaluation and a trial. I get professionally nervous when everything falls in my favor in court, but I don't want to ruin her moment by telling her. "We need to work out the logistics for you to pick up Dawn."

Glancing down the hall at Geraldine, I can see she is doing damage control with Patty. At one point I hear Geraldine tell Patty to keep her voice down.

"I never expected this to happen today," Karen confesses. "I don't even have groceries in the house." I suggest that she put her house in order today and pick up Dawn tomorrow. I think it will also give Patty a chance to simmer down, pack up Dawn's things and create an orderly transfer. Karen readily agrees.

Looking back on it – as I have so many times since -- I wish I hadn't rushed out of the courtroom before the judge could grant visitation rights to Patty.

I ask Karen to stay on the bench while I go down the hall to talk with Geraldine. I walk noisily toward them to alert her and ask if I can speak with her. She gives me the only unguarded, beleaguered look I'd ever seen on her face. "Excuse me, Patty," she said as she followed me to a place out of earshot of both of our clients.

"Well, that was unexpected!" She laughs ruefully. "I should have disqualified him."

"When I heard 'Shotkill' I thought of doing it myself," I tell her to soften the blow. I propose that Karen pick up Dawn the next afternoon to allow her time to say goodbye and pack up Dawn's things.

"Thank you," she says as if she means it and walks back to Patty to arrange the details.

I file the order and return to where Karen sits. She has wiped her eyes and collected herself.

"You know, you hardly had to say anything at all. The judge did everything. I might have overpaid you." I take it as a good sign that she is able to tease me.

"Good preparation," I say, with mock smugness.

When Geraldine returns, she agrees that Karen can pick up Dawn at two the next afternoon. I shake her hand, and we all say goodbye.

On the drive back to my office, I turn on Bruce Springsteen and sing at the top of my lungs. I have a terrible voice and only sing when I'm alone in the car. When the CD ends, I start to rethink the morning's events. It has gone too well. The judge had nearly used the wrong legal standard, which would have given Patty a good appeal. But he did have evidence to support his ruling. Still, with Geraldine on the other side, something else is likely to happen unless Karen can pacify Patty. I decide to call Karen when I get back to the office to make sure she is diplomatic with Patty in the transition. I will encourage her to arrange for Patty to be able to visit with Dawn.

But I have a new client appointment, several calls from distressed clients, and then a tricky negotiation with another lawyer over child support that had us at our computers comparing guideline calculations for nearly an hour. I forget to call Karen.

11

KAREN

I am afraid to look up at this fearsome judge. But when I hear him say, "the guardianship is terminated," I can't help myself and my eyes lock with his for just a second. I see understanding. I see compassion. I wonder for a second whether he has ever stumbled in his life. I want to sit there a moment longer and bask in this understanding, but Analee is antsy to get out of the courtroom.

I walk out of the courtroom in such a strange state that I forget my case folder on the table. The bailiff comes out and hands it to me very nicely, as if it were a diploma.

Dawn is coming home! I am suddenly in a surge of joy. I throw my arms around Analee to thank her, but her body feels solid and unmoved. I can't even tease her into joy. She asks me to wait until tomorrow afternoon to pick up Dawn. I've waited this long; I can wait one more day. I will fill the house with flowers, I am so happy.

I have no memory of driving home from court. But then I am parked in front of my house and I realize I should have stopped for groceries on the way home. I don't feel like grocery shopping at this moment. I'm too amped. I just want to celebrate. I call Megan on my cell, but I get only her voicemail message. Then I call Jenny, with the same result. I leave each of them a message that practically screams my joy and asks her to call me as soon as she can. I fish around in my bag for my house key and can't find it. Instead of getting frantic as I might on other days, I try the door and it's unlocked; my keys are on the kitchen table. Tossing off my shoes at the door and walking into Dawn's room, I want to make it perfect. I want to make her as happy as I am. In twenty-some hours, I'll be able to nuzzle her sweet little neck and welcome her home.

In my bare feet, I feel how dusty the floors are. I should scrub all the floors of the house. They'll be clean and sweet-smelling, and I'll burn off some of this energy. Time to buy Dawn a real bed and a dresser for her clothes.

I should sit down and collect my thoughts about what to do for the next day, but I am too antsy, so I change out of my one good dress, put on my jeans and hiking shoes and take off down the path behind my house. Euphoria – when's the last time I'd felt euphoric? I know the bottom range of the emotional register, not the top. But I do remember feeling something like this when I took Dawn home from the hospital. Right after she emerged I was in some altered state, exhausted and just anxious to know she was okay. But when I walked out of the hospital I wanted to yell, "I'm a mother!" Patty was there too, of course; she drove me home. She was as excited as I was, but she practically had to pry Dawn out of my arms to put her into the car seat. "You have to face it backwards for the first six months," she taught me. Dawn was so tiny we had to stuff padding all around her so that she fit snugly into the car seat.

I did it! I did it! I am saying it out loud now, but I was also saying it in my head that day we drove her home. Patty wondered why I wasn't talking on the way home, but my heart and veins were so full of emotion I couldn't even string words together. Meanwhile she babbled on about sterilizing bottles, making sure to burp the baby over my shoulder and holding Dawn's head when I bathed her. I wasn't really listening; the doctor had explained most of that to me and, besides, I was intent on nursing rather than on using formula. I don't know if she'd assumed I couldn't nurse because I'd borrowed her eggs or because I'm so small or because she herself had felt uncomfortable about nursing. "It made me feel aroused," she'd admitted years earlier when Sandra was born, and nursing had given her a bad conscience. But her way wasn't my way, and I couldn't wait to get home and have her leave us alone.

Of course, soon after she left and I put Dawn to my swollen little tit, I fell into a panic. Dawn sucked so hard that my nipple began to bleed. I flinched and she let go, but started to wail inconsolably. She cried so much I thought the neighbors would report me to Children's Protective Services. I offered it to her again. She clamped down again and I tried not to wince as she sucked and sucked without yielding anything but tears for us both. But the next morning, after she started to suck, I felt the most amazing surge in my breast. The milk came in like many rivulets flowing downhill after a hard rain, and I could feel the flow. It still hurt, but I was ecstatic, and so was Dawn. Her face transformed into placid contentment.

Today feels almost as good as if my milk had come in again. Tomorrow afternoon she'll be back for good, and we'll find again that perfect responsiveness to each other. Maybe I'll take her down to the river, in that shallow, slow place near the bridge that doesn't require a long hike. I'll cook macaroni and cheese, her favorite dish, just the way she likes it, with mild cheddar and sundried tomatoes. By the time I get back to the house, I have a mental grocery list and plan for the perfect first afternoon. After the river, we'll stop in town for ice cream and a new book.

I leave early to avoid any problems. I've emptied the trunk of my car to make room for Dawn's clothing and toys. In an excess of efficiency, I've even washed the car, hauling the hose around from the back of the house, uncoiling the kinks, and spraying off weeks of accumulated dust.

I've cleaned the closets, all two of them in the house, the one that serves as a makeshift pantry in the kitchen and the one in my room that holds both Dawn's and my clothes and shoes. The pantry disgorged a three-year old box of baby formula and some other foodstuffs with ancient use-by dates, which I threw out. The closet yielded up a small cache of five-year-old condoms that I took straight out to the garbage, a couple of my dresses and a college sweatshirt I never expected to wear again, and sandals that Dawn had outgrown by the end of last summer, which I put into a Goodwill box. I feel so *ready.*

Not ten miles down the road, I see a red light flash on my dashboard, like a capital U with its sides bulging and an exclamation mark in the middle. I slow down. A squirrel darts out in front of the car, stops, runs forward and then backward, before running out of my way just in time. Nothing feels abnormal; my red lights have never gone on before. What does this one mean? It looks vaguely like a tire, but I am not sure of the symbols. I pull over to the side of the road and walk around looking at my tires, which seem normal to me. I decide to check the manual that I store in the trunk of my car, only to find I'd removed it yesterday along with the spare tire, in my zeal to make room for Dawn. Should I go back to the house to get them? Is this some other emergency I am misinterpreting? I try to call Megan on my cell phone but stop before I finish dialing; I remember she has rehearsals today. Should I drive to the Toyota shop in Roseville? Go to the local garage, now about five miles back up the road? Return home for the spare tire and the manual? Any choice will make me late.

Gaping into the empty space of my trunk, I come undone. First tears, then sobs rip from me. I collapse onto the trunk rim and heave sobs until my sides ache. I cannot be late today; the lawyers have negotiated the pickup time and I'm not supposed to call Patty. I am echoing Patty's judgment that I am incompetent and inadequate to the task.

Just sitting there will also make me late, I tell myself, and get back into the car to drive to the Toyota place in Roseville. But I have not gone a mile before I tell myself how busy they always are, and if this were really an emergency the car could break down on the way. So I make a U turn and head for the familiar garage in Grass Valley, where a sturdy young woman (*a woman, thank god!*) named Gemma comes out to ask if she can help me. I tell her about the red emergency light. After taking one look at it herself, she confirms that tires are the problem and walks around with the air gauge testing each one. "Here's the culprit," she pronounces, as she shows me a nail in my front right tire.

"I left the spare at home," I confessed.

"No worries; we can patch that." She vanishes into the garage and returns with a vial of glue and a small tool that resembles an oversized wine bottle opener. As soon as she pries out the nail, the tire hisses air, but she plugs it with what looks like a little rubber plug, surrounded by glue, at the tip of the bottle opener tool. She tops off the air pressure, shows me how to reset the red light, takes my fifteen dollars and waves me on my way. The whole process consumes no more than twenty minutes. Giving thanks for the resourceful women of my county, I am back on the road, speeding just a little to make up for my lost time.

Just outside Roseville, I notice a highway patrol car immediately behind me and instinctively lift my foot from the gas pedal. At seventy-two, I am at the speed of the other cars on the road. *Please don't,* I say to myself, and pull over one lane to the right. The patrol car passes without turning on its light. A second near miss. I shudder.

After all that negative prelude, I get to Roseville early and decide on a whim to bring ice cream for all three children – a cup of outrageously blue bubble gum for Ian, orange sherbet with vanilla for Sandra and chocolate for Dawn. Patty and I have bought ice cream with all the children together so many times that knowing their flavors is second nature. It will be my token goodwill gesture. I carry the three little cups stacked inside a freezer bag as I walk up to the front door. I can hear the children playing in the back yard; the swing squeaks and Ian calls "catch!" to one of the girls. In the old days I would have walked around the house to join them, but decide today I should ring the bell.

"I'll get it," Ian yells and runs around the side of the house.

"I *knew* it was you!" He comes at me as if about to tackle me, and throws his arms around my hips. I lean over to kiss him and tell him I have ice cream for him and the girls.

"What color?"

"Are you testing me? It's blue, of course." He grabs for the bag.

Sandra is on the swing, pumping as if for the sky. "Hi," she calls out half-heartedly.

"Ice cream!" Ian yells, holding up the bag. Sandra slows down and gets off the swing, not wanting to look too eager. She comes over to me as if forewarned that I am the enemy.

"Dawn and Mom are inside," she says, looking away from me. She takes her cup and its plastic spoon and walks over to the backyard table without saying another word to me.

"What's doin'?" I ask Ian, still at my side. He tells me about the birthday party he is going to later this afternoon, a swim party for his friend Dan, just turning six. I start to ask him more about the party when I glimpse the back door start to open. Patty walks out holding Dawn's hand, but I can only see Dawn's hand and her legs behind my sister.

"I got him a giant water gun," Ian tells me as I stand wondering why Dawn hasn't run over to greet me. "Pshew! Pshew! Pshew!" Ian yells, pumping his arm and spewing imaginary water from his gun as he twirls around me.

Finally Patty lets go of Dawn's hand. She walks toward me shyly. Her reticence is so out of whack that I am slow to notice what is odd about her head. Instead of the wild curly fluff that usually encircles her head, she has a short, straight bob. I blink and shake my head. "It's me," she says and wraps herself around me. I kneel down and hold her tight. "We're going home, sweetie," I whisper into her hair. It smells like the sort of spot remover you'd spray on a rug and bleach it for life. When I touch her head, it feels unnaturally smooth. I want to smell *her*, not this chemical on her head, and nuzzle her neck.

"You're coming home," I repeat. As good as she feels, I can't stifle a surge of anger.

"What did you do to her hair?" I yell at Patty, who stands with her hands on her hips, looking officious. Her posture alone infuriates me.

"It *hurt* her…. Every time I combed her hair, it hurt her." She speaks slowly, accusingly. "So I took her to the hairdresser's to get it professionally cut and straightened." She stands defiantly. "There's some product you should put on her hair every five weeks or so, when it starts to curl up again. I packed it in her bag."

"*Product!* On Dawn's hair?" A tornado swirls inside me. "How could you touch… *my*… daughter's hair – without even asking me? What about her curls? You *ruined* her hair – can't you see that?"

Dawn starts to cry. She wilts at my feet, but I am so furious I walk away from her to confront Patty.

"When did you do this?" I practically spit in her face.

Patty turns her back to me and returns to the house. "I'll put her bag into the car," she announces coolly. I stand glaring at the door for a long minute before turning around slowly. Sandra sits at the table looking down at her ice cream. Ian hands Dawn her cup of ice cream but she isn't taking it. She lies curled on the ground.

"I don't want to be ugly," she moans, as I lean over to pick her up. She hides her head on my chest and snuffles into my shirt. Ian stands next to us, the ice cream cup indented in his hand and dribbling melted chocolate over his thumb. "It happened yesterday," he tells me softly. "She was worried you wouldn't like it," he explains, putting his own free hand on her shoulder.

"Honey, I love you. Stop crying. You're the most beautiful little girl I ever saw." Dawn is limp in my arms. "You'll get your curls back, don't worry." She starts to cry harder, hiccupping in my arms.

I carry her to the car, put her into the child seat in the back and ask her to wait for me. I go to the front door to have some more words with Patty, but she has locked it. She stands in the window next to the door, staring at me coldly.

"I won't forget this. You bitch!" I yell through the door.

When I get back to the car I see only one small suitcase in the back seat.

"Where are your toys?" I ask Dawn, in not the best tone of voice.

"In the house," she mumbles. "Aunt Patty told me I needed to leave them there 'til I get back."

"Get back!" I yell. "She'll be lucky if she ever sees you again!" At which she starts to cry again. I start to get out of the car to go to her side to comfort her again, but I see Patty in the window watching us. I gun the engine, skidding on the gravel as I pull out of her driveway, and speed down the block.

Dawn cries quietly all the way home. Every time I glance back at her, I catch sight of what Patty has done to her hair, and I get furious again. As many times as I said to myself I would not let Patty poison my time with Dawn, I cannot find a place in me to comfort my daughter.

Finally, as I open the door for her and she stands before me, I kneel down, wipe her eyes and nose with some Kleenex, and tell her I love her more than anything, no matter what Patty did to her hair. I suddenly remember something, and begin to giggle.

"Remember, a year or two ago, when Sam dyed her hair purple, how mad Megan got?" Dawn begins to smile. She takes my hand and we walk into our house together. Together we unpack her tiny suitcase and put her clothing into the bins in her room. We agree it's time to get her a dresser for her room, and a proper bed. We'll drive to Ikea's and she can choose them herself.

"I want white ones," she pronounces. Her dresser at Patty's was white.

"We'll find you a white one, if that's what you want." I can do this.

We make our ritual trip to the outhouse, and eat strawberries together. I pick the greens off hers but don't bother for myself. She asks for one with the leaves still on, and I pick one with no stem and a tiny span of leaves. After chewing it carefully, she asks me to take the greens off the next ones.

A bit later, in the middle of our simple dinner, she asks me why Aunt Patty 'did this' to her hair.

I put down my fork. "She said you cried when she combed your hair and she wanted to make it easier for you." I use every bit of will power not to ask what Patty has told her.

"I think she wanted to make you mad." She looks at me searchingly.

"Well, she succeeded." I begin to laugh, and she does too. "I am so sorry I hurt your feelings. I wasn't mad at you."

After I wash the dishes, she comes out of her room with the can of 'product' in her hand.

"Can I throw this away?"

"Only if you want to."

She tosses it into the garbage.

Within a week, my euphoria gives way to practical concerns. I am used to carrying on an internal conversation of 'rationing resources' whenever significant expenses arise, but now I am really, truly responsible for two of us in a way I have not been since Dawn's first year. She and I have picked out and assembled her new white dresser, and the bed frame is to arrive soon. While her room takes on an orderly and cheerful new aspect, my finances do not. My royalties have fallen off without new books in the pipeline, and my 'time out of life' in the hospital and rehab (as my therapist and I reframed it) interrupted the flow of books from me. I am not quite finished with a new book, and I have irregular income from illustrations. I phone my agent to ask about new assignments for illustrations, and she says she will try, but that my best opportunities depend on my publishing a new illustrated book of my own. When I first told her about it, she liked the idea and 'couldn't wait' to see it. She thought "Where Does the Ketchup Grow?" would be a clever title and concept. Now that

I am one or two illustrations short of sending it to her, she seems dubious that it even exists.

Dawn gave me the idea for this book. A year or so ago, we were driving past a brilliantly yellow field of mustard in flower. "Look, honey, it's a field of mustard in bloom." She glanced searchingly at the bright yellow field and asked me where the ketchup grows.

I have painted several fields of tomatoes but haven't yet been able to convert this into a field of ketchup fit for four-year-olds. I need time to finish the book. Since Dawn too loves to paint – and I now have my idea for the concluding illustrations – I should be able to finish and send off the book before school starts. Ketchup starts as tomatoes, but it 'grows' in the kitchen. I will make that happen.

In ten days she will start kindergarten in Grass Valley, at the same school where I will teach art to the older students. I wish we were both back in Nevada City, but I can't afford to move back now. She and I are each excited about her starting school.

When I registered Dawn for kindergarten in Grass Valley, I asked if the school might have an opening for an art teacher. With luck, I find myself with an art teaching assignment for grades two through five, three days a week. I will have a small, predictable salary within a month, and my workday will end only a short time after her school day, with free day care for her. She and I shop for school clothes at the second-hand children's store in Nevada City, and she picks out her own boldly colored array of leggings, skirts and tops. She dresses herself these days, with a combination of patterns and colors that Patty would never have permitted. Even I try to tell her some combinations clash, but she insists on her own choices.

I worry about finding friends for her, since Megan's daughter Sam and Jenny's sons are much older than Dawn, but they adopt each other, and I rationalize that with school starting soon, she will find new friends her own age. She asks about Ian several times, but I am vague about when she might see him again.

12

KAREN

People say that fear crouches in the pit of one's stomach. Not so for me. Fear clenches my chest, so tightly that I have to steal tiny, shallow breaths from it.

I smelled smoke from the moment I awoke this morning. A pink haze coats the view outside my window. The treetops have a vague outline and the rising sun is a brilliant orange. From the local radio station I hear there are fires on the eastern slopes of the San Juan Ridge, not twenty miles from here. The fire updates are so frequent that music creates the intervals rather than the other way around. The air is hazardous from particulate smoke; children and seniors are to be kept inside. The radio is periodically drowned out by the over-flight of firefighting planes, which sound like WWII movie planes to me. There is no wind. That's good from a firefighting perspective, but we will have to live with this thick, gauzy air for a while.

Jenny lives up on the Ridge, not where the fires are, but still closer than we are. It's only eight by my watch, but I call her to invite her and the boys to spend the day with us down here. School has been canceled for today at least. She is already up and eager to leave. "The air here is nasty," she reports.

Dawn awakes with a different reaction. She's never seen pink air before and it's cotton candy to her. She is all delight, her nose pressing the window. It's been two months since I fetched her from Patty, and her hair has recovered its curl.

"Can I taste it?" she asks eagerly.

"Yes, just once so you know what it is, and then we need to stay inside. You won't like the taste."

We walk out to the moon house. "Ick!"

Breathing the air outside is like eating a mohair sweater in campfire smoke. I explain that there is a forest fire far away, that it will not come here but the air is very dirty and we need to stay inside. Jenny and the boys will come. We'll have an inside picnic.

After breakfast we paint. I have an assignment and Dawn loves to work, as she calls it. She has her own small easel. "Make it flat," she tells me as I set it up, "so the colors don't run." She already knows this about watercolors, and she knows how to mix her colors. She fetches her own bowl of water while I adjust her easel.

"How do you make pink?"

"Add water to the red."

When I hear the car door shut and the doorbell ring, I call out for Jenny to just come in, but it rings a second time.

A man I have never seen before stands at the door. My first thought is that he has been sent to tell us to evacuate because of the fire. But he is just a man in jeans with a manila envelope in his hand.

"Are you Karen Haskins?"

"Yes…" Before I can ask him anything, he thrusts the envelope at me. A rattlesnake tattoo coils around the arm with the envelope. He turns and leaves without another word.

I look down stupidly. The envelope is addressed to me, and it bears the logo of a Sacramento law firm. From working in high school at my dad's old law office, I guess that I have just been served with some legal papers. But I am afraid to find out what lies inside. I put the envelope on my bed.

When Dawn asks who it was, I tell her it was the mailman.

I sit down in front of my own easel. I can see my own sketches from the other day of the little boy on a big rock, leaning over the water. But I cannot paint. I feel as if I have just touched the wrong wire when I changed the ceiling light.

Dawn, on the other hand, is busy. She has created a pink wash over the entire sheet of paper.

"Can I paint on it while it's wet?"

"Sure, but everything will be fuzzy." That seems to please her, and she lays down bold strokes of brown tree trunks.

When the doorbell rings again, I jump, even as Jenny, Jonas and Gulliver stream into the room. Gulliver, who also likes to paint, immediately inspects Dawn's painting. "Cool!" Jonas carries a loaded grocery bag. "For our indoor picnic." And Jenny thrusts an iced coffee into my hand before giving me a hug.

After we get the children set up and the groceries put away, I pull Jenny into my bedroom.

"So what's up?" She knows me. I push the envelope toward her and tell her I think it's from Patty, but I'm afraid to look. I ask her to read it for me.

She stays in my bedroom while I go back out to the children. Jonas has set up a huge puzzle that looks too difficult for him, but he lets me join him and we look together for edge pieces. After what feels like a long time, I go back and check on Jenny, who sits on the bed with an odd expression on her face. She doesn't want to tell me whatever it is.

"Don't react when I tell you." I start to laugh, that insane kind of laugh that takes over at just the wrong moment.

I sit down next to her. She takes my left hand with hers.

"I don't understand all the legalese, but Patty is asking to be Dawn's mother."

Jenny doesn't mince words.

"That can't be," I say as I reach for the papers, but she puts them behind her back.

"If it's that bad, I'd better read it now while you're here." She hands them to me and leaves the room.

I think that from my one summer working in my dad's law office I know how to read legal papers, but what I read so stuns me that I almost can't see. Patty alleges that she is a second mother to Dawn based on her egg donation. That's what's in the petition, but there is also a request for order form seeking a hearing on custody – in one month! – and a declaration in Patty's own words that recites Dawn's genetic history, that I have no biological connection to this child, that I was hospitalized for depression and she had to care for Dawn for nearly two years, and, finally, that Dawn is not safe with me. I want to scream, but there are three children in the next room, and I must hold it together.

Jenny gives me a searching look as I return to the main room. I take her hand, and she wraps me into a hug. I cave in to the solace of her empathy, which wrings the anger out of me, but now I want to cry. I can't run outside because I have told the children we can't go out today, so I stand here trying to squelch my emotion.

Gulliver wants help with his painting, so Jenny releases me to see to him. "Call Analee," she whispers.

Still fortified by Jenny's hug, I go back into the bedroom and dial Analee from my cell phone. She had trounced Patty in that one short hearing, and I need her to tell me she can do it again. Only to learn from Gerta that Analee is in San Francisco for a five-day holiday, not to return until next Tuesday. I tell Gerta what I have received, and she responds that she has received a 'courtesy copy' of the same document this afternoon. She will tell Analee about it as soon as possible. Even she sounds abashed, as if someone had thrown a rock through the front window of her office. I ask how soon I can get an appointment with Analee, and she gives me a time on Wednesday morning when Dawn will be in school. Today is only Thursday, I don't know how I can wait. I ask if she can have Analee give me a call before Wednesday. She promises she will try. Then, she adds in a strong but caring voice (and I am stunned because she was so stern when I first met her) that this must be very hard, and she will try to get Analee to call me as soon as she can.

In the most peculiar of coincidences, KVMR is playing "Bridge Over Troubled Water" as I come back to the main room, and Jenny sings the refrain to me, "I will ease your mind."

Dawn's brown trees have bled into the pink background as predicted, but she has created an effect not unlike our day, when everything is seen through a thick haze. "It looks like today," I tell her, and she agrees, satisfied with herself. Gulliver has taken an entirely different approach, keeping his paper dry and creating a colorful bird with a long tail in precise brushstrokes.

13

ANALEE

I was just toasting Adam with a glass of sauvignon blanc, thinking this will be the perfect San Francisco getaway long weekend. We had dropped off the boys with Adam's parents this morning and got to the City in time for an extravagant lunch at Boulevard. In front of each of us sits a wide shallow bowl with seared scallops at the center. Our waiter is in the process of pouring lemon grass cucumber soup into Adam's bowl when my cell phone rings. The waiter casts me a dark look and Adam also glances at me quizzically, as if asking whether I can allow myself to be on vacation.

"It's from Gerta. She wouldn't call if it weren't important." Adam shrugs. The waiter looks down at me and asks me to take my call outside. Leaving my seat, I autodial Gerta as I move toward the front of the restaurant. "What's up?"

I can't hear her voice until I stand outside, facing the water across the Embarcadero. "Say it again."

"I wouldn't call you if it wasn't urgent, but Karen was just served with a parentage action from Patty, and she's come unglued. I think you need to talk to her."

"A parentage action?" I can't believe it. "Have you seen it?"

"Yes, we received our own copy from her lawyer. Patty claims that she is Dawn's genetic mother and seeks custody as Dawn's second mother."

"Oh, no." I start to rub my forehead with my one free hand.

"And she's hired a new lawyer, too – Stephen Petrakis."

"Huh. At least someone I can work with. But I can't believe she'd do this. I'm stunned. Can you fax the pleadings to me at the hotel? I don't have my computer with me."

"Sure. I'm sorry to ruin your weekend. But I'm glad you're going to call her. She needs to talk to you."

"Thanks, Gerta, for being on top of this. You did the right thing."

Adam hasn't touched his soup. "I saw you from the window. What's wrong?"

"You remember the woman I visited in Rough and Ready? The guardianship termination?"

"Yeah, I thought that was over."

"It was. But now her sister filed a parentage action, claiming she is the little girl's second mom. Because of the ovum donation, the little girl is her genetic child."

"I thought that only happened with same-sex couples."

"So far, that's been true."

"Taste this; it's out of this world." Adam tries to distract me. "It's amazing. I wonder what's in here besides lemon grass and cucumber."

"Do you think you could replicate this?" I ask him.

"I'm going to ask for the recipe, if our waiter is still on speaking terms with us. But I'm curious about this lawsuit. If the other woman wins, is her husband the child's father? Will the child have three parents?"

"I don't know which is weirder: a child with two mothers and one father/uncle or a child with two mothers, one of whom she always thought was her aunt."

"You presume this child understands what an aunt is."

"Good point. And I don't even know whether she's trying to replace my client as the mother. I don't think so, from what Gerta said. Also, she can't prove abandonment. But I need to read it before I call my client."

"So it sounds like I'm going to the MOMA by myself this afternoon, while you take care of this."

"'Fraid so. I'm sorry." I give him an apologetic look, but he can see I'm distracted.

"Constitutionally, can a child have one parent at birth and then the court designate another parent to replace her later if it's better for the child?" The legal question has bitten Adam, the constitutional law professor.

"Not without proof of abandonment. But can you add other parents later? Especially when that wasn't what was intended when the child was conceived?" I eat my soup between questions.

"Wasn't there a case like that?"

"Yeah, one of the three lesbian mom cases involved an ovum donation. I know they both ended up as parents but I can't remember the Supreme Court's reasons without going back to read it."

"I got it!" Adam holds a spoonful of soup in his mouth as if he is winetasting. "Lemon cucumber."

I laugh. "I bet you're right. Now if you can help me figure out the issues in this lawsuit as well as you did the soup…"

"We'll be cookin'."

By the time I return to the hotel, the package awaits me at the desk. I rip it open and read it quickly before even getting to the room. Then I sit down and read it again, as slowly as I can. The petition is as plain vanilla as such a thing can be. Patty alleges that she and Karen are Dawn's two parents – she genetically through her ovum donation and Karen by giving birth. She doesn't list her husband as another parent. But she has also filed a motion for access to the child, alleging in full detail how Karen had stormed out of the driveway with tires screeching, because she didn't like Dawn's haircut. Ever since then, Karen has prevented Patty from seeing Dawn, even though Dawn had lived with her and her husband and two children for over nineteen months. The supporting declaration makes Karen sound vindictive, a little crazy and certainly oblivious to Dawn's interests. No wonder Karen feels unhinged. I sat for a moment trying to organize my thoughts before calling Karen.

Karen answers somewhat breathlessly on the first ring. I can hear Dawn in the background, as if she is singing softly or reading.

"Karen, it's Analee. I'm so sorry to see what Patty has filed. Are you able to talk?"

"I have to talk to you. I'll go into the other room." Her voice rejoins after a moment, and I can no longer hear Dawn in the background. "Can she do this?" Her voice breaks.

"I'm afraid anyone can file a lawsuit. But this is really a strange one. You know how surprised I was when she didn't do anything after the guardianship termination? The court lost jurisdiction after sixty days to grant her visitation. So now this." I think but do not say that this might not have happened if Karen had allowed Patty to visit with Dawn, as I had urged her to do a few days after the hearing. I know I need to keep any blame out of my voice; it would only make matters much worse.

"But can she win?"

"I wish I could tell you that this lawsuit is nonsense and will be dismissed as soon as we ask the court to do that. But this is very strange new territory, and I can't give you that reassurance. I know of only one other case involving an ovum donor claiming to be a parent."

"What happened in that one?"

"The ovum donor was found to be the second legal parent. It was a lesbian couple who had lived together and reared the children together. I haven't read the decision in a few years, and I don't remember the court's reasoning. Obviously, I'll research it as soon as I get back."

"But that wasn't what we planned. She has children of her own. This child was supposed to be mine."

"You're right. And then a lot of other things happened that make this a tougher question. She's also filed a motion to have visitation rights. Are you willing to reconsider on that point?"

"No way! Not after she's done this to me. She doesn't deserve to see Dawn."

I can see it would be pointless for me to try to persuade her to do anything right now. I promise her I will research this as soon as I get back, and that we will sit down together and try to figure out what to do. I tell her I will call the other attorney and ask him to postpone the hearing a few weeks.

"Analee. Be straight with me: am I going to lose this? Am I going to have to share Dawn with Patty?"

"Karen. If I knew the answer, or even a likely answer, I would tell you straight out. But this is new territory. I can only promise you I'll do my best for you if you want me to represent you."

"How can I afford you? This sounds like it'll be expensive."

"We'll talk about that too."

I pace the hotel room for some time, grinding my memory for how I had neglected to make sure that Karen would maintain contact between Dawn and Patty and her family. Surely that haircutting fiasco should have been avoidable. How could I have managed this differently after that hearing? I remember how lucky I felt, how Karen and I had 'skated' through it and escaped a more pressing examination of Karen's circumstances. Now I castigate myself for having taken such a limited view. Instead of just calendaring the deadline for Patty's appeal and waiting for it to pass, I should have spent some time with Karen, counseling her on the adjustment.

Now everything in this case has the potential for becoming infinitely worse.

"Stephen, it's Analee Meriwether. How are you?"

"Hi, Sharon and I are just back from visiting our youngest daughter. She's about to start with Teach for America. So we're feeling good."

"Congratulations! You're way ahead of us. Our youngest just started kindergarten."

"Enjoy every minute of that; it goes way too fast. But I'm sure you didn't call me for advice on being a parent."

"Well, maybe I did, in an indirect way. I'm calling you on *Ward and Haskins*. I represented Karen in the guardianship termination, and I'll probably be representing her in your parentage action. I'm on vacation this week, and there's no time for me to prepare with her for the RFO you set in three weeks. May we have a month's continuance? I'd like to think we could work out some access arrangements in the interim."

"Well, they have to go to mediation anyway; it would probably have to go over for that reason alone. So I'll say yes without even consulting my client. But if you think you can work out access arrangements, you are a wonder worker. From what I've heard, Karen won't even talk to her sister."

"The sad thing is; they used to be close, all their lives. When Karen got sick, Patty was there for her. And they coordinated well throughout Karen's recovery. Only when Karen wanted Dawn back, Patty balked. And then there was that stupid incident when Karen came to pick up Dawn."

"Do you think Patty knew how to push Karen's buttons?"

"Thank you, Stephen. I won't repeat that." I paused. "This little girl shouldn't lose contact with her aunt and uncle and cousins. Karen and Patty need to mend fences more than they need this cutting-edge lawsuit. If we could somehow restore normal relations in the family, if Patty knew she had enforceable visitation, do you think we could make this lawsuit go away?"

Stephen sighed audibly, as if he were thinking it over. "Look, if we could restore normal relations in this family, we'd all be miracle workers. The lawsuit would fall of its own weight. When you get back to the office, we should work on getting them to see the best mediator around."

"Matt or Joanne?"

"Yeah. Those are the first names that came to me also. But I have to tell you, I think there's too much water over the dam in this family. It's gone too far for us to put things back together again."

"You mean you're looking for a test case in the Supreme Court?"

"No, Analee; I've been around too long to look at it that way. Everyone will lose if we have to take it that far."

"Well, you give me some hope."

"Analee, one more thing. I'm glad you're on the other side."

"Just tell me one thing. You're not going back to the office this week." Adam has returned from the new MOMA, ebullient about the exhibits.

"I'm not going back to the office before Tuesday. Stephen gave us an extension."

So we rent bikes and ride along the Embarcadero, across Crissy Field and through the Presidio, working up our appetites for another special meal, this time at Poggio in Sausalito, where we eat at an outside table, facing the ferry dock and marina.

"Whatever happened to our dream of living here?" I wonder aloud.

"Reality intervened. I was lucky to get a position teaching con law at McGeorge. I'm more than willing to start a new search, but it will take time, and you can imagine how seldom positions open up in the Bay Area. I have enough seniority now that I could take a year's guest teaching assignment somewhere here. That's the best way to get an invitation to join the faculty here, but is it worth it to disrupt our lives to do that? I'd either have a killer commute or we'd all have to relocate for a year or two. What about your practice?"

"You know I'd relocate my practice in a heartbeat, but I admit it wouldn't work for just a year or two."

"And think about real estate prices. We'd have a hard time buying a home with two little bedrooms in San Francisco; there's no way we could replicate our four-bedroom home and big yard if we moved here."

"Yeah, we'd be defeating our purpose if we could only afford a home in Vallejo and had to commute to San Francisco every day."

"Besides, what about your judicial ambitions?"

"Yeah. And it's cold here in the summertime. So should we just say we're lucky where we are and give up?"

"I know how much you like giving up."

"Let's look at homes in Marin on Sunday."

I awake Sunday morning to Adam's fingers caressing my back, his wordless sexual invitation that usually hypnotizes me. But I swing out of bed instead, eager to fetch a Sunday *Chronicle* with its real estate section. Adam sighs and rolls more reluctantly out of his side of the bed, scratching his neck. I am already partially dressed.

"Can you get a *New York Times* too?"

"Of course." Then I'm out the door before he can tell me this will be an exercise in frustration. I can hear him sighing as I leave.

I sit in the lobby with a cup of black coffee and the real estate section before even going back to the room. It is obvious that anything we could even remotely hope to afford would be a big step backward from where we now live. So I go back to the room proposing that we ignore reality altogether and just look at fantasy homes in Marin. We visit a hilltop home in Tiburon with views in three directions, oblivious to its eight million dollar price tag. Adam jokes about not being able to concentrate on cooking from the kitchen because of its breathtaking views of San Francisco. Exploring every bedroom and closet takes me that much further away from what is already starting to preoccupy me.

14

ANALEE

"DECLARATION OF PATRICIA HASKINS WARD IN SUPPORT OF PETITION FOR PARENTAGE AND REQUEST FOR ORDER FOR TEMPORARY CUSTODY

I, Patricia Haskins Ward, declare:

I bring this action to secure the legal parentage, custody and welfare of my daughter, Dawn Haskins, age four. Dawn was conceived from my ovum and sperm from an anonymous donor. The resulting zygote was implanted in the womb of my sister Karen Haskins, who gestated and gave birth to Dawn. As a consequence, I am Dawn's genetic mother and Karen is her gestational mother.

As we had planned, Dawn initially lived with Karen, though she visited frequently with my family. When Dawn was twenty months old, Karen descended into a deep depression that required her hospitalization and led to a prolonged period of psychiatric disability. With Karen's consent, I became Dawn's legal guardian on March 30, 201_, and Dawn came to live with my husband Doug and me, and our two children, Sandra (age 9) and Ian (age 6) at our home in Roseville. Dawn lived with us continuously for nineteen months, thriving in the supportive atmosphere of my family, until Karen obtained a court order on July 18, 201__, terminating the guardianship.

Ever since Karen picked up Dawn from our home on July 19, 201_, Karen has prevented Dawn from having any contact with the rest of her family. On that occasion, Karen provoked an argument over my having cut and conditioned Dawn's hair (she has very curly hair and it used to hurt her to have me comb it). Karen yelled at me in front of all three children, seized Dawn and drove off with the tires screeching on her car. To the best of my knowledge, she did not even take the time to secure Dawn in her car seat. I do not know if Dawn is either safe or secure in Karen's custody, and it is not in Dawn's best interests to be torn from her other parents and her siblings.

Karen has a history of depression going back to adolescence. She experimented with drugs in high school and suffered long "blue periods." Until her collapse in 201_, she never sought professional treatment. Although she was sometimes employed as an art teacher in Nevada City and wrote and illustrated children's books prior to her collapse, Karen's personal life has been erratic and relatively unstable. I do not know what, if any, employment she now has. Karen has had a series of short relationships with inappropriate men throughout her adulthood and has never married. She now lives in Rough and Ready in an old house where, according to Dawn, she goes to the bathroom in an outhouse. I believe Karen lives alone with Dawn, although I have no way of knowing what sorts of people visit her.

By contrast, when Dawn lived with our family, she had two loving and attentive parents and a sister and brother of similar age who were her constant playmates. She attended preschool here in Roseville three mornings a week. She lived with us in our four-bedroom, three-bathroom home where she has her own bedroom (we had a "Dawn Sky" with a rising sun painted on one wall for her). We have a one-acre lot with a play structure in our enclosed back yard. I am a full-time mom who can give Dawn the loving attention she deserves and needs. My husband Doug is an attorney in Sacramento, who is home every night for dinner with our children and me.

For the sake of Dawn, I ask that this court declare that I am her mother (along with Karen), grant physical custody of Dawn to me and permit Karen regular weekend visitation such as she had during the guardianship period.

I declare under penalty of perjury under the laws of the State of California that the foregoing is true and correct. Executed at Roseville, California on September 28, 201_."

By noon on Wednesday, I had read and reread this declaration and the parentage petition, jotted a disjointed list of questions and issues, reread two family law treatises on parentage, and started reading some of the parentage cases. I am becoming more and more agitated and less focused as the hours flee. Karen is coming in at two, and I haven't even begun to figure out what I will say to her.

Parentage is another legal realm altogether from child custody. I know the realm of custody well, but have had few parentage actions. The ones I had involved unmarried biological fathers, and the question of parentage hung on the outcome of genetics and blood tests. Custody actions depend on the best interests of the child, and begin with the parents participating in mediation to explore whether they can resolve their disputes themselves, with the help of a trained mental health professional. Parentage is altogether different; the issues of mediation and custody aren't even on the table until one is determined to be a legal parent. The reported cases arise from widely disparate backdrops and contain no bright-line rules. Our codes and cases identify natural, gestational, presumed and legal parents. Presumed parents rank higher than natural parents, but this ranking relates mainly to males and the history of men conceiving children but then either abandoning the mother or taking an active parenting role. We have statutory presumptions, but exceptions to most of them. A child born to a married couple is presumed to be the child of both spouses, regardless of biology, but there are exceptions to that when, for example, the mother leaves the marriage to be with the biological father and the biological father maintains a parenting relationship with the child.

We have a statute governing parentage of a child born from a sperm donation but none for an ovum donation. Social policy arising from marriage collides with biological facts, and the intention factor in assisted reproduction is not always honored.

My mind is muddling. A walk and lunch are my remedies or excuses, but I need to clear my head before talking with Karen.

As soon as I have walked a couple blocks, glancing up at the sheltering trees, I start to think of the people involved instead of the confusing state of the law. Whatever else is true, Patty and Karen remain sisters. Patty had been of immense help to Karen in many ways, and to Dawn as well. They had been close. Their children were close. To fight to maintain a complete alienation must hurt them all.

I have learned over the course of the morning that, while mediation is mandatory for disputing parents, it is not required between a parent and someone who is only alleging to be a parent. I had assured Stephen that mediation would happen, but I have to tell Karen that, at this stage, she can say no and prevent it. Given her state of mind on Friday, she might not agree at all to mediation. Should I try to persuade her? She would not be legally harmed by even an unsuccessful mediation because it is entirely confidential, but she has a right to say no.

15

KAREN

I've waited from Friday until Wednesday afternoon to meet with Analee and have her tell me how I can dig myself out of this legal pit I have tumbled into. Jenny helped distract me over the weekend; we drove with our kids to Lake Tahoe, took a short hike, grilled chicken and – all of us holding hands -- dashed into and out of the water. Whenever I brought up the subject with her – out the children's earshot – she reassured me that my attorney would help me figure it out.

On Monday I took Dawn with me to Rock Creek Farm, where I help out twice a week in exchange for my Friday box of fresh vegetables. The owners Sarah and Paul, a couple in their fifties transplanted from Minnesota, not only consented earlier to my bringing Dawn but seem to enjoy it when I do. They hand us our straw farmer's hats on arrival and assign me to trimming green beans at a table and tagging them for the subscription boxes. Earlier in the summer, when I asked Sarah how they managed to provide a miniature hat, Sarah laughed and told me they have had visiting children before. From the way she put the hat onto Dawn's head and asked her how tight to pull the neck cord, I realized this is a treat for her also. My guess is that it's been a while since she has done this with her own children and she either has grandchildren who live far away or she's waiting for grandchildren.

Sarah asks Dawn if she wants to work with her today. Dawn takes her hand and they walk to a patch of sungold tomatoes, arching over their metal braces, with beckoning strings of orange, marble-sized fruit. Dawn is just the right height to pick them. They start working close to my table, and I can hear them talking to each other.

"They match your hair," Sarah tells Dawn, who announces that these are her favorite tomatoes. I watch as Sarah hands Dawn several plastic pint boxes and explains that, each time Dawn fills a box, she can eat two sungolds. I look around me with a sense of pleasure and wholeness. Everything is green and healthy and thriving in the sunlight. Around me are ripening heirloom tomato patches, vines of lemon cucumbers, and fence rows filled with green beans. A huge pile of untrimmed green beans lies next to me on the table, their stems entangled, and Dawn is not more than a dozen feet away, starting to fill her first basket. My task of trimming the green beans and bagging them is repetitive but satisfying in a way I cannot explain. My fingers are busy but my mind is free and open.

"Ian loves these too. I should bring some home to him," I hear Dawn tell Sarah, who understandably asks who Ian is.

"He's, like, my brother."

Why didn't she say cousin? She knows he is her cousin. Sarah has the good sense to leave the subject alone and compliments Dawn on how many baskets she is filling.

Dawn lasts the full four hours of my stint, though she spends part of the time wandering among the rows of zinnias, admiring all their color. Sarah sends us home with a small handful of them, magenta and orange and yellow. Dawn carries her little basket of earned sungolds. Just as we start walking to our car, Sarah waves goodbye and invites me, in the friendliest Midwestern way, to bring Ian the next time. All the day's pleasure evaporates in this instant.

When we get home, Dawn puts her basket of sungolds into the refrigerator and asks me for a particular vase that I haven't used in a long time. It is a circle of flutes, not more than six inches tall. How Dawn remembers this, I cannot fathom.

Halfway through a cheerful dinner, she puts down her hamburger, studies my face and asks whether her donor has red curly hair. I have told her before that she has a donor instead of a regular father, but this is a difficult concept and she keeps asking. Of course Patty is a donor too, but I hope never to have to explain that to her. I tell her honestly that I've never met him but that I read that he is a musician with red, curly hair.

"Do you wish you could meet him?" she asks wistfully, as if this family picture is missing a member.

"No, honey, I'm just thrilled to have you." As if this will stop this conversation. But then I ask the next question.

"Has anyone ever asked you that before?"

Dawn looks wistful. "Once, when Aunt Patty took me to the grocery store, a lady asked me the same question."

"What did Aunt Patty say?"

"She said 'no, he has straight brown hair.'"

I want to hurl something at the wall but hold my tongue. Patty's husband Doug has straight brown hair. I try to keep my face expressionless.

"Why did she say that if it isn't true?"

"Maybe she forgot." I try hard to keep my voice civil.

She asks if she can sleep in my bed, which she does occasionally, and I say yes. Later, as I am reading her "The Giant in the Bean Stalk," she interrupts to ask what a donor is.

"A child is formed from the genes ..."

"I know," she interrupts, "not blue jeans but some tiny, tiny things."

"Yes, exactly, from the genes of a man and a woman. Since I did not have a husband, I had to use someone else's genes to make you. There was a catalogue, and I got to choose your donor from that catalogue."

"Like choosing vegetable seeds from a catalogue?"

"Yes," I say, excited by her analogy. "And I chose a musician with red hair, although I didn't know at the time that it was curly."

"Will I be a musician too?"

"Maybe. I don't know."

With that, she stops asking, and I return to reading her book. But after she lies asleep, I ask myself what burden I have laid on her by not giving her a real father. While I can tell myself that she is better off by not having some kinds of fathers, I know it is still a burden, and I cannot lift it from her.

I wonder how she thinks of Patty and Doug. She knows they are not her parents, but still they cared for her. I can't answer this question. And now it has become infinitely more complicated by Patty's suing me to become Dawn's mother, or other mother. It is more than I can comprehend. It would be even more terrible if Dawn were to find out about the lawsuit. Who could possibly explain that to her? I shudder. My anger at Patty now consumes the gratitude I had for her taking in Dawn while I was down. I wonder if she is doing this just to see if she can make me break down again, so she can take Dawn back. That will *never* happen; I am determined.

Finally, Wednesday arrives and I am in Analee's office. She is infuriatingly calm, which only agitates me further. She tries explaining to me the law on parentage, but it gets hopelessly tangled. Even she cannot explain it well. Finally, I just butt in.

"Just tell me if she can win."

"It's possible." For a long moment, she says nothing further. "It's possible she just wants the ability to share time with Dawn. It's possible she wants to have Dawn come back to live with her most of the time. We don't yet know. Part of the question is whether you can live with the prolonged uncertainty of this lawsuit; it can be long, expensive, painful and unpredictable."

I want to throw things at her from the top of her desk, like the State Bar Award or her glass candy jar. The vision of jelly beans raining over her desk tempts me. But I sit on my hands, chewing the inside of my gums until I taste blood, while Analee draws what she calls a decision tree.

As a tree, it is both upside down and entirely lopsided, with one short, blunt limb on one side and a labyrinth of limbs and branches on the other. While Analee is painstakingly drawing it, explaining it with maddening slowness, I drift into a fantasy of moving to Canada with Dawn, living in a cabin in the North woods and writing children's books from there. The cabin would be tiny but look out on endless forest through square windows. Dawn's room would be sunny, mine pale blue. Too soon, I realize I'd miss Megan and Jenny and their children, and I could be located through my agent, and probably deported.

Analee looks at me expectantly, holding the decision tree before me so that I can read it.

"Tell me about the short limb," I blurt. It is labeled mediation.

Analee explains that Patty and I could meet with a trained mediator to see if we can agree on a human solution rather than a legal solution. If we agree, the lawsuit will go away. If we don't, the mediation will die a silent death and the lawsuit will go forward (into that labyrinth of limbs on the opposite side of her tree). Mediation would be entirely confidential. The mediator she has in mind has worked successfully with many bitter parents.

"But Patty's *not* Dawn's parent!" Even before these words are out of my mouth, I can see Analee trying to choke back her words and substitute "family members."

"Your agreeing to participate in mediation doesn't mean you admit Patty is a parent."

"What do I have to do?"

"Keep an open mind that allowing Dawn to see Patty and her cousins again might be good for her -- and even for you."

Matt Shipley, the mediator, gazes at me with protruding, mournful eyes, whose lower lids droop slightly, creating half-moons underneath that I can easily imagine welling with sympathetic tears, their arc mirrored by pale but subtly active eyebrows that move separately from each other and ask their own questions as they flicker. He sips tea from a mug next to the upright chair where he sits cross-legged, but his eyes never leave mine as I tell him the history of Dawn's conception, birth and life so far. He does not interrupt or ask me any questions.

Patty sits in a chair across from me. Dr. Shipley has us sit facing each other, him at my left and her across from me. His eyes hold mine, and I do not even glance at her until he finishes listening to my history. When he turns his eyes to Patty to hear from her, I sense the same lock of eyes between them. I watch and listen as they speak. Her own rendition of Dawn's life is similar to mine at the beginning, but she lays it on thick about how deeply Dawn has become "part of her family." At the third or fourth time she uses that phrase, he asks her his first question.

"When you say 'part of your family,' does that family include Karen?"

Patty shifts in her seat, smoothing her skirt underneath her, as she tries to shift her narrative accordingly. "I mean part of our nuclear family – Doug, Sandra, Ian and me – but of course Karen is my sister and part of my larger family." Her slight smile betrays her satisfaction at dodging his bullet.

Dr. Shipley falls silent again, until Patty finishes her story. Then he asks each of us separately – Patty first – whether she thinks it is good for the family – "I mean your whole family, not just your nuclear family" – for Patty and me to be alienated from each other, and for Dawn not to see both of us. Instead of saying the obvious – "of course not" – Patty rambles on about how I can't be trusted with Dawn's safety, how I focus on my own needs rather than Dawn's, how my 'avant-garde lifestyle' is more important to me than Dawn's welfare, and how she can't be certain I won't fall into another depression.

He follows her on each of those trails, the depression first, getting her to acknowledge that she could seek a new guardianship if I were ever to sink into a 'deep, clinical depression' again. About my lifestyle being more important than Dawn's welfare, she latches onto Dawn's hair, of all things.

"Dawn has very, very curly hair, and it hurts her when I comb it. Sometimes she would cry and beg me not to comb it. Finally, I asked her whether she would like to have smooth hair so that it wouldn't hurt when I comb it, and she said yes. She was excited about the prospect of getting her hair 'smoothed,' as she said. After I had her hair straightened, it didn't hurt her to comb it and she liked her new look. But when Karen first saw it, she lost her temper and made Dawn feel ugly and scared."

"Did you ever talk to Karen about how much it hurt Dawn to comb her hair and whether it would be good to straighten it?"

"No, by that time we weren't talking to each other, so I just did it, so that Dawn wouldn't have to cry every time Karen combed her hair."

"But what about months earlier, while Dawn was living with you and Karen was visiting each weekend?"

Patty admits she had not thought of it then.

Dr. Shipley turns his riveting gaze to me. I want to yell: did you ever think of using a soft brush? But I wait for his question, which is "did you like Dawn's new look with straight hair?"

"No, I hated it, and Patty knew I would. That's why she did it. I am very, very sorry I got so angry that evening, because Dawn was afraid and she did think I thought she looked bad. I lost my temper and I shouldn't have. I've talked this through with Dawn since then."

"Does Dawn cry when you comb her hair?"

"No, I use a soft brush. If I used a comb, her hair would get all tangled, and I imagine she would cry. But Patty never asked."

This time he does not ask a question; he makes an observation. "So it strikes me that this was one issue that might have been resolved if you two could have talked it over." Patty and I each nod.

"And isn't it likely that there will be other issues that may come up in Dawn's childhood where one of you has an idea or a solution that might be useful to the other?"

I leap in first.

"Sure, but she can't force her solution on my child. Just as I couldn't force mine on her children."

"Might you two agree on that as a general proposition?" I nod. Patty began, "yes, but...."

Dr. Shipley acknowledges that we have other issues but that our first session has come to an end. Would we be willing to come back? To my surprise, we each say yes immediately.

I sail home with the euphoric notion that Dr. Shipley will end this nightmare. I phone Jenny, who has Dawn with her, to offer to cook dinner, and on the way I buy chicken and corn to grill, and a bunch of flowers for Jenny. When I burst into her kitchen with the grocery bag, she hustles the children out of the room to hear my report.

"This is going to work!" I hug her as I try not to yell my news.

Jenny wants details before she will share in my jubilation. Even after I tell her what happened, she is cautious, which irritates me. I want company for my misplaced optimism, and she won't go there with me. But she helps create a festive dinner for the kids and us. Her son Jonas challenges the rest of us with how many ears of corn we can eat, and I cut Dawn's in half so that she can claim two.

The next morning, when I call Analee to report to her, I am more subdued, reporting just that it had gone well and that we will meet again in two days. She surprises me with her own excitement, telling me I could create my own solution through mediation and 'cut her out of a big fee' (that she knew she could trust me with this joke pleases me too).

But as I mentally prepare for the next session, I wonder what Patty must be thinking. Clearly Dr. Shipley is leading us toward trying to normalize our family again, but I struggle to find a period of time of happy normalcy after Dawn was born. In her first year, we were all close and happy, and I drew heavily on Patty's help and knowledge. By the beginning of her second year I had collapsed and she took over. After that, I saw Dawn only on weekends and holidays, and she was in charge. She would probably say that she had always been in charge of Dawn until I took her to court to end the guardianship. It occurs to me that Patty really feels she was losing her own child, and that I was the one who had started the legal battle. She would always have the claim of her 'special attachment' to Dawn due to biology and this period of time that I was truly down. But couldn't she see that I am now able to parent on my own? I certainly have no insight into how to approach her, but I hope that Dr. Shipley will.

He begins our second session by observing that we had left off agreeing that it would be good to 'restart' communication with each other over Dawn's needs. I jump in prematurely and tell him I had tried to do that when Dawn and then others in Patty's family had had strep throat, but that I had been rebuffed.

The mournful eyes roll toward me with a pale rebuke.

"I know you each likely have stories of how you have failed in the past, but we're trying to create a template for your future with this child you both care for deeply."

I feel hushed and put in my place, but then he tries to draw me out.

"Do you have any suggestions, Karen, about how you might create a new future?"

"I don't think that Patty's and my just talking to each other – other than here – is going to 'restart' our family, but I do have a suggestion." I glance at Patty's skeptical face, then away before it can shut me down. "What if Patty and Ian and Dawn and I create a sort of play date together, a picnic in the park or something?" I can feel deflation in my voice tone as I end the question, as if I too doubt this would work.

Dr. Shipley asks why I didn't include Patty's other child, and I tell him as tactfully as I can that Sandra is a bit older than Ian and Dawn and tends to look down on them a little. He glances at Patty, who actually nods, with a hint of a smile.

"A picnic in the park with Ian and Dawn might be a good start. They have a special closeness to each other."

My heart begins to pound. "How about the park in Sacramento along the American River? There's a wading beach there."

"That park is unsafe. It's a Mexican gangland."

"Wherever you like." I try to keep it positive, and when she suggests the little park closest to her home in Roseville I agree.

Dr. Shipley tries to help us structure this event, recognizing that the last time the children had seen each other was when I picked up Dawn and we had that big fight.

"Dawn really loves her cousin Ian," I burble stupidly.

"*Cousin?*" Patty puts on the brakes.

"Do the children know the difference between cousins and siblings?" Even Dr. Shipley has wandered into the labyrinth.

"Dawn knows that Patty is Sandra and Ian's mother and that I am her mother. She knows that Patty is my sister. I assume Ian and Sandra know the same thing."

"We've all become so much one family that I doubt the children are that binary. Surely Sandra and Ian see me as their mother, as they have known no other, but Dawn probably thinks of both of us as a mother to her, and Ian treats Dawn as his 'one, true sister.' His words, although he hasn't said it in front of Sandra."

"I am Dawn's mother, and she is quite clear about that, regardless of whatever you might have told her." My tone is acidic.

"I've never told her that I'm her genetic mother, if that's what you're driving at, but she surely knows who has taken care of her as a mother for almost two years."

We are both practically snarling.

"Well, you got quickly to the heart of it, haven't you?" Dr. Shipley injects. "Can you create this picnic without having to get to who is Dawn's mother or whether you both are?"

"If we are going to have this picnic, it has to be with the ground rule that I make the decisions about Dawn and you make them about Ian. I'm not going to have you tell Dawn – or me – what is safe or not."

"Well, there you have it, don't you?" Patty says as if she has just revealed my weakest rib.

"Can you create a venue where safety isn't likely to become a flash point between you two?"

I tell him that Patty had chosen just such a place. "Everything in her neighborhood is safe."

"Folks, you put me at a fork here: should I just help you with the logistics of this picnic, or should we go down the road of your different conceptions of safety and precise relationships?"

Why is he turning it over to us? Isn't he supposed to help us?

"I think we need to go down the path of what is or isn't safe and who gets to decide for Dawn." Patty says these words, but I agree with her and nod. We both look to Dr. Shipley, who seems to have much preferred just to plan the picnic.

"This goes deep," I begin. "I don't know how to convince Patty that I'm ready to parent Dawn on my own. It's what led me finally to end the guardianship, when she wouldn't agree to Dawn's coming back to live with me."

"Has Patty seen Dawn since the guardianship ended?" I think he knows the answer but is just opening the line of questions. "Would you be willing to let Dawn visit with Patty, or with Patty and Ian, without you there?"

"Yes, but what happened to the picnic? And how would I know that she would return Dawn, when I had so much trouble before?"

"I hear the two of you verging on non-starters over ground rules for the picnic. As for a return time, we could have a written agreement if you like."

"I will bring Dawn to Patty's home in Roseville for a visit and pick her up the next day. How's that?" Now, both Dr. Shipley and I look at Patty.

"I'll even pack her hairbrush," slithers out of my mouth.

Patty has the good sense not to reply to my last comment. We agree to the upcoming Saturday morning to Sunday morning. We agree that I will not go into Patty's home unless she invites me in, and that she will have Dawn ready at the door, with no provocations, on Sunday morning. We also agree to another mediation session in a week.

The visit itself was uneventful. Jenny told me I needed to be the Model Citizen, and I played my role well. Until the ride home.

I ask Dawn if she had a good weekend, and she answers enthusiastically.

"It was great! Daddy Too taught me to throw a football with Ian, and ..."

"*Who?*"

"Daddy Too – Uncle Doug. It was a little football, and he showed me how to hold it when I throw."

"What about Aunt Patty?"

"She and Sandra baked a pecan pie."

"That sounds delicious," I say, though my words must sound like poison. She hasn't told me what she calls Patty, and I know I shouldn't ask.

But I do in the next mediation session, and I hear more than I can take. Patty has just finished answering Dr. Shipley's question about how the visit went. She is obviously pleased and tries not to gloat. Dr. Shipley turns to me with the same question, and I blurt to Patty, "since when is Doug Daddy Two? And who is Daddy One?"

She pauses, looks down, and replies in a voice you would use in telling your child the family dog has died.

"It's Daddy 'T-o-o,' not 'Two.' Ian started it. I'm sorry, Karen, but you missed out on a whole period of Dawn's life, when she was learning to talk. She started to call Doug Daddy, and Sandra objected, saying 'he's *my* daddy.' Ian came to Dawn's defense, saying 'he's her daddy too,' and Dawn started saying Daddy Too and Mommy Too. That's what she calls us."

I try not to crumble. I can't even look into Dr. Shipley's eyes.

"That must be difficult for you to hear."

I just nod. I can't look up. We three sit in silence for a long time. Finally, I say, "Then why didn't Doug join your lawsuit?"

It is Patty's turn to grow quiet. "He didn't think it was right."

More long silence. I can feel Patty and I are both waiting for Dr. Shipley to rescue us.

Finally, he asks, in a voice that is not a question, "Is a lawsuit the best way to solve this."

We all know the answer. I break the silence.

"I'm willing to resume normal family relations. Only we have to be clear that I'm in charge of Dawn, just as you're in charge of Sandra and Ian. And the lawsuit needs to be dropped."

"But how can I be sure that you won't cut off contact with Dawn and the rest of us?"

"You know me. I don't do revenge. I only filed to end the guardianship because you wouldn't allow me to live with my own daughter."

"I worry," she says after a long pause. "I'm afraid of losing her, and she's become part of me too." She looks at me almost pleadingly.

"I won't cut you out. Not you or Doug or Ian – or even Sandra." I smile, and I can see her fighting a smile too at the allusion to Sandra.

"I need to think about it."

On that note we end our session, scheduling another in a week. But the next session is canceled, and it is Analee who tells me that Patty has decided to proceed with the lawsuit.

On impulse, I phone Doug at work as soon as I get off the phone with Analee. His assistant seems to recognize me, sounds friendly and tells me more than she has to, that he is in a deposition this morning but is expected back in the afternoon. She suggests I phone him back after two.

But he calls me back even before then. I thank him for calling me back, and he acknowledges I am probably wondering what is going on. Each of us pauses, waiting to see if the other would begin. He does.

"This is hard on all of us. I was hoping she wouldn't do this, but she couldn't see another way." He stops, and I just wait for him.

"Your hospitalization undid her – more than anyone would have imagined. After your mother lost her mentation and your dad went off the rails, your falling apart left her feeling that she was the only one standing, the one who had to carry all the burden of the family. She's the one who manages your mother's care and visits her every week. She's the one who handled your dad's funeral, emptied his house and cleaned up all the loose ends after he died, and executed his little estate. That feeling of being the only one responsible has only hardened, even though you've returned to normal life. She feels that Dawn is in jeopardy unless she's the one responsible for her. I've tried to dissuade her, tried to persuade her to go into therapy to lighten her load, but now with Sandra in therapy, there's no way I can convince her to do it."

"*Sandra's* in therapy?"

"This is all more than I should tell you, and I hope you'll keep it to yourself, but Sandra is jealous of attention paid to anyone but herself. She was verging on nasty to Dawn when she was here recently; she is tough on Ian; she has no friends herself; and she wants all of Patty's and my attention. We're trying to uncover what makes her so threatened."

"I had no idea."

"I'm not surprised. There's no way you would know, and it's not like Dawn to complain."

"Doug, is there anything I can do to convince Patty that I can take care of Dawn myself?"

"Not that I know of. I've tried to talk to her, but with no luck."

Unexpectedly, tears well up, and my throat blocks my speaking. He's reminded me that I still have a mother, lying in oblivion, and that I'd missed the death and funeral of my father. I can't even *try* to think of them right now, my morass with Patty and Dawn consumes all of me.

"Karen, I have one thing to ask of you: please leave me out of this. I don't want anything to do with this lawsuit, which is bound to be ugly.

"And, if possible, please treat this conversation as if it never happened. I don't expect there will be another until this is over, whatever that means."

"I hear you." I am crying now. "Doug, thanks; I mean it."

I wake up the next morning seeing my mother's face – not as it might be now, not even as it was when I last saw her that day when Dawn was still a baby, but a much younger face -- looking down at me disapprovingly in my bed. I am sixteen, it is late on a Sunday morning, and I had come in well past my midnight curfew after having had sex with my then boyfriend Zack. What has she seen or heard while I lay there asleep? But my waking now is with a different guilt. I have not seen or even consciously thought of her much since coming out of the hospital and rehab center. To me, she was effectively dead, even if not actually so. To Patty, she has apparently been our living and breathing mother, even if not capable of much of anything. Patty has always been the dutiful daughter, I the irresponsible one. Before Dawn was born, Patty would try to bring me on her weekly visits to the memory care center, and I would usually go with her as a compliant observer. After that incident with Dawn, I refused to go back. I try to imagine the spirit in which Patty visits her, but I can't. Until I remember how Patty sometimes appeared to me in the early days that I was in the hospital or rehab center. Although she always warmed to me, I sometimes caught that same disapproving look at the start of her visit. Her face mirrored my mother's so long ago. It made me anxious, then and now. I try to banish the thought, but the anxiety remains.

I show up in Analee's office with my check for her $20,000 retainer in hand. In my mind, this was part of Dawn's college tuition money, and it stings to part with it.

"This must really hurt," she echoes. "Both Patty's decision and the money." But then she brusquely gets up to take the check out to Gerta. When she returns, I tell her I have spoken to Doug. Before I even begin, she blurts, "I can't wait to question him." I flinch, and she immediately changes her tone. "What was that conversation like?"

"Analee, he spoke to me in confidence. I don't want to ruin that."

Analee sits back and reminds me, with what feels like deigned patience, that everything said between us is confidential, and that she will not use information without my consent. I tell her first about Sandra, because even I can see how useful this could be and I have never had any sympathy for that child. She agrees that this information could be usefully damaging to Patty's description of her tight, happy nuclear family. She also volunteers that we should not use this now, in my response to the initial papers, but wait to question Patty about Sandra. I absorb how immediately strategic she is with this information. Is a person trained to be that way, or are some people just like that? I don't know whether to be repelled or grateful, but I feel both.

Gradually, I tell her what else Doug had told me about Patty's need to take control. Although I think I render it as Doug had to me, Analee's response is quite different.

"How arrogant! Only *she* can rule the universe?" I sit with this sarcastic response for some moments before correcting her.

"Actually, I think Doug was describing something else, a heavy responsibility. Not that she thinks she is the best in the world, but that she's the only one left to carry the burden. I'm not saying it very well, but he was describing her dealing with the notion that she had to hold it together because everyone else in her family had failed."

She stares at me for some moments before responding.

"You may be right, that she's operating under a deep sense of responsibility, but either way, it's going to be tough for us to shake. This lawsuit is not going to be easy."

With that said, we get down to the task of preparing a response to the petition and a declaration for me to sign. Her fingers charge furiously over her laptop as we speak, and she has a draft declaration for me to review before I leave her office.

"Take it home and mull it over. I will too. Call me tomorrow with anything you want to add or change."

I hold the pages as if they are tainted. I know I don't want them in the same room with Dawn.

"Can I just go over it now with you?"

Analee seems surprised but agrees. When we finish, she has Gerta print it on legal paper and I sign it. She explains that this will be part of our reply to the motion filed by Patty but that she also wants to file our own motion to dismiss on legal grounds, that Patty cannot legally be Dawn's mother. Her taking that initiative encourages me. I need her to think for me.

16

ANALEE

Before Karen leaves my office, she asks if she can read the only Supreme Court case in California regarding an ovum donor as parent. I lead her into my library and pull it down for her.

I had forgotten completely the half-completed jigsaw puzzle spread out on the table. I never let clients see my puzzles; they may think I play frivolous games on their time. But Karen gravitates toward it immediately, bending over it intently as if searching for a piece that fits. After a long silent moment, she stands upright and looks at me thoughtfully.

"Jigsaw puzzles helped me get back to normal when I was in the rehab center," she confesses. "I'll always be grateful for them."

"I come in here to do them when I feel stuck mentally. If I approach them with humility and curiosity, I make progress, and work through my mental block."

Karen shoots me a grateful smile. "My case must be giving you plenty of puzzle time." I grin at her and nod. I had never confessed this simple fact to a client. Her reaction made me like her all the more. If I hadn't accidentally let her see it, I never would have discovered this connection.

My mind is streaking. I uncurl myself from Adam as gently as I can, trying not to wake him, and glance at my watch. Nearly five; I'd had almost seven hours of sleep and can make it through the day even if I don't return to bed. I unplug my laptop and take it to the kitchen table to release what has overtaken my mind.

SUMMARY OF ARGUMENT

Parentage is not an Olympic sport: the judge's task is not to rank the contestants' relative skill, performance or grace. A slip on the balance beam is not a disqualifying event. The judge's function is not to decide who has the bigger or better home, the more money or more family members. The judge's task is to determine whether legally – not as a factual matter – this child has more than one parent. That Karen is Dawn's parent is incontestable: she gave birth to this child and her parentage is not challenged. Patty claims to be this child's second mother, as if she needs one, which she does not. Whatever preference the law has for two parents, it does not require a second parent – especially where, as here, the single parent is fully capable. Patty's quasi-parental rights as Dawn's legal guardian have been legally and finally terminated, and she did not seek visitation rights for Dawn in that action. She cannot, by filing a second action to seek comparable rights, undermine the finality of the prior judicial determination.

By putting a summary in writing, I can now organize my argument and recite the authorities. I worry most about the second parent part; the cases seem to stretch to find a second parent except in the most desperate of circumstances where there is no one available. I have to reject what I know in my core as a parent, that I would be lost without Adam, and I wonder how Karen manages; but I remind myself that Adam and I set out to co-parent. A single parent does not have another parent engrafted without serious misstep. Karen's temporary disability should not justify such a graft, especially when there has already been a judicial determination ending the guardianship.

My goal with this motion to dismiss is to preclude a trial. I am convinced this case should be dismissed as a legal matter, without getting into expensive discovery and a trial. I will rely as heavily as I can on the prior legal determination.

I hear a toilet flush from our bedroom and glance again at my watch. Six-thirty: Adam is predictably up, without an alarm, at nearly the same time each morning, ready to awaken our two boys, who would sleep until nine every day if they could. I save the argument summary, close the computer and return to our bedroom to dress.

Adam emerges wet and naked from the bathroom to embrace me. He whispers in my ear, "Streaking?" I nod. He named this trait in me, and now we just use the one word to convey what is happening. I cup his butt appreciatively. "Don't think I don't know what I'm missing." With that he grins, returns to the bathroom to dry off and we each prepare for our respective days.

The two competing preliminary motions are to be heard today, both Patty's for visitation and ours to dismiss. Patty filed hers first, but I will ask the court to hear ours first, since it contests the court's power to make any orders on what Patty has filed.

I am disgruntled that Karen will not even attend. She is not legally required to attend, but her presence would both give the court its first look at her and demonstrate that she cares. Karen's excuse is that she doesn't want to miss her work and wants to be able to take Dawn home from school. I almost never get to pick up my children from school. Also, I will bet good money that Patty will be there. Karen's absence will only allow the court to conjure up the irresponsible character that Patty describes in her papers.

I dress as plainly and seriously as I can, in my charcoal gray suit, which will be too warm for today's surprisingly warm November day, but I have no lightweight counterpart, and I want to match Stephen's gravitas, even though his comes with gray hair and more years of experience. He will predictably wear also a red bowtie, his own old-fashioned trademark. I will wear simple pearls under my open white shirt.

I can hear Adam in the other room, verbally wrestling the boys to the breakfast table. He is on duty this morning, since I will be in court, and all three of them know the routine, know not to bother me before court. They can hear me tromping down the hall in my heels and they fall into a quiet mode as I come into the kitchen. No one wants to provoke me. I kiss Alex on the side of his head and tousle his short hair. He mumbles 'hi, Mom' between his gulps of cheerios. Andy, our picky eater, is removing the offending yellow fruit loops from his bowl before he pours milk over them, and he doesn't even respond to my hand on his shoulder and kiss on the side of his head. Alex, my stalwart supporter, hugs me, whispers "formidable" into my ear appreciatively, and sits down with his dad and Andy. He heard his dad describe me this way and he has adopted the word as his own; he pronounces it perfectly though I doubt he knows what it means. I pull a glass from the cupboard and pour myself a glass of milk, all I will allow myself until after the hearing.

Adam is in shorts and a tee shirt, since he has no classes to teach today, but the two boys are spiffed. I admire them all with my eyes, a comfortable trio of guys chowing down together. I wish the boys a good day in school.

Traffic is worse than usual, but I have allowed extra time. I keep the radio off as my way of keeping my thoughts clear and focused. The air is unusually dense, and in a short while I see the source of the backup as a brush fire along the highway, fire trucks blocking the right lane. I get only a glance but note the fire is spreading away from the highway across a desiccated field of grass. I silently curse the careless smoker who likely caused this damage.

As I pull into a space in the courthouse parking lot, I sit for a moment and try to retrieve a clear head. I conjure Adam at the front of a law class, my epitome of a calm and clear authority on the law. It works. I know how he thinks and reasons, though how he keeps his calm under pressure still defies my comprehension.

Outside the courtroom, which is still locked, Stephen stands with an imperious-looking Patty. Though she wears loose curls in her pale brown hair and a feminine, appropriate dress, there is something rigid in her posture that implies to me someone accustomed to being in charge. I have won my private bet that Patty is here. Stephen catches my eye but nods slightly as though to warn me against approaching him now. He is explaining something to his client, who has her arms crossed in front of her.

I look at the calendar and see that we are set last. Of course, the judge sets the longest hearings for last on the calendar. In theory, that affords her more time for them, but in practice the toughest cases are sometimes accorded the least time, and we cannot keep the court into the lunch hour. I sit in the back of the courtroom where I can watch everyone else. The calendar call reveals a shorter calendar than first appears, two stipulations for continuances and one no-show.

Judge Bremmer is in good humor this morning, always a good sign. The first matter entails a child support calculation for two parents who dispute the level of the father's income, and the judge jokes about how the designers of the statewide child support calculations thought the process would be simpler with their formula. The judge resolves it expeditiously and moves onto the second and then the third matter, after which I zone out of her calendar and into my own arguments.

At the morning break, I approach Stephen to ask if he will consent that my matter be heard before his since mine is pivotal to the future of the lawsuit, but he shakes his head solemnly and says only, "I cannot agree to your going out of order." I wonder if he would have taken the same stance if Patty were not standing at his side.

I renew my request when our case is called, but our judge comes to the same conclusion, though assuring me that she will not rule on visitation until she rules on my pivotal request, thus signaling that she quite well understands that if she grants my request, there is no power to grant visitation. Stephen is eloquent as always, describing the close connection Patty has had to Dawn and how, with only one exception, contact has been severed between them, which is not in 'little Dawn's' best interest. I explain that with the termination of the guardianship and no visitation orders in that matter – none requested, none granted – the decision to allow visitation rests with my client, and that she permitted a mediated visit but that Patty had terminated mediation. Judge Bremmer states she will take that request under submission pending decision on my request. As I stand to make my argument, she asks me how I believe the guardianship disposes of the parentage question. I explain that if Patty believed at the outset she was a second parent, she could have brought a parentage action rather than a guardianship action, which determines only the -- usually temporary -- rights to care for a child. Likewise, she could have but did not request visitation at the hearing to terminate the guardianship. That hearing resolved my client's capacity as a parent, and this new action – to interject a second parent into a nearly-five-year-old's life – is not only an impermissible 'second bite at the apple' but is also ill-conceived and inherently confusing to the child, who knows Karen is her mother and never thought she had two mothers.

"But aren't those factual determinations for the trial court to make?" the judge interjects.

"Exactly!" Stephen interjects as I pause, recognizing I have already lost. Stephen proceeds to inform the court that it would have been cruel and abusive for Patty to have sought parentage when Karen was "incompetent" in the hospital and that the grounds for establishing parentage arose partly in the nearly two years that Dawn lived with Patty and her family 'as another daughter'.

I return to the finality of the guardianship termination but recognize the probable futility of this effort. Even though the judge announces she will take the matter under submission because she wants to read the cases cited and consider the legal issues, I can predict her decision. I am now relieved that Karen was not present to have to hear herself termed incompetent.

17

KAREN

I'm glad that I told Analee I would not come to the hearing. I watch Dawn almost skip into her classroom as if expecting the wonders of Disneyland. I remind her that I will be teaching 'just down the hall' and will come for her at the end of the day. She says 'bye, Mom' as casually as if I were going into the other room of our little house and turns to the attractions of her kindergarten room.

I will have an hour before any students come to my art room. I know there will be 21 third graders at 9:40, 19 fourth graders at 11:40, 17 fifth graders at 12:40, and 16 six graders at 1:40. I will start with acrylic painting, easy-to-mix colors, water-based for easy washing up, and thick enough to paint over anything the students don't like. I cover the large art tables with paper and set up small pots of paint, brushes and painting paper for the first students. After I show them how to mix colors, I will ask each of them to paint their favorite place from their summer break. I smile as I think of asking them to paint where the ketchup grows but keep that antic thought to myself. I've posted a large color wheel at the front of the room. By the 9:30 bell, my classroom is in order. I have donned my own painting apron and hung enough aprons for each student just inside the entrance to the room.

The eight- and nine-year-olds stream in with the energy of soccer players. I let them group themselves at the tables rather than assign them seats. There are six tables for four each, which is more room than we need. While most of the students jam to sit near each other, one boy moves to the furthest table to sit alone. Although my initial instinct is to place him near others, I decide to watch and wait. At the 9:40 bell, I welcome them and describe our activity. I ask the class as a group what is the favorite place each has visited last summer, and hands shoot up. "The river" is the most common refrain, and I tell them it is mine also, but one student mentions Las Vegas and another Mt. Rainier. I ask each of them to sketch in pencil just an outline of his or her favorite place for five minutes and then give them a short talk and demonstration of mixing paint colors. When I let them loose on their task, there is an unbridled energy at some of the tables, with the expected tipping of at least one of the paint pots, which I explain is their responsibility to wipe up, but at the back, the solitary boy is slow, quiet and deliberate. After they settle down, I walk around to provide help and suggestions. The girl who has seen Mt. Rainier wants to know how to paint white, and I explain the trick of leaving blank spaces for what she wants to be white. When I finally reach the loner in the back, I see that he is painting, with patience and some skill, what looks like an abandoned cabin. I praise his effort and ask him where it is. He tells me it is a gold miner's cabin in Washington and asks me if I know where that is. I nod and tell him it is a little town at the bottom of a huge hill east of Nevada City. He gives me a small nod and a hint of a smile. I want to ask him if he lives there, but I don't. No need to dredge up any unwanted memories of Abe.

The class hour, which isn't a full hour, zips to its end. I give each of them a five-minute warning, as ask them to put their names on a large folder I have put at each place, to store his and her artwork for the semester. Since it will take a little while for each of their paintings to dry, I ask them to put their painting on top of but not inside the folder. By the end of the semester, I promise them, each will have a portfolio of artwork to show off – and it will be worth showing off.

I do the same exercise with each class, partly to give them an easy outlet and partly to assess their skill levels with mixing colors and handling paints. At lunch, I make a point to sit with Dawn's kindergarten teacher. She is the only one of all of the teachers who is in her first year of teaching.

By the closing bell, I am physically tired but stimulated by contact with so many children. As I walk down the hall to pick up Dawn, I catch a glimpse of her hugging a girl with light brown skin and a cascade of reddish-yellow hair, before she runs over to hug me. I practically trip over her grasp of my legs and grab a desk to balance myself. "I'm going to learn to read!" she proclaims as if I'd never told her so. (Maybe I hadn't.) In the jumble of parents reclaiming their children, I wave over my shoulder to Ms. Joyner and feel the pulse of my cell phone. I reach for it as Dawn continues to rave about her day. As soon as I see it is from Analee, I put the phone back into my pocket until we get into the car. Dawn prides herself on fastening herself into her own car seat, and I glance at my phone while she does so.

"No decision today. Will send it to you as soon as I receive it from the court. Analee."

I sit for a moment with a tumble of reactions. I have spent a full day without even thinking of the threat of the lawsuit; now it comes back like a punch in the jaw. Analee texted me instead of calling. Does she not want to talk to me about what happened? Should I phone her back?

"Mom" comes to me as if from another place. "Can we get ice cream on the way back home?"

"Absolutely. Comin' up." I vow to stay in Dawn's reality as much as I can.

As I reflect back, my time at school that first semester was one of the few respites I have had from my preoccupation with the lawsuit since it was filed. All the good developments of that semester seem too often to get lost in the misery of preparing for trial. I did manage to get a book contract for "Where Does the Ketchup Grow?" but the whole advance went directly to Analee for attorney fees. Dawn loves kindergarten, she quickly learned to read, and she made friends – especially with the biracial Alana with the luxuriant hair – but she still misses Ian and asks why she can't visit with him.

18

ANALEE

The decision arrived on Friday of the same week as the hearing. The court decided it could not determine the merits of Patty's claim to parentage without hearing the facts. Nor could it grant visitation to Patty without a prior determination of parentage, since the guardianship had been concluded. As soon as I finished reading it, I e-mailed it to Karen, inviting her to call me.

Since this was the outcome I had expected, I had been strategizing in my head – while cleaning up after dinner, running in the morning or even working on more routine cases – on what discovery to conduct and when. I was eager to take the deposition of Doug, Patty's husband, since we already knew he didn't want this lawsuit. I want to depose him even before I depose Patty, and I was already composing questions to get under her skin.

By the time Karen called, I had already moved to this eager phase and had almost forgotten my role in trying to assuage her disappointment at the lawsuit going forward. Fortunately, she leapt in with her questions before I could blunder into my discovery lust. Did the court think Patty was going to win; is that why it did not dismiss her action? No, not at all, I explained, but the court recognized it would need to know the facts before it could rule on the merits. I gave her my canned rendition of decisions on the law versus decisions on facts. As I spoke, I could almost hear my own eagerness to get into the meat of this lawsuit, which surprised me even as I began to recognize it.

Karen seemed prepared to accept the reality of going forward, but when I mentioned taking Doug's deposition, I hit a wall with her.

"No. He confided in me and said he wanted no part of this lawsuit."

"Did you promise to keep him out of it?"

"I'm not sure. I didn't know if he could be kept out of it, but I want to respect his wishes."

We went back and forth on this before I abandoned the effort in this conversation, but she did give me her clear permission to take Patty's deposition, and I sent out the notice the following day. Ideally, I would take his before taking hers, or at least immediately afterward; but I wanted to make sure I would depose Patty before Stephen would depose Karen. I did send Karen a lengthy e-mail explanation of what Doug could add factually to the whole background, including the period of time while she was in the hospital and rehab and had no way of knowing what was going on in Doug and Patty's home. I told her how the court would want to know Doug's stance in this unusual parentage suit, what he could contribute to the question of how the children got along with each other, and more. I wanted to let her sit with this note and digest the advantages.

Stephen phoned me the next day to request a different date for Patty's deposition, since he had a trial set for the day I had it scheduled. We reviewed our respective calendars and found a new date we were both available, subject to his clearing the new date with Patty.

"Stephen, one more thing: I want to take Doug's deposition."

I didn't yet have Karen's authorization for this, but I hoped I could persuade her.

The line went silent for a long moment before he replied.

"What about the spousal privilege not to testify?"

"Let's see if he claims it. Patty can't claim it for him."

"Do you really want to go down that path?"

"I think I have to. Can you imagine if I don't take his deposition and he appears at the trial to testify? I can't let that happen."

"I hear you, but there's another solution. Will you back off if I can give you a stipulation that he won't testify at all in this proceeding?"

We left it at that, with his obvious need to discuss this issue and its ramifications with both Patty and Doug, and my need to talk to Karen about it too. As I thought about it afterward, this stipulation could be the best solution. Karen would not have to violate whatever promise she may have made to Doug, and the court would be left wondering what role Patty's husband has to play in this family. Her going forward without him by her side would leave the impression with the court that he wanted no part of this effort. What kind of family would Patty be creating where Dawn would have two mothers, an uncle married to one of them, and two siblings, one of whom resents her?

Stephen got back to me within a day to say that Patty and Doug would agree to the proposed stipulation keeping him out of the whole action. When I spoke to Karen, she agreed immediately. She really wanted to honor Doug's request. Stephen had found a way to do that without our prejudicing our case.

Which is not to say I don't have some litigator's regrets about this. I have, in my periodic wakeful stages in the middle of the night, thought of brilliant, razor-sharp questions to ask him. But causing him pain on the stand might not advance my cause, and I have to keep telling myself that destroying one witness on the stand is not the same as winning the case.

19

KAREN

Analee told me I would need to attend Patty's deposition so that I could help her correct any misstatements Patty might make. I told her I would be there even though it entailed my taking a day off teaching. I didn't tell her how badly I wanted to be there to see Patty suffer under her questioning.

Sitting across a conference table from Analee and me, Patty wears a navy business suit with a sheer, lemon-colored blouse underneath, her hair so clean it glistens, pulled back into a bun. I wonder for the first time if Patty tints her hair; it has auburn highlights I have never noticed before. When Analee asks her to describe her educational background, she mentions first her law degree from UC-Davis. Asked if she'd ever practiced law, she says, "No, I wanted to be a full-time mother first."

"How many children do you have?"

"Counting Dawn, three." Analee had trained me not to react, and even I recognize this as calculated bait. I sit impassively next to Analee, gripping the pen she has provided me to jot down any notes to her.

"Did you consider yourself Dawn's mother when you agreed to donate your ovum to Karen?"

"No, Dawn didn't yet exist." Patty tries to squelch a smile, but I can see her trying to mess with Analee.

"I'll rephrase my question," Analee says quietly, apparently unruffled. "When you agreed with your sister Karen to donate your ovum to her, were you planning to become the mother of that child?"

"Not at that time."

"When you obtained Karen's consent to be named as Dawn's guardian, were you then planning to become Dawn's mother?"

"Not right away. It was something of an emergency. Dawn and Karen both needed immediate care. After we settled into the situation, it became gradually obvious that I was as much a parent to Dawn as to Sandra and Ian."

"And did you consider yourself Dawn's parent when Karen left the hospital?"

"I would say yes; Dawn still needed my full-time care."

"When Karen left the rehab facility and returned home, did you consider yourself Dawn's parent then?"

"Yes."

"And that sense of parenthood was something you took very seriously?"

"Yes, definitely."

"Then why didn't you assert that you were Dawn's other parent when Karen filed her petition to end the guardianship?"

I can tell she hadn't thought of it then at all. Her expression begins to dissolve like a pattern in sand rinsed by a wave, and her face takes a tilt toward her lawyer, but she rallies.

"I didn't assert it then because it seemed obvious to me that the guardianship needed to be maintained, and I didn't want to add to Karen's troubles because at that time she still had so many."

"And now she doesn't have so many troubles?"

There is a long pause, and I wish a video could capture the tics crossing her face.

"Karen is still troubled, and she has made it more difficult for the whole family by not letting me spend time with Dawn. Dawn needs her whole family, not just her birth mother." She spits out the words 'birth mother' and glares at me as she does so. I give her as vacant a stare as I can muster.

"Does Doug regard himself as Dawn's father?" Analee is shifting her tack. "I notice he's not a party plaintiff."

"He doesn't feel as strongly as I do about this and chose not to be a party." Patty says this with such pursed lips that I can imagine what a hard time she must have given him.

"But answer my question: does Doug regard himself as Dawn's father?"

"He's been a real father to her ever since she came to live with us, even though he doesn't think of himself as her father."

"So if you prevail in this lawsuit, Dawn will have two legal mothers and no legal relationship to your husband?"

"Calls for a legal conclusion," interjects her lawyer.

Analee reminds Patty she should still answer the question.

"Yes. Doug will still be Dawn's uncle. Dawn will have two loving parents, and I will be there to ensure her physical and emotional safety."

"You believe Karen will not ensure Dawn's physical and emotional safety?"

"That's exactly what I'm worried about."

"What makes you think that Karen will not take care of Dawn's physical and emotional safety?"

"Well, just a few months ago, she apparently accidentally dropped Dawn into the river. Dawn nearly suffered a concussion and could easily have drowned. Karen thinks nothing of taking Dawn on hikes where there are rattlesnakes and mountain lions."

I suddenly recall Analee and the rattlesnake and suppress my own smile.

"Are there rattlesnakes in your community?"

"I don't think so. I've never seen one."

"And no mountain lions, I suppose." We had all read the article about the suburban woman who discovered a mountain lion attacking her six-year-old son in the backyard.

"Not that I know of."

"Do you ever take your children to the river to swim?"

"No, I don't think it's safe. We have a pool in our back yard."

I watch Patty as if she were a person I had never seen before. Had I ever noticed how prim she looks and sounds? It occurs to me for the first time that she probably thinks the river is too dirty; her kids could drag mud into the house.

"Do any of your friends take their children to the river to swim?"

"Maybe; I don't know."

"Are there other ways in which you believe Karen jeopardizes Dawn's safety?"

"I have no sense of security that Karen will not again sink into a deep depression, like she did before. She's always been moody."

"With Karen's having always been moody, why did you decide to entrust her with your eggs?"

"I thought becoming a parent might make her a happier person. I had no idea she would become so depressed that she needed to be hospitalized."

"How would you be better able to protect Dawn in such an emergency as a legal parent rather than as a guardian?"

"We'd be able to rescue Dawn immediately, without having to seek a legal remedy first."

"When you say Karen has always been moody, what do you mean?"

"Sometimes she is very withdrawn and doesn't want other people around her. When we were growing up, sometimes she went for days without speaking to me."

"Do you know that this is a current problem?"

"Well, I haven't seen her much since she cut off contact."

"You mean, since you filed this lawsuit?"

"No, since she terminated the guardianship."

"So, for the last five or six months, you have not seen Karen at all?"

"Only in the mediation sessions."

"You haven't had any regular contact with Karen in the last year, have you?"

"No."

"How would you describe Dawn's relationship with Ian and Sandra?"

"Ian and Dawn have always been close; they love each other's company. Ian misses Dawn and asks when he can see her again. He is a protective, slightly older brother to her."

"What about Sandra? How does she relate Dawn?"

"Well, Sandra is three years older and not that interested in her younger siblings."

"Would you describe Sandra as sisterly toward Dawn?"

"No. Well, maybe as a jealous sister." As soon as these words come out, Patty bites her lip.

"Please describe how she is jealous."

"She doesn't want her younger siblings to have anything she doesn't have."

"Does she treat Ian the same as she treated Dawn?"

"Not really. I mean, he's a boy and she's a girl."

"How did Sandra treat Dawn? Was she ever friendly toward her?"

"Sandra treated Dawn as an unwelcome outsider. She resented her presence in our home. With Ian, she's just a bossy older sister."

"How, if at all, do you think it might be better if Dawn were imposed on Sandra as a sister?"

"I wouldn't use the word 'imposed.'"

"How, if at all, do you think it might be better if Dawn were determined by the court to be Sandra's sister?"

"I think Sandra would have to make an adjustment."

"How, if at all, would it be better *for Dawn* to have Sandra as her sister?"

"It would be better for Dawn to know that she has the security of two parents."

"Not my question. How would it be better for Dawn to have Sandra as her sister?"

"I don't know."

"Is Sandra in therapy now?" At this, Patty glares at Analee.

"Objection; privacy," Stephen interjects. I think, how can he object if this is all the same family? But Analee doesn't argue.

"Answer the question."

At this, Patty glances at her lawyer for direction, but with the faintest of nod from him, she understands she needs to answer.

"Yes."

"For how long?"

"About eight months."

"What behaviors led you to put her into therapy?"

"She was demanding all of Doug's and my attention, was not getting along well with other children...."

"Sandra was never kind to Dawn when she was in your home, was she?"

"Sandra ignored Dawn when she could. The age difference made that easy for a while, since they had different skills and interests."

"What about when she couldn't ignore Dawn, such as at the family dinner table?"

"She would try to talk over Dawn and keep the attention on herself. We had to remind her it's rude to interrupt others. We're working on it."

"Sandra is now ten, am I right?" Patty nods, and her lawyer nudges her to answer out loud. But Analee has gone on to her next question.

"Does Sandra know about this lawsuit?"

"I intend not to tell her or Ian abut it."

"But, if she did learn of it, what do you think would be her reaction?"

"She would be upset."

"So, if you are found to be Dawn's parent, how will you present this to Sandra?"

"We will deal with that in her therapy."

"What does your husband Doug think of your having brought this lawsuit?"

"He respects my right to protect Dawn in the way I have chosen." She has practiced this answer.

"Do you think it may be confusing for Dawn to have you as a second mother, Doug as her uncle and Ian and Sandra as her cousins and brother and sister?"

"Not at all. She has her own names for Doug and me that the children found themselves. Doug is 'Daddy Too' – t-o-o – and I am "Mommy Too.' Dawn is already comfortable with this family construct."

"Have you and Doug ever disagreed over the family structure you are trying to create?"

"What I have described to you is a family structure that already exists." Patty insists.

"Have you and Doug ever disagreed over your seeking to be legally determined to be Dawn's second mother?"

Patty shrugs.

"You need to answer verbally." This time it is Analee reminding her.

"Yes."

"What did he say?"

"I don't want to answer that question."

Patty's lawyer asks Analee if they can step outside the room for a moment, and Analee consents. While they are out of the room, I ask Analee if this is part of the agreement she made about Doug not being a witness. She tells me it is related but not the same.

When Patty and her lawyer come back, he speaks up.

"My client claims the spousal privilege and will not answer the question."

"The privilege belongs to Doug, not to Patty." She asks the

reporter to certify the question so that she can pursue it with the court.

"Do you recognize that, if you are determined to be a second parent of Dawn, that you will be legally responsible for her support and may have to pay child support?"

"Of course." Patty is well prepared on this one. "In fact, I have already set up a Scholar Share account for her as well as for Sandra and Ian."

"What money did you use for this account for Dawn?"

"Doug and I pool all our money, so we used our joint funds."

"Am I correct that you have no earned income?"

"Yes; we agreed that I would not work while our children are young."

"So if you were ordered to pay child support for Dawn, you would be using joint funds which are actually Doug's income?"

"Yes."

After Analee finishes Patty's deposition, she signals me to follow her as she struts back to her office. She sinks dramatically into her chair, throws me a beaming smile and all but gestures with her hands to praise her performance.

"You did a great job," I tell her with what little spirit I can muster. I had felt early in the day how thoroughly she had debunked Patty's grounds for the lawsuit, but as the day wore on, what struck me was how destructive this whole process is becoming. I want no part of it, but I am mired in its center. While I know I am lucky to have Analee defending me, I just want to run as far as I can from all these personal attacks. How could anyone reconstruct a life after this?

I thank Analee and tell her I need to pick up Dawn. Before I leave, she reminds me that my own deposition is scheduled soon – on the Wednesday before Thanksgiving – and that I should make an appointment with Gerta for preparation. I obey. Gerta gives me a half-day appointment on the preceding Tuesday, when I have no classes.

I drive as if released to vacation. Dawn is visiting Alana at her home for the first time. Alana has come to our home after school once before, and I have spoken to her mother Zara on the telephone, but I have not yet met her. Their home is somewhere north of Nevada City off one of those roads that seem to trail off into wilderness, but I have directions drawn by Alana's mother or father. As I pull off the Interstate onto Highway 49, I start to relax. When I weave into the woods north of Nevada City I feel a deep relief, emanating from the very scent and sway of the trees. My directions tell me to pull off onto Ray Lane just past a row of ten mailboxes. As soon as I do, I catch sight of a beautiful log cabin, with a larger home structure going up behind it. I lower my window and just close my eyes for a moment, to listen to the calm rustle of the trees.

"Karen? Are you okay?"

Startled by the voice next to me, I jump in my seat. To my left stands one of the most astonishingly beautiful women I have ever seen, with smooth skin the color of medjool dates, a compact flat nose, eyes the color of amber, and a head of African hair a foot long, descending in every direction from the top of her graceful head.

"I'm sorry. I just drove from a meeting in Sacramento and closed my eyes for a moment to rest them in this lovely quiet. You must be Zara."

"Welcome. The girls are inside."

As I follow her into the cabin, I notice a woven scarf looped around her neck, with reds, oranges and yellows of varying hues in a loose pattern. When I admire it, she tells me she made it. "That's what I do."

"Mommy!" Dawn throws herself at me. "Alana and I are counting freckles. She has as many as I do. See?" She holds up a piece of paper with lines and hatch marks on it, seven groups of five.

"How did you learn to do that?" Before letting her answer, I turn to Alana and introduce myself as Karen.

"Ms. Haskins," Zara corrects, and Alana stands up and says, "good to meet you, Ms. Haskins." She then explains that her dad has taught her to count by lines and hatches. "He told me I only need to be able to count to five, and then he can count how many fives."

I see now for the first time that Alana's face and forearms are covered in freckles, though not as noticeable as Dawn's because her skin is tawny.

"Did you get them all?" I ask.

"No, that's impossible." We all laugh. Zara offers me some iced tea, and we go sit in the living room while the girls return to their freckle counting. I admire the rocking chair she offers me, with graceful curved spokes and a silky woven seat that looks like it might be Zara's work. She explains that her husband John is a master wood craftsman and furniture maker and that she has indeed woven the seat, I ask if I had seen his work in the gallery on Broad Street, and she tells me they both exhibit there.

"He uses his own name, John Reinholdt, but I use Alana's middle name, Sahar, because there is already a clothing line named Zara."

Zara shifts the conversation to me, telling me that Alana says I am an artist who paints illustrations for children's books.

I laugh. "I see I have a good agent in my daughter."

She laughs too, revealing a huge, bright smile. I already want to paint her portrait and am beginning to wonder how I could ask. She explains that Dawn had told Alana she already knows how to paint and Alana wants to learn. I offer to have Alana come over some Saturday for lessons, and she leaps at the invitation.

John walks in from a back door, brushing sawdust off his overalls. Unlike Zara, he is tall and robust, with short blonde hair and a pale mustache. He could be a Swede or German.

"Hi," he greets me warmly, with a smile nearly as bright as Zara's. They invite Dawn and me to stay for dinner, which is already heating in the oven. Zara allows me to help construct a salad, into which she breaks small pieces of flatbread. "Fattoush," she explains. She quickly mixes lemon juice and olive oil to dress the salad, and places the casserole on the table. It is an aromatic concoction of chicken, black olives and lemons, accompanied by a bowl of rice. All the food is delicious and new to me. Dawn eats with as much enthusiasm as the rest of us. Conversation is easy, and I cannot resist asking John and Zara how they had met.

They exchange a quick look, which I read as their decision to let John tell the story. He explains that seven years ago he had spent six months in Ethiopia, partly learning some ancient carpentry techniques and partly with an aid organization, where Zara was also donating her time. At this point, Zara picks up the story. Originally from Tunis, the daughter of a banker and his wife, she found herself at loose ends after graduating from university. She and John fell in love in Ethiopia and he persuaded her to move to the United States with him, first to Santa Cruz, where he had gone to college, and then here, where he had grown up.

"It was much easier for me to fit in in Ethiopia than in Nevada City," she explains. "When we go to crafts fairs in the Bay Area or Chicago, I fit in just fine, and I can even get Tunisian food, but here I am a strange one."

"I grew up here. You don't have to explain." I add, thinking how my teen-aged differences pale by comparison to hers.

"I'm glad our girls made friends with each other so quickly."

John asks me if I am married, and I tell him no, I've always been single.

"I have a donor," Dawn pipes up unbidden.

"She's right," I acknowledge. I have never heard this social admission from her.

"What's a donor?" Alana asks, and her parents pause to give me the first go at it.

"A donor is a man who allows a single woman like me to use his genes so that I can become a mother." That is apparently enough information for her, for she does not ask another question.

Before we leave, we make arrangements for Zara to bring Alana to our little house in Rough and Ready the following Saturday for painting lessons. On the drive home, I feel excited. I revel in this unfamiliar emotion all evening, to the point that I can hardly get to sleep.

20

ANALEE

Karen was already twenty minutes late for her dep prep session when I asked Gerta to call her, but there was no answer. I still have to pick up the turkey and brine it, not to mention clean my house before family arrives tomorrow. I am becoming cranky about all the other things I could be doing besides waiting for Karen.

When she arrives five minutes later, she apologizes profusely, complaining of traffic on the road. When I ask why she didn't call to let me know, she explains that she didn't want to phone while driving, both her phone and car are too old for a Bluetooth connection. Trying to let go of my irritation, I ask her plans for Thanksgiving. Expecting to hear of a miniature dinner for two, I am happily surprised to hear she will be part of a celebration of twelve people – old friends since high school and their children, plus a new family and their child who is in kindergarten with Dawn.

"Take lots of pictures," I tell her. "We can use them at the trial."

Although she agrees, she casts me a peculiar look. *Is trial all there is?* I have occasionally read the same look on Adam's face at home.

I explain that we will role-play questions and answers this morning as if I were Patty's attorney and she were answering on the record. When we need to make corrections, I will stop to tell her. I

161

began with innocuous history: her education and occupations since college. When I ask what books she has written and illustrated, I suddenly remember that she had given me one for the boys but that I had never taken it out to read to them. I can't even remember where it is, but make a mental note to find it. I review with her the places she has lived since Dawn was born, covering her hospitalization and rehab only by periods of time, and ask her to describe her present home.

"It's an old cabin from the mining era, with a pump next to the sink and what used to be an ice box, and an outhouse. We have a real kitchen sink with faucets and running water, of course, and a refrigerator, and a working indoor bathroom, but the relics are part of the atmosphere. We have two bedrooms and a living room/studio for our painting."

I ask her about the nature of her relationship with Patty, as they were children, in high school, college and throughout their adulthood. Her descriptions of early life with her sister are tender. In high school, even though Patty led the life of a popular girl in groups and Karen had been an artist with purple streaks in her hair, Patty had made time for the two of them to be together alone and compare their lives. Karen's answers were good: short, real and sympathetic.

I begin to test her gently.

"What traditions have you developed with Dawn?"

"Traditions? She's five years old." We share a look of recognition that this is a bad answer. I toss out a prompt.

"For example, what do you do on Thanksgiving?"

Karen glances off to the side, as if recovering memories.

"For Dawn's first and second Thanksgiving, we went to Jenny or Megan's, which I always did before she was born. For the next two years, she was staying at Patty and Doug's and I went there to be with her. For the first of those I had to be released from rehab for the holiday. This year, Alana, Zara and John are joining us at Megan and Jeff's home."

"I know I'm not supposed to volunteer, but I remember one

lovely thing about the Thanksgivings at Patty and Doug's. His parents were there, and he clearly made them understand that Dawn is my daughter, even though she was staying with them at the time. He always respected me, even when I was down." Karen lowers her head.

"It's too bad he couldn't convince her not to bring this action," I remind her. She looks at me plaintively.

"Isn't there any way you can convince Patty's lawyer that she's welcome to see Dawn, but only if she's not suing me to become her parent?"

I tell her I will talk to Stephen once again, but wonder if this is the best time. "He might think we are just trying to get out of having your deposition taken."

She pleads with me to talk to him, doesn't care about appearing weak. I promise her I will, and we go back on task. I tell her that, if asked about traditions, she should say something to the effect that she and Dawn are developing them over time.

Gerta knocks and opens the door.

'It's Mr. Petrakis on the line. He wants to continue Karen's deposition."

As I grab the phone, I see Karen's expression lift.

"I'm sorry to do this at the last minute, but I'm going to have to postpone taking Karen's deposition. My wife's family arrives tonight, and she wants me home tomorrow."

Relieved myself, I tell him this is his prerogative, and we can pick a new date now or talk next week. He opts for talking next week. My own spirits lift with Karen's, and I begin to think of holiday preparations again.

"You're sprung for tomorrow. We can pick a new date next week. Will you be around for the next several weeks?" She assures me she isn't going anywhere and asks that we set this during the Christmas school break.

We wish each other a hurried happy Thanksgiving. She says the same to Gerta on her way out. Gerta and I leave early too.

I brine the turkey as soon as I get home, grateful to be early enough to start before dinner. It requires an ice chest to hold the several giant plastic garbage bags surrounding the turkey in its salty-sweet bath. After I close the lid on it and wash my hands, I go into my home study to find the book Karen had given me several months earlier, when I visited her in Rough and Ready. Rummaging through stacks of papers, I reflect on my irritation with Karen today, at her loss of energy for this lawsuit. I regard it as nearly life or death for her, as she had seemed to at the beginning. Now I have become so immersed in the complex legal issues that I have an extra layer of attachment to it. Karen, by contrast, has lapsed into complacency because normal life is good and the lawsuit has lost its immediacy to her. Trial is set for February, and I can only hope she will re-engage productively.

I find the slim book under some legal journals I had set aside for later reading. On the cover, a baboon with a jaunty, teasing humanoid expression hangs from a tree limb above a menacing leopard. I read it first, as I do with all books my boys receive, and decide to try it out on them before bed tonight.

Cleo and the Leopard

Cleo and the Leopard lived in the same neighborhood, sometimes even in the same tree, but never at the same time, because they were not friends.

But they understood each other's speech and sometimes spoke to each other. As a baboon, Cleo spoke more than the Leopard. Words came to her readily because she was always talking with the other baboons. The Leopard was usually silent.

When the Leopard tried to sneak up on some tasty little mongoose under Cleo's tree, she and her brothers started a horrible screeching. "Yak, yak,

yak, yak!" They scared away the Leopard's meal. The Leopard was annoyed.

"You make too much noise," he snarled.

"We protect our friends," Cleo retorted. "You don't have any friends," she taunted.

"I don't need any friends," said the Leopard. "I am enough for me."

"My friends help groom me, and it feels good." One of Cleo's brothers was picking ticks out of her ears.

"I have a nice long tongue and I can groom myself," said the Leopard.

"I have a thumb that lets me hold onto branches and swing from them," bragged Cleo as she flung herself from one limb to another.

"So you can," said the Leopard, "but I have excellent claws for climbing," and he leapt up so suddenly and so close to Cleo that she shrieked and swung away as fast as she could.

"You have an ugly bare rump," said Leopard, staring at Cleo's bare pink behind. "I have nice fur all over my body."

"Talk about ugly," Cleo shot back, "your fur is all spotted, as if you had sat under the weeping tree when it was dripping black juice. Mine is a nice even brown."

None of their talk was pleasant.

One night Cleo disappeared. The Leopard did not see her for three days. When Cleo reappeared, she had a tiny baby tucked in her arm. She moved more slowly and carefully with only one arm free. She no longer taunted the Leopard. She was too busy feeding and grooming her baby. The Leopard paced below, consumed with curiosity. Despite himself, he admired how tender and attentive Cleo was with her baby.

When Cleo looked down at the Leopard looking up at her baby, she became nervous. She became so nervous that her milk stopped flowing on one side. She switched her baby to the other arm, but something happened in the way she shifted her body and she lost her balance for a second.

Cleo's baby fell out of the tree. It landed with a soft plomp on the leafy ground and lay still. A nearby jackal lifted its nose and trotted toward the baby.

The leopard sprang out of the tree before the jackal could get to the baby. "Stay away!" he hissed loudly, and the jackal slunk away.

Cleo held both hands in her mouth, paralyzed by fear.

The Leopard sniffed the baby and nudged it with its paw. The baby opened its round black eyes but did not move.

The Leopard grasped the baby's neck in its jaw, but very gently. He leapt onto the tree trunk with the baby dangling from his mouth. Cleo looked on in horror. The Leopard climbed to the limb where Cleo sat frozen in place. Very gently, he set the baby down in front of Cleo. The baby quickly crawled back into Cleo's arm, where it belonged.

The Leopard crawled back down the tree trunk and sat still.

Cleo did not know what to say. For a long time, she was unusually quiet.

Finally, she said, "Leopard, I thought you would eat my baby, but you didn't. I was wrong about you. You may have ugly fur, but you are beautiful inside."

"Don't mention it," said the Leopard, as he slunk into the bush.

I read it twice, admiring what Karen had written. I glance at its publication date five years ago and surmise that Karen had written it while pregnant with Dawn. I wonder how my own boys will receive this story.

At dinner we allocate chores for Thanksgiving Day. My dad and both of Adam's parents will join us. Since they are all local, they will come just for the afternoon. Adam reminds us all that he is in charge of roasting and carving the turkey. I will prepare the stuffing – "please, no oysters this year" from my picky eater Andy, who favors only red and green foods. I promise to leave out the oysters and to include apples and celery, but I remind him this is an occasion on which there is no getting around a brown bird and mostly brown stuffing. But I tell him I want his help in making cranberry sauce and green beans, which satisfies him. I remind Alex that he will have to set the table and arrange appetizers on plates. He groans but agrees when his father gives him a stern look.

At bedtime, I tell the boys I have a new book to read them, about a leopard and baboon in Africa.

"Not another Kipling story," Alex gripes, our literary critic.

"No, a more modern author, and it's short," I assure him. Adam decides to join us. I had privately mentioned the book to him without showing it to him.

I read it slowly, with different voices for the two animals, and everyone listens raptly. When I finish, I glance at Andy, whose eyes are wet.

"That's completely unrealistic!" Alex exclaims. "Animals have no empathy. That leopard would have eaten that baboon in a hot second."

"Yes, that's what we would expect," I tell him, "but that wouldn't be a story."

Adam reminds Alex that there are videos of real wild animals befriending one another under improbable circumstances. He has seen a nature film about a young lion that befriended an abandoned gazelle fawn. "I think animals do have emotions, but we may not know how to read them."

Adam asks Andy what he thinks.

"Animals have feelings too. The leopard knew this baby needed its mom, and he did the right thing." He takes the book from me so that he can look at the pictures again.

After we say goodnight to the boys, Adam tells me he admires the book.

"If we had a dog, Alex would know that dogs have great empathy." He slaps me on my butt, knowing my aversion to dogs.

After we get into bed, I realize it has been weeks since I have seen my dad, and I miss him. Mom died not long after he retired three years ago and he has often seemed to regret having left the practice. It still bears his name, Meriwether & Meriwether, even though only I am left to carry it on. Carter (we called each other by our first names in the office) trained and mentored me, and I crave talking to him about Karen's case. I decide to ask him to come early tomorrow so that we can talk.

I call him the next morning.

"Carter," I begin. In this way he will know my subject is business, not family. My dad reminds me of the obvious, that Thanksgiving is a poor time to have our conversation, and we agree to meet for coffee on Friday morning.

Over pumpkin lattes on Friday morning I bleed out all my concerns about the case, the legal obstacles, Karen's avoidance and request that I try to persuade Patty's attorney to drop the lawsuit if Karen will grant ready access to Dawn, and my reluctance to do what she asked.

"Don't you think that would be the better outcome?" he asks, typically trenchant.

"Yes, but if Patty couldn't be persuaded in mediation, why

should she now, and doesn't it empower Patty to ask just before Karen is deposed?"

"You and Stephen know it's the better outcome. That is reason enough. You can make it your idea rather than Karen's if you're worried about appearances."

"I bet you could persuade him," I tease.

"He's not the one who needs to be persuaded. I imagine he is struggling with his own client."

"Thanks, Dad. As always, you lift my load." I feel so relieved, lighter and clear-headed. "How are things with you?"

He smiles ruefully, his lips forming a strained 'S' shape, one side down and the other up. I don't remember seeing this smile when he was younger and working. "Not enough on my plate," he admits quietly.

"Would you like to come back and help on this case? I bet you could persuade Petrakis."

This time his smile is open. "No, I'm past that. I need to find new water to wade in."

Full of resolve and new energy, I speak with Stephen the Monday after Thanksgiving. He has called to set a new time for Karen's deposition, and we agree on a date during the week after Christmas. "Normally, I don't work then, but with a trial date of February 1, I've got no choice."

"Stephen, as much as I love the challenges of this case, I wonder whether we're leading our clients in the wrong direction. I'm pretty sure that Karen would still give Patty regular access to Dawn if Patty didn't insist on being named as Dawn's parent. If we try this case, no matter the outcome, these sisters will hate each other, and Patty may never see Dawn again."

He reminds me that this was what we had told each other at the outset of the case. "Recognition as a parent is a do-or-die issue for Patty, and I haven't been able to dissuade her, no matter what I say." He sighs. "I don't like being just a tool, and I suspect you don't either.

I know your dad complained bitterly when he had to recognize he couldn't persuade his own client. He coined the term, 'being a tool'."

I thank him. Dad had never used the term in talking to me, but certainly I recognize his values. Without telling him so, I love that Stephen has provided me a new detail about my dad.

21

KAREN

Tradition? Me? The question comes back to me as soon as I get on the road home. Was I supposed to have traditions? All my life I have regarded them with something bordering on contempt. To me, tradition connotes boredom, stagnation and a failure of creativity. Patty is the one who respects traditions; I am the one who flouts them. To her, traditions are likely a source of comfort and strength; by re-enacting them, she does her duty without having to think about what it means. I can name a list of traditions for Patty and Doug, but none come to mind for myself. They have the same menu every Thanksgiving and Christmas Day; they spend a week every summer at Lake Tahoe at the same lodge; they host a Labor Day barbeque and pool party for their neighbors every year; they spend a weekend at the same hotel in San Francisco every year for their anniversary. Patty visits our mother every week on Sunday, usually after she drops the family home from church. The family goes to All Souls Parish most Sundays; I went with them once while I was staying with them after my release from the hospital. All I can remember is my misreading the church name as "All Souls Perish," which seemed fitting enough to me at the time but an unlikely name for a church. Patty's values lie in following the rules and traditions.

The problem has always been the same for me in our family. I like things that are wayward. I like things taking an unexpected turn and going their own way. I love Dawn's unruly hair. Part of what makes me so uncomfortable about Patty is that she is *so relentlessly proper*. Her straightening Dawn's hair was her own message to me and she knew exactly how I would react. I can't stand the thought of Dawn turning out like Patty.

I think I have values in place of traditions. I value Dawn above all else, and nothing is more important to me. I am only starting to forgive myself for failing her in her second year, but I know I can make up for that time only in the present and future. I value Megan and Jenny, who have been my good friends since high school, and their families. I go to the opening of each play that Megan directs. A tradition? No, to me it is a way of honoring her achievement. I respect and love the world of nature; it gives me more comfort than any church ever will. I respect growing plants. Aha! I am building a garden tradition with Dawn, who wanted to plant the flowers she first saw at Rock Creek Farm. We have created our own raised bed of tomatoes and lettuce and herbs, out of the rubble of our little back yard.

Tomorrow I will bring sweet potatoes to Thanksgiving dinner at Megan and Jeff's. Online, I found an interesting recipe including apples and brown sugar. If I had to make the same dishes each year, I would be bored and resentful. Tomorrow we will have new friends at the feast --Zara and John and Alana. Adding them to our circle is a blessing.

Tomorrow we will celebrate our connection, our friendships and our larger family and good fortune. I will put the lawsuit out of mind for the holiday. Dawn is back. Nothing could make me more thankful.

In that spirit, I fetch Dawn from school and, after a simple supper, begin to prepare the sweet potatoes. Dawn asks why I am cooking after dinner, and when I explain I am bringing a dish to

Megan's for Thanksgiving, she asks what she can bring. I tell her that if she make a drawing or painting and gives it to Megan that it will be a great addition to the celebration. As I slice the sweet potatoes and lay them in the dish with apple slices, she sets up her own paints, jar of water and large sheet of paper. By the time my concoction comes out of the oven, with an aroma of baked apples, Dawn has finished her own -- two rows of people holding hands, one row upside down because, she explains, we are all in a circle and the paper isn't large enough to show us all across the page. She proudly identifies us all – she and I in the center, Alana holding her other hand, Alana's parents together, Ian holding my other hand, Megan's husband Jeff next to her and Sam next, Jenny and her sons below. All of us smiling, all of us connected. Ian is near the center even though I know she knows he will not be with us tomorrow.

Thanksgiving Day warms enough that we can all mingle outside on the deck Jeff had built at the back of their home, above Deer Creek. We can hear the gurgle of the water just below our own conversations. It turns out that Jeff, who does construction of high-end homes, knows of John's furniture work, though they hadn't met before, and they talk woodworking, while I loop arms with Zara and bring her into the kitchen with Jenny and Megan. She carries John's contribution to the meal, a steaming blue bowl of red cabbage slices, with a rich sweet-sour fragrance. I admit I have never seen or heard of such a dish, and Zara explains that it has been part of John's family dinner celebrations for as long as he can remember, originally cooked by his grandmother to accompany roast pork. "Every time he bites into this, he says the same thing: 'this brings back my family.' Watch him, and tell me if he doesn't do the same tonight." We all laugh, and she fetches two glasses of cider to take out to John and Alana.

After Zara leaves the kitchen, Jenny confesses she experiences every Thanksgiving as a loss since her divorce three years ago; Daniel had been part of a huge family that had two large dining tables and two turkeys to feed them all. For eleven years that had been their celebration. Megan assures her she will always have us as family. I hug Jenny and tell her I am grateful each year to be back in this family.

Megan tapes Dawn's drawing to the wall adjacent to the large dining table. As we eat dinner, John sits directly across from me next to Zara. When the red cabbage comes around, he bends to inhale its vapor and exclaims how it brings back memories of feasts with his grandparents, now gone, and his parents. "I'm always amazed at how a particular taste, or a particular scent, can bring back such powerful memories." Zara winks at me across the table.

Unbidden, I suddenly remember pan-fried trout with lemon and a touch of vinegar that Abe often prepared after catching fish in the river. I push back that memory by inhaling the food in front of me.

On the day of my deposition I face Patty's lawyer for the first time. He sits across his conference table with a porcelain teacup and saucer in front of him. The rest of us have coffee in mugs. He is a man who will have hair all of his life; it is like sod atop his head, thick and erect, but gray. Unruly eyebrows mark his face; on the left side the hairs jut outward, pushing his horn-rimmed glasses away from his forehead, and on the right the hairs jut upward. Even those eyebrows can't overwhelm his black, penetrating eyes. I imagine him as a brilliant law professor.

To his left sits Patty. Her head is down and she is furiously writing something. Too late, I want to tell her. Her hair is uncharacteristically loose today, parted in the middle, and I can see the narrow dye line between her part and the vibrant auburn of the rest of her hair. She passes the note to her attorney but still does not look up at me.

At the end of the table, between him and me, is the court reporter, a friendly young Asian woman with an array of equipment before her — a computer with at least three cords attached and a tiny extra keyboard with only a few keys, from which she is poised to begin. Distracted by it, I wonder how its few keys can capture whatever will be said.

"Good morning, Ms. Haskins. I am Stephen Petrakis, your sister's attorney." His voice is deep and steady. He launches into a rote set of instructions, not to answer a question if I do not understand it, to ask him if I do not understand a question, and so on, as if I am an idiot. He tells me our dialogue will be printed into a book (*as if* this were book-worthy), which I will be tasked to read and to correct any errors. He asks me to recite my full name and address, and I obey. It proves to be my first and last good answer of the day.

"Rough and Ready, is that a real place?" He asks with some sarcasm and a trace of a smile.

"Haven't you ever been to the Gold country?" Analee kicks my foot, her signal for me to behave. "Yes, it's the name of a real town."

He wastes no further time in preliminaries.

"Was your sister Patricia involved in your decision to become pregnant?"

"No. I decided that myself."

"Was she involved in your choice of a sperm donor?"

"Yes. I previewed the choices with her and my friend Megan." That day again. And so he walks me through that worst decision of my life, to have my sister donate her eggs so I could become pregnant.

"Why did you use your sister's eggs?"

I pause for a moment here. I could rant for days about why this was a terrible decision.

"One of the fertility nurses gave me the idea, and when I asked Patty, she said yes."

"Was Patricia present at Dawn's birth?"

"At the moment of her birth, no, but she and my friend Megan were at the hospital with me." I notice Patty's furious writing has begun again.

He asks why, at that very moment, Patty was not there. I have not thought about this at all since then, but it floods back. There is a reason in nature that women forget the details of their labor and birth; it is simply too painful to replicate. I had wanted no drugs, which was not Patty's way of giving birth; she'd had a spinal both times and apparently had had relatively short labors (I wasn't there). When I was in my fifth or sixth hour of hard labor, groaning like a wounded elephant while I stood in a shower under a relieving stream of hot water, Megan gripped my hand and reassured me I could do this, just stick with it. Patty paced outside the shower, haranguing me to take some drugs and be done with it. When the doctor popped in, Patty quizzed her as to why she wasn't doing something to relieve the labor. The doctor made it clear that it was my decision to make. I couldn't stand in the shower all night, I had to return to the hard, narrow pallet of the delivery table, but the doctor offered to cut the amniotic sac to relieve the pressure. My water had not broken and I was nowhere near fully dilated. As soon as I said yes, a momentary, relieving flood of warm water bathed my legs, and then, soon after, my labor became more intense. Patty kept telling me I was doing this to myself and that I was foolish not to take drugs to relieve the pain. I yelled at her to shut up or get the fuck out of the room. She paced around a bit more, grumbling, and then left. Megan was the only person with me as Dawn emerged, at five eleven in the morning.

"Ms. Haskins, I asked why your sister left the delivery room." Apparently I had answered the question only in my own head.

"She kept badgering me to take drugs to relieve the pain, and I wanted a natural childbirth, so I told her to leave the room."

"Did Patricia take you home from the hospital?"

"Yes."

"Did Patricia help you out frequently during the first weeks and months of Dawn's life?"

"Yes, as did my friends Megan and Jenny. They all knew more about new babies than I did. They were all helpful."

He continues in this vein, and I am beginning to get a feel for answering these questions. As I am starting to relax, I notice more of the room. Behind him on a credenza are about fifty Christmas cards. I can even see the faces on some of them, no doubt satisfied clients. I randomly focus on one card with a couple and their three children seated in front of a fireplace with three stockings hung from the mantel. I am answering questions on automatic pilot. The youngest child in the photo has red hair remarkably like Dawn's and it is curly like hers. I stare more closely and finally recognize it is Patty and Doug, with their children and Dawn in the photo. *Unbelievable!* How did they do this? How could they!

"I need to take a break," I blurt. I nearly topple the chair as I get up, and unavoidably see Patty staring at me. Analee follows me to the hall. There is a window to the conference room, and I have to get as far away from it as I can. Analee leads me outside, where no one can see or hear me. I burst into tears. She understands immediately, says it is psychological warfare on Patty's part, and tells me that I have to put it out of mind and resume. She walks me around the parking lot, telling me to take deep, long yoga breaths, and to know that I am strong enough to get through this. It works for a little while, and then I think of all the people they must have sent that card to, with its misleading photo of their tidy family. They must have made that card back in June, when she still had Dawn with them. What a fraud! I burn at the sneakiness of it. I tell her I can't go back into that room and stare at that card another time.

"Tell them it was a cheap shot and they need to take it down before I will come back. Go do that."

I can tell this is not what Analee wants to do, but she goes back into the building while I hang out in the parking lot fuming.

When she fetches me back into the room, all the cards are gone.

"I want to know when that photo was taken. It's a theft and a fraud." Analee forcibly takes my arm and pulls me into my seat. I sit but won't let it go.

"When did you take that photo?" I snarl at Patty, who looks ever so slightly daunted. I have never seen this expression on her before.

"Ms. Haskins, today is the day for your deposition. I ask the questions and you answer them."

"When you finish asking them, I want to see that card and know when the photograph was taken." I barely recognize the person in me who makes this demand.

I have no sooner sat down than he asks me whether I have always had a competitive relationship with my sister. Huh? I've never thought about it that way. Is that how Patty sees it? It's not about competition; she has her family and I have mine. My mind drifts back to the summer before my senior year of high school, when I worked for my father in his law office. I was only vaguely aware at the time that she resented my going to work with him every day and learning the details of his work life. At the end of that summer he took Patty away for Labor Day weekend to one of the lakes in the Sierras, just the two of them, something our family had never done before, and I didn't understand at the time why they were doing it. Mother explained to me that Patty had felt left out with all the time I had spent with Dad, and in the way she told me I gleaned that Mother had also felt left out. Only she did not get the vacation alone with Dad.

"Ms. Haskins." His voice penetrates. "I'm waiting for your answer."

I am beginning to lose track of what I answer in my mind and what I say out loud. I tell him I had not seen our relationship as a competition. He perseveres.

"Do you consider yourself a competent mother?"

"Yes."

"Do you consider Patty a competent mother?" Aha, I think, he has started to call her Patty.

"Yes."

"As between you, who is the better mother?" Analee objects that it is irrelevant (*how I love to hear her object!*) but I have to answer the question anyway.

"Patty is the better mother for her children and I'm the better mother for my child."

"Did you consider yourself a competent mother when you were hospitalized for depression?"

"No, I didn't. I definitely needed help then."

"How would you describe your state of mind then?"

"Confused, profoundly fatigued, depressed, foggy." Completely demoralized, sorry I had been born, undone, fearful, ashamed, hopeless …. Analee had told me beforehand that many people forget things in the pressure of a deposition, and that it was okay to say I don't recall or I don't know. But it is having the opposite effect on me. I could run on and on with my answers. The questions spark memories I wish I didn't have.

It was a cloudy day in March when I was taken to the hospital. I lie in bed without the energy to get up. Dawn darts around the house with the energy of a squirrel, chattering as she goes. "Berries," I hear her say, and she is out the door into the yard before I can stop her. In slow motion, my brain tells me to get her, but I can't rouse myself. It's not long before she is back, standing beside my bed with one hand in the air, clutching some early white flower. I burst into tears. She tries to climb up onto my bed, and I am able to lift her to lie next to me. I spoon her hot, hungry little body, rest my nose in her springy curls and weep until my body is heaving. She needs breakfast and I cannot even get out of bed to get it for her.

At this moment Patty comes into the house. She has been worried about me and has been checking on me every day.

"Karen, did you know your door is unlocked? Anyone could come in," she says in her admonitory, superior way.

"I'm glad it's you." She gives me a look as if I am mocking her but I ignore it. Her tone allows me to stop crying. "Can you get cereal for Dawn? She hasn't had breakfast yet."

"No breakfast? It's nine o'clock." From her incredulous tone, you'd think I had tied Dawn to a chair and starved her for three days. She bustles efficiently around and fixes Dawn a bowl of Kix with milk and strawberries.

I can hear Dawn slurping by herself in the kitchen when Patty materializes at my bedside.

"What's wrong with you?" This time there is a little fear and even some kindness in her voice.

"I can't….I can't…seem to do anything. It's hopeless."

"Oh, Karen." She actually puts her hand gently on my cheek. "We need to get you some help."

She gets me a clean set of underpants, a bra, a tee-shirt and my jeans, along with a fleece. She helps me to sit up, and once up, I know I need to get up and get dressed and follow her. By the time I am ready she has packed a small bag of Dawn's clothes and her floppy kitty, she has dressed Dawn, closed my windows and locked my doors. She lifts Dawn into her arms, and I see how readily Dawn wraps herself around her Aunt Patty. I follow them out the door.

"How long were you in that state of mind?" It is the lawyer again, back in my deposition.

"I don't exactly know. I got better gradually. I'm fine now." I feel Analee's foot again, knocking mine under the table.

"Were you fine when you ripped Dawn out of Patricia's arms last July?"

"I did not *rip* Dawn out of Patricia's arms, then or any other time." This is only half-true, I realize immediately. I did rip Dawn away from Patty, who was holding her hand. I think her lawyer sees me shift in my chair. One of those eyebrows has lifted and his glasses slip slightly down his nose. He pushes them back up with his left hand. Patty looks at me for the first time, a smirk on her face.

"How, exactly, did you take Dawn away from Patricia that day?"

"I took Dawn's hand and told her to come with me."

"Were you yelling at the time?"

"Not at Dawn."

"What did you yell at Patricia?"

"I said, 'what did you do to her hair!'"

"What if anything did Patricia say to you?"

"She told me she had straightened Dawn's hair, which was obvious. She told me it used to hurt when she combed Dawn's hair."

"What did you reply?"

"I told her she had no right to do that."

"Was Dawn witness to this conversation?"

"Yes."

"What did she do or say?"

"She started to cry."

"Do you believe Patricia's straightening Dawn's hair justifies your cutting off all contact between them?"

Of course not; how could it? "I believe everything Patty has done since the judge gave my daughter back justifies my cutting off contact. She was never Dawn's mother or other mother or whatever you want to call her. Her filing this lawsuit is outrageous, and on some level she must know it." Patty's eyes have reverted to the tabletop, her expression hidden from me.

"Do you think it's in Dawn's best interests for you to deny her contact with other members of her family?"

"I think this whole lawsuit is not in her best interests."

He shifts tactics, this eel of a lawyer.

"When you were in the hospital, did Patricia deny you contact with Dawn?"

Taking me back to the hospital is painful for me, and he knows it. Patty brought Dawn to me whenever I was able to muster myself to see her presentably. At first, I could not even show my face to anyone, let alone her. I would have lain in bed, just starting at the ceiling if the hospital attendants hadn't prevented me from doing so. Patty came to the hospital often. I remember her telling me that Dawn missed me. It made me feel worse every time she said it. One day I pulled the covers over my head and refused to talk to her or to anyone else. When I finally told one of the doctors what she had said and how I knew I was a terrible mother, Patty stopped saying it. Instead, she began to bring Dawn to the hospital to visit. Dawn would crawl into bed with me and we would just cuddle for as long as we were allowed.

I look up and everyone in the room, it seems, is staring at me.

"What was your question?"

"When you were in the hospital, did Patricia deny you contact with Dawn?"

"No. That started later." Analee foot hits mine again.

He announces that it's nearly noon and we'll take our lunch break now. The two lawyers agree to come back at 1:00. I know I am not hungry, but I feel as if we have been at this for more than a day. Analee takes my arm as I get up and leads me out to the parking lot, where she offers to drive me to a local salad place. I'm not hungry at all, I just want to take a walk. She tells me that often clients have no appetite during depositions or trials. She tells me there is a walk along the river just a couple blocks away, pointing up one of the streets.

"But I want to talk with you a bit before we go into the afternoon session; meet me back here at 12:45."

I am so relieved to be walking; it is like a release from inquisition. Soon I am at the river itself, in a parkway with a wide, winding pathway that I follow. Willows lean into the river, their leaves like fingers tracing the slow current. A pair of mallards shelter close to the shore. This is how I imagine walking meditation, slow paces and a cleared mind. It is cold enough that I can see my breath as I exhale but the air refreshes me. I feel I could go like this for a long time. There is an open field on the opposite side of the river, and a white-tailed kite hovers over it, poised in one space for a long moment, before it dives like a bomber. But it rises without a catch and soon hovers again in a slightly different place. I watch it until it flies to a further location. In the distance, I see a coyote pace through a gap in the field. I marvel to see this much wildness so close to the city. At a curve in the river, there is a bench, and I sit in the sun. Its warmth soothes the tension from my neck. I close my eyes. Voices lift me from my reverie. Two joggers pass, and I ask them the time. 12:35. Now I have to hurry back. My reverie is replaced with the anxiety of knowing I will be late. My anger at the card returns also. I need to see that card.

By the time I leave the parkway and cross the boulevard that leads back to the lawyer's office, I am burning. Analee is there in the parking lot, pacing in an agitated manner as I approach.

"*Where have you been*! It's almost one fifteen. We were due back at one, and I needed to talk to you about this morning."

She glances at my left wrist, where there is no watch, and I swear she almost rolls her eyes but catches herself.

"Do you know that you spaced out several times this morning before answering questions?"

"I'll do better this afternoon." I am determined now. "And I need to see that card."

She looks at me, totally perplexed, then paces some more. "Let me be the one to ask for it."

"I didn't prepare you enough for this deposition. I think I should go back in there and tell them we need to continue this to another time."

This time I took her wrist. "I can do this. I'm focused. Now that I know what this is and I've had a break, I can do this. I don't want you to postpone it to another day. That would only be harder."

When we return to the conference room, Patty's lawyer looks at his watch with a pointed expression. "Let the record reflect it is 1:25 that deponent returns to the room. We were scheduled to begin at 1:00."

Analee asks a word with him outside the room and off the record. He consents. Patty and I are alone in the room with the court reporter, whose hands are now in her lap.

"That card tells me more about you than I wanted to know. Isn't your own family enough without needing my child also? What's wrong with you?"

At this moment, I hear Analee's raised voice outside the door. That gives me strength. I trust she is making the same complaint.

"Dawn is as much part of our family as she is yours," Patty answers coolly. She gets up and walks out of the room.

In a moment, Analee gestures me to join her outside the room, and we go into an adjacent smaller room where we can be alone. She explains that Stephen didn't even know the card was there. He told her he would not have put it there had he known. He promised to give her a photocopy of the card at the end of the day. Staring at me pointedly, she tells me to stay present, give brief answers and leave the card alone. I agree.

He begins by asking how often I had allowed Patty to visit with Dawn since the guardianship was terminated.

"She hasn't asked."

"My question was: how many times?"

"Once, while we were in mediation, but Patty broke that off."

"Before the guardianship was terminated, how often did Patty allow you to visit with Dawn?"

"Usually, it was every weekend, but Patty started interfering with that toward the end, and Patty wouldn't even allow me to come to Ian's birthday party."

"Did she give you any explanation for the birthday party?"

"Yes. She told me it was for *her* family."

For the first time, I see him shift in his chair and glance at Patty's notecard, on which she has written nothing. She stares in another direction.

He shifts rapidly to another subject.

"On the day that Dawn fell into the river, what injuries did she sustain?"

"She had a big bruise on her head. We were worried about a concussion, but the doctor ruled that out."

"Were you supposed to return Dawn to Patty at the end of that day?"

"Either the end of that day or the following morning, I can't remember now."

"Did you return her on time?"

"No, I called Patty and told her I would keep her some extra time because the doctor wanted me to keep watch on her to make sure she didn't have a concussion."

"How long after that accident did you return Dawn?"

"Three days. And then Patty told me I couldn't have the next weekend because I had kept Dawn too long."

He returns to the scene of the accident, asking me to describe the terrain in detail, as if I had decided to climb Everest with Dawn on my back. I stay calm. I describe accurately. I do not ramble. He seems to wind down a bit himself by the end of the afternoon. Finally, he calls a break and invites Patty out of the room. They come back in a few minutes and he declares the deposition over. I go outside to wait in the parking lot while Analee waits for the copy of the Christmas card.

She comes out with it and hands it to me. "I don't think he knew about this before. He seemed pretty unhappy about it."

I stare at the photocopy of the card. Sandra stands between her parents, their hands on her shoulders, while Ian and Dawn hold hands on the chair in front of them. It bears a current date and contains a note in Patty's handwriting with her holiday wishes and thanks for his good work. I can't tell when they had posed the picture, but it is less than a year old; that much I can tell from just looking at Dawn's face and legs. I hand it back as if it were slime.

"Why does she think she needs my daughter?"

Analee sympathizes, tells me she has no answer. I'm eager to get into my car and drive home. The ride itself gives me a chance to think.

Until I was thirty-eight, I didn't even know that every woman is born with all the eggs she will ever have, and, starting with her first menstrual cycle, she loses one every month until menstruation itself ends. Before I even had my first period, I expected it to be a nuisance. Aside from the welcome marker of growing up, which came late for me, it was always an unexpected handicap. All through my teen-aged years, I never had a regular period, and it always came at an inconvenient time, like just before swim class, when I worried I would leave a red trail behind me in the water. As a young woman, I gained a modicum of predictability by taking the pill. Along with the regularity, I could rely on not becoming pregnant. When Patty had Sandra, I was almost thirty. Though I was curious about having a niece, I was completely disinterested in 'settling down,' as my parents phrased it, or in having any children. I never even thought of menstruation as an accumulation of losses. Now that it has stopped for me altogether, and I realize how I wasted whatever fertile years I had, I feel the accumulation of losses.

I may have been peri-menopausal when the idea of having a child first occurred to me. I was having uncontainably heavy periods, which fooled me into thinking I might be especially fertile. My moods ranged dramatically, and I began to feel, for the first time, that I had wasted my life. Even though I would not have traded Patty's husband or children or mode of life for my own, I began to envy her the surrounding of family. She'd married at twenty-seven, had Sandra immediately, and now had a yard full of swing sets and a pool full of floating children's toys that made me sad in a way I could not describe. I found relief in my painting, in sitting at the easel totally focused on the colors I intended to create, but even reading my stories to an audience of children sometimes left me feeling I had lost something, something had washed out of me. I sometimes wonder how much my menopausal stage contributed to the depression that sent me to the hospital.

I know the difference between sadness and depression, and that itself gives me a measure of comfort. I'm sad that I never had my own biological child, if only because no one else could then have claimed her. But I have Dawn – she is her own, completely unique and wonderful self, regardless of whose genes combined to create her. Still, I profoundly regret having relied on Patty for her eggs. As much as I was grateful then, and for her saving Dawn and me when I was depressed, I resent her now. I hate her. I don't know how to end this misery. I don't want to destroy her; I just want her to leave us alone. She seems to want to destroy me, both financially and by taking Dawn from me. I don't understand what propels her. Even if I did, it might not give me the tools to make this trouble end.

22

ANALEE

It's a chilly Sunday in January a week before trial is scheduled to begin, and I have come to the office, where it is totally deserted, to complete my trial brief. Adam has taken the boys to Tahoe to play in the snow, which will occupy them all day. In theory, I could do the same work at home, but my office creates the mental space for me to get my work done.

I have finished my recitation of facts, after obsessing about how to designate Patty and Karen. Instead of genetic mother, Patty is the 'ovum donor' and Karen is simply 'Dawn's mother,' not 'birth mother.' How many iterations have I written and deleted before landing on these simple descriptions? I am now trying to outline and prioritize the legal principles, borrowing partly from my earlier, unsuccessful motion to dismiss. I have got as far as articulating the state's public policy of establishing a child's parentage as early as possible, so as to provide stability and consistency for the child. But it is obvious to me that Dawn has had no consistency, through no one's fault or neglect. She has spent the first twenty months of her life with Karen, then almost the same period of time with Patty and her family, first visiting her mother in the hospital and then on weekends. Remarkably, this child does not seem troubled or confused, and her first semester in school has been a happy one. The legal principles sound so cold and abstract. I have to bring them to life to compel a judgment for Karen.

I hear a key in the door and freeze. Who could be here at this hour? So far as I knew, the cleaning people come on Friday evenings. The door opens and closes loudly, without stealth. As soon as I hear the step, I know it is my dad. I fly up from my chair.

"Carter!" I fling my arms around him.

"How did I know where to find you," he jokes, kissing me lightly on the forehead. "Are you ready?"

"I'm slogging through my trial brief," I moan. "I can't bring it to life." It is a child's voice inside me chanting *I can't, I can't*. He hears it too.

He doffs his jacket and sits down in the client's chair facing my desk. He grabs a pen and tablet from my desk and looks at me fixedly.

"Why shouldn't Dawn go back to live with Patty and her family? It's part of what she knows as family, and she's been well nurtured there."

"She belongs with her mother," I begin, but his skeptical look matches my own recognition that this isn't even an adequate beginning. I begin again, and he keeps asking me hard questions, until I finally begin to weave together a more powerful beginning.

"Can I take you to lunch?" he asks, but my pleading look is his answer. "Okay, tell me what to bring back for you."

By the time he returns with my tuna melt and coke, I am well into my legal argument.

"What would I do without you?" I look at his wiry frame. Still healthy and in full possession of his penetrating mind at seventy-four, he invigorates me every time he revisits what used to be his office. But someday he will be gone.

"You'll figure it out," he tells me with a grin and locks the door as he leaves.

With the 'juice' he has provided me, I finish the trial brief by four and have enough energy to concoct a robust chili and toasted cheese sandwiches for Adam and the boys when they tumble in after their day in the snow. Andy is so hungry he abandons his reservations about eating food that isn't red or green. Their banter carries me through the evening, and I fall asleep curled around the sturdy warmth of Adam's body.

I awake at six on Monday, fueled by the challenge of preparing Karen to testify. She will be in today for what I hope will be far better, more thorough preparation than I provided her for her deposition. Strange, how some witnesses rally under pressure, giving better answers than during prep sessions, and others seem to decompose, getting angry, forgetful or pre-occupied with spooling out their life story. Sitting beside her helplessly as Karen went into a kind of reverie as she pondered the questions at her deposition and then paused unnaturally long before answering, was a strange new experience for me. I felt that day that Karen had presented herself as a zombie to Stephen, who must have thought me inept. I must find out from Karen how she experienced that session and discover the clue to her becoming a good witness.

23

KAREN

Trial has completely disarranged what remains of my family, and it has not even yet begun. I awake at 6:13, just before the alarm is to go off at 6:15 on Monday morning. I turn it off. The day is not yet light, but raucous jays and a distant rooster have disturbed the silence.

Megan, amazing friend that she is, has spent the night on an air mattress in my living room. She will take Dawn to school this morning and will pick her up after school. Sam has remained at home to take her younger brother to school. And Jenny, my other best friend, will arrive at 7:00 sharp to drive me to Roseville, where I will meet Analee at 8:00 at the courthouse (never again to be late for Analee!), and trial will start this morning at 9:00 and go all this first week of February. Jenny will attend the whole trial with me.

A trial against my sister. Two practical orphans, she and I, now enemies in a courtroom. I cannot even comprehend this, although I have started to live this enmity in pieces, as we prepared for trial.

I am alert to the point of vigilance. At Analee's instruction, I have purchased and put on a dress in a soft color, a blue the color of a lake with no sun shining on it, that the saleswoman called teal.

Last night I bristled at having to put on a costume, but Megan stopped me cold.

"Why do you think we pay so much attention to costume in the theater? People get to see a character for only a couple of hours, at most, and I need to create an impression through costume. Don't underestimate it."

When I told her this isn't theater, she practically shouted at me.

"Get real. This *is* theater – with consequences!"

When I go in to wake Dawn, she is on her back with her stuffed river otter under one arm, her halo of red curls splayed around her. Yes, I say to myself, this is why I must do this, so that she can remain at home here, where she belongs. I kiss her on the forehead, but this is not enough to wake her. "Wake up, my girl," I say, and she opens her eyes.

"When do you have to go?" She knows I must spend the week in court, whatever that means to her, but she does not know why, has not asked.

"Soon, but if you get up now, we can have breakfast together." She rolls out of bed quickly, asking for berries on her cereal. She saw me buy strawberries yesterday, out of season, for this week.

I leave the room, knowing she will insist on dressing herself anyway, in a colorful, mismatched fashion that makes sense only to her. I tell her to dress for a cold day.

Megan is up and dressed herself, making coffee in the kitchen. She glances at me approvingly, and notes I have put on the right 'good mother costume'.

"It had better not last more than a week," I tell her. "I have only four of these."

"Well, you picked the right one to start."

I pour two bowls of cheerios and cut bananas and strawberries for them. Megan, who hates cereal, has toasted two slices of bread for herself. Dawn bounds into the kitchen, wearing a bright red sweater, blue skirt and orange tights. She gives Megan a hug. Megan knows better than to comment on Dawn's choice of clothes.

Jenny arrives right on time, announcing that it is cold and clear, no ice on the roads. She too gives Dawn a big hug, but she compliments Dawn on her beautiful red sweater. Dawn twirls, announcing that she will warm up the day.

"So you will," Jenny says as we leave. I kiss Dawn goodbye as if it were just another school day.

When I see how crowded the highway is, I thank Jenny for driving, for "doing this," which means much more than the driving. We are almost silent in the car on the way in, and she pulls up to the courthouse as if she drives this route every day. We find the meeting place in the cafeteria and arrive early. Analee, already seated at a table with a cup of coffee, glances at her watch and smiles approvingly at us both. I introduce her to Jenny, and Analee thanks her for driving me. As she gets up to get coffee for us both, I notice she wears a suit the color of some dark red wine, a white blouse with no collar, a single string of big pearls, and simple black heels. One day when we were preparing for trial, she told me she always wears 'sincere pearls'.

"Remember that Patty, as the Petitioner, gets to go first in everything at trial, opening statements, witnesses…. She could call you first, though I doubt she will, but don't be shocked if it happens. Just trust that you are ready." She takes another sip of coffee, gulps it, and looks at me very closely.

"You will hear lots of things that are hard to listen to, that may be lies, but don't react to them. Trust me that you will get your turn to set them right."

"Yes," I repeat obediently. We have spent many hours rehearsing for my testimony at trial, and I know it has helped me to stand here without my hands shaking. I show her the small tablet I have brought to write down reminders. She nods her approval.

When we enter the courtroom, Patty and her lawyer are already at their counsel table, notebooks arranged in front of them. The two lawyers shake hands and greet each other, but Patty and I do not. Patty is dressed almost identically to Analee, with her own 'sincere pearls' and gray suit. Her attorney keeps bobbing up, to re-arrange this or that, a man who seems more at ease standing than in a chair. He is decked out in a charcoal suit with a white shirt and neat, small red bowtie. I don't know whether it is Megan, the theater director, or Analee who has made me so conscious of everyone's courtroom costumes, but I seem pre-occupied with these details today. It is not my world. I know performance counts here, and I will try to be attentive to every detail I can catch.

The judge's nameplate sits atop the wall around the desk: Graciela Garcia. I lean over to Analee and whisper, "our judge is a woman?"

"Yes, and she's a smart, no-nonsense judge. Also a single mother," she whispers the last part very softly.

When the judge walks in, we all stand. Everyone in the courtroom is taller than she is, and slimmer by a significant margin. Judge Garcia has a double chin, round cheeks that have not yet begun to sink, and a smile that would calm a frightened child. And curly brown hair that falls forward over her face; she brushes it back behind her ears before she even sits down. I will see her do this many times over the course of this trial.

After the attorneys have announced their names and ours, the judge tells us all that she has read counsel's 'excellent' briefs. Looking piercingly at Patty and me alternatively, she says, "this trial is about a small child who is lucky to have family members who care about her deeply, but unlucky to have family members who are fighting over her." She asks if counsel wish to make opening statements, and Stephen Petrakis rises as if about to take the oath of office. His sense of control over the courtroom is palpable.

"This lucky/unlucky child to whom you refer," he pauses for emphasis, "could not have been conceived or born without the two women in this courtroom. They are each, in their own way, this child's mother. When one faltered, the other was able to take charge and rear this child. Each of her mothers has spent substantial time in her rearing, and each deserves to be recognized as one of Dawn's parents."

So he has decided to begin by not attacking me. I recognize his elegance, his skill, even as I recoil from his guile. Beside me, Analee is writing as fast as she can.

When Analee's turn comes, she rises slowly and begins by describing my own efforts to have a child before Patty offered her eggs, the playful discussion we had together about my choice of a sperm donor, Patty's assistance to me as a new mother and her considerable assistance to Dawn and me as her guardian. I have never before heard her speak this slowly, but her pace quickens as she describes how Dawn has always known me as her mother and Patty as her aunt, how constant I was with my visits and my requests to have Dawn come back home. She describes the clarity of roles within Patty's family, how Doug is Dawn's uncle and the children are Dawn's cousins. "Dawn knows only one mother," she concluded, "and that is my client."

As predicted, Patty is called as the first witness, and she takes the stand confidently, as if this were a daily role for her. She describes how involved she was from the outset, how she helped choose the donor and how important it was to me that we use her eggs. I wonder if she has made this up because I don't remember that at all. She provides painstaking detail of the "ordeal" of generating her eggs, first taking hormone pills and then enduring a "surgical procedure" to harvest them for fertilization and implanting them into my body. She describes my descent into depression and inability to care for Dawn properly, my hospitalization, my initial apathy toward everyone and everything, and gradual recovery. She describes her concern about Dawn's safety in my care, how I kept Dawn beyond the allotted weekend when her family was sick. She describes my fall into the river as if I had deliberately risked Dawn's life and my own, as well as my refusal for a second time to return Dawn on time. Strangely, she says nothing at all about the termination of the guardianship proceeding, but she describes in vivid detail my hostility when I came to pick up Dawn and how my tires "screeched" as I drove away with her. She ends with how sad her whole family has been since I terminated contact with them and Dawn, and how Dawn needs two parents.

Analee rises to begin her cross-examination. I can feel her taking a deep breath, as if preparing to dive underwater. She walks slowly around our table to approach the witness stand, and her heels stab the floor loudly.

She carries a sheet of paper, which she asks the clerk to mark for identification.

"You volunteered to be the egg donor, did you not?" was her first question, and Patty said yes almost proudly.

"And as the egg donor," she emphasizes the word 'donor' slightly, "you were informed, were you not, that you gave up all claims to being a parent of any child born of the process?"

"Informed by whom?" Patty asks her own question.

"Please read the document in front of you," Analee instructs, as she hands the document to Patty.

Patty glances at the paper dismissively and then looks up at Analee silently.

"Did you read this document at the time?"

"Probably not. There were so many things we had to sign at the hospital that I couldn't take the time to read them all before signing them." Patty glances up at Analee, the glint of a challenge in her eye.

"Did anyone at the clinic discuss this document with you at the time?" I myself have a vivid memory of the woman who painstakingly explained to Patty and me that she would have no claims to the eggs or to any child born from them. But Patty claims not to remember.

Analee slows down, backs up, asks whether we had a counselor at the clinic, establishes that we did and that there was at least one discussion of the process, and that Patty was asked to sign a sheet of paper, which she says she did without reading at the time.

"The process was termed an ovum donation, was it not?"

"Yes. I gave my eggs to my sister; I didn't try to sell them." There is a hint of triumph in her sarcasm.

"And you understood at the time, did you not, that your donation meant giving up any rights to claim parentage?"

"I understood that the clinic wanted to know I would make no claim against them for ownership of the eggs; in that sense, it was a donation, and I willingly signed a paper to that effect." She nodded toward the sheet of paper Analee held in her hand. "It had nothing to do with what Karen's and my own roles were."

Even I can feel Patty's cockiness, but Analee holds her slow, steady pace of questions. I glance at the judge, who is attentive but impassive, and at Patty's attorney, who appears to be communicating with Patty with his furled eyebrows.

Even when Analee confronts Patty with the language of the ovum donation contract that stated Patty would make no claim of parentage, Patty still holds to her account that she signed what the agency required in order to use her eggs, but that parentage was a question between her and me. After the ovum donation contract becomes Exhibit A in evidence, Analee asks Patty about her and my plans at the time.

"Did Karen ever tell you that she wanted you to be a second mother to Dawn?"

"Not in those words." She seems about to go on, but glances at her lawyer and then closes her mouth. By the time I glance at him, he is looking down at his papers.

"My question calls for a yes or no answer. Did Karen ever tell you that she wanted you to be a second mother to Dawn?"

Patty now turns to the judge. "Your honor, I can't answer that yes or no without putting it into context."

The judge faces Patty. "You must answer yes or no. If counsel does not give you a chance to explain now, your own counsel will be able to do so on redirect." Her tone is kind but firm.

"Did Karen ever tell you that she wanted you to be a second mother to Dawn?"

Patty strangles out a "no."

Analee lifts several more papers from the table and has them each marked by the clerk.

"I show you Dawn's birth certificate. Who is listed as Dawn's mother?"

"Karen."

"Who is listed as Dawn's other parent?"

"Unknown."

"I show you the registration forms for Dawn's initial pediatrician. Who is listed as the mother?"

"Karen."

"Who is listed as the other parent?"

"N/A. Not applicable."

"When Dawn came to live with you, you took her to your own pediatrician, did you not?"

"Yes."

"And on those forms you are listed as 'legal guardian,' not 'mother,' are you not?"

"Yes."

"After Karen was hospitalized, you asked her to sign guardianship papers so that you could make medical and other decisions for Dawn, yes?"

"Yes."

I am beginning to like Patty's more obedient chorus of yesses when her attorney asks if we can take the morning recess. Analee asks the judge for permission to ask a few more questions before the recess and the judge allows her five more minutes.

"You realize a guardian is not a parent, do you not?"

"Objection: calls for a legal conclusion."

"Your Honor, the witness is a California attorney."

"Overruled."

"Ms. Ward, you are a licensed California attorney, are you not?"

"Yes, but I've never practiced."

"You are aware, are you not, that a guardian is not the same as a parent?"

"Well, a guardian acts in the place of a parent," Patty answers almost proudly.

"You did not answer my question: are you aware that a guardian is not the same as a parent?"

Patty yields a grudging yes.

"A guardian can be nominated by a parent, isn't that correct?"

"Yes."

"Karen, as Dawn's mother, nominated you as guardian, did she not?"

"Yes."

Here the judge herself calls the morning recess.

In the hall, I can see Patty's attorney ushering her quickly to one end, where they turn a corner to talk. Analee practically emits sparks; her eyes burn with intention. I try to tell her she is doing brilliantly, but she tells me it is too early. She counsels me to show no emotion in the courtroom or as we are exiting. Jenny takes my arm and leads me to a bench in the hallway so that Analee can think by herself. Analee paces back and forth intently, while we sit for the recess. Jenny firmly holds my hand. We say nothing to each other.

Back in the courtroom, Analee begins with a different line of questions, about Patty's allowing me regular weekend visits after I left the halfway house, without any supervision, and that this went well for over a year. Patty notes the two exceptions, of my keeping Dawn an extra two days when she had strep throat, and my falling into the river with Dawn. Analee gets Patty to admit that I treated Dawn appropriately when she had strep throat. About the river incident Patty said that I "tend to take unreasonable risks." Apparently, just taking a small child to the river is an unreasonable risk.

24

ANALEE

After Petrakis led Patty through her rendition of Karen's sinking into a depression that finally caused her to hospitalize her sister, he asked, "What was that like for you?"

I should have objected, interjected anything – "vague," or "calls for a narrative" – anything to have interrupted her, but I didn't.

I now sit at home staring at the partial transcript, and I *still* don't know what I should have asked her on cross. I just slid past it, as if it didn't exist, hadn't happened, hadn't drowned us, but here it is in black and white.

"It was frightening. It hadn't been that much earlier that I had lost both my parents, in different ways – my father abandoning us and then dying of a heart attack and my mother leaving us via Alzheimer's – and now my sister seemed to be falling apart too. I didn't know why she was so listless, so depressed, so totally without any energy. I wanted to get her help -- if she could be helped -- and then there was her baby also. So we took Dawn into our household, and we took Karen to the hospital. The first days were frantic, with us going back and forth to the hospital and trying to manage with a new child in the household. Then when Karen was discharged, it wasn't as if she was well; the hospitals keep people now only until they are out of crisis. We thought we could take her in, but that proved unworkable. We found a rehab facility for Karen, where she stabilized, and we made a home for Dawn.

"How did you relate to Dawn while she lived with you?"

"At first it was clear that she was my sister's baby. I had spent a lot of time with her and Karen, so she was already quite used to us. But over time the relationship became much deeper and more attached. Knowing that she was as much my child as Sandra or Ian created a deep sense of her belonging with us, a sense of protection and love and attachment that I feel only for Sandra and Ian. I can't quite explain it, but the connection of being a parent is not like any other relationship on earth. I didn't expect it at first, but once it came on I couldn't let go of it. Dawn and I are bonded as mother and child, and we shouldn't be separated."

Counsel: "What were your feelings for Dawn when she was born?"

"I loved her as my sister's child, of course, but I was curious, too, since I knew she was biologically my child. I looked for physical resemblances. I think she has my eyes. But when Dawn came to live with us, the sense of her as my own child grew. I noticed small gestures that were like mine; I watched her with her siblings. I developed a sense of protection for her that one has only for one's own children. It's very deep – and hard to explain at the same time. The first time she fell down and hit her head on the bookcase, I realized how strong this was. She wasn't hurt for more than the few moments she cried, but I felt the fear, the worry, the need to comfort that one really feels only for one's own child. This sense of connection only grew deeper the longer Dawn lived with us. By the time she had been with us for a year it was as if she had always been one of us, and we were her family. When Karen started asking to take Dawn back to her home, I felt worried on so many different levels – whether she would be safe, whether she would adapt to being in a family of only herself and Karen, whether Ian and Sandra could adapt to not living with their little sister.... I worried about how much we would all miss her, and how much she would miss us. We had become her primary family.

Every child needs two parents – for the other to fill in when one is sick or too busy or too preoccupied to attend to what the child needs. Or when the other can't exercise good judgment. I love Dawn as much as I love Sandra and Ian, and they love her as a sister. I want to restore the rest of Dawn's family to her."

By the time I objected that she had gone beyond answering the question, the damage had already been done. The judge overruled my objection without a second's hesitation. I could feel Petrakis' satisfaction. I glanced at Karen next to me, who blinked hard but did not move or make any faces. The judge was attentive but opaque. I felt how insidious this was, to have one's parenting siphoned away over time. An anger I hadn't felt before, along with an anxiety I couldn't identify, built within me. Petrakis had rehearsed Patty very, very well.

I tried, however lamely, to dissect this speech on cross, by recalling how strictly she had limited Karen's time with Dawn after Karen's recovery, but Patty portrayed concern that she not 'overburden' Karen with parenting responsibilities after her 'ordeal' in the hospital. Her veneer of compassion for her 'troubled' sister survived all my questions. I focused on the day when she was to transfer Dawn to her sister and tried to get her to acknowledge that straightening Dawn's hair was something she knew would provoke her sister. I failed, even when I asked why she had waited until the last day she would have Dawn living with her. "It was my last chance to do it," she'd said simply.

When I read Patty's statement to Adam at dinner, his only reply was a legal one: why hadn't she appealed the guardianship termination? He responded like the law professor he is, but I felt our judge was taking this in as a fellow parent, and human being. He let me off the hook of dish duty and encouraged me to play with the boys after dinner. Was he trying to make the same point as Patty in her testimony, that my kids now needed the 'other parent'? I need to stop asking such questions, I tell myself, or I will overthink my life.

Alex asked me to build with him and his Legos, a good distraction, I thought. I let him give me orders and I followed them, building pillars for whatever structure he had concocted in his mind, while he erected the structure. I knew better than to ask him what it was, for he lacks the words to describe the elaborate shapes in his head. But he seemed satisfied with what we built together. When I put him to bed, he asked me to read him "The Little House in the Big Woods," a tattered Golden Book left over from my own childhood. "I want to build my own house," he told me before falling asleep, and I assured him that he would build a beautiful one someday.

I was reading Patty's deposition transcript when Adam came to bed at nearly eleven. He climbed in, naked as usual, and laid one warm hand on my arm. I tried not to be distracted by the sheer warmth of him.

"You always torture yourself with the worst that happened. What was the best thing that happened today?"

"I violated a rule," I said, without missing a beat. "I asked a question for which I didn't know the answer. Petrakis called the doctor who had treated Karen and Dawn after they fell in the river. She seemed to want to say more than answering Petrakis' questions, so I asked her if she had any independent recollection of her encounter with Karen and Dawn."

"What did she say?"

"That what struck her about the whole encounter was that this mother, whose injuries were much more serious than that of her child, was focused only on her child, and on tending to her."

"What made you ask the question?"

"Instinct."

"Trust that, Analee. It's one of your best trial skills." He gently pried the transcript from my hands, put it on my nightstand, and curled up around me. I swear I could feel the beat of his heart through my own body, as the rhythm of mine slowed and I fell asleep in his warmth.

25

KAREN

I must have fallen asleep in the car on the way home from the courthouse, and I woke up when Jenny pulled into the driveway of Megan's house. Through the front window I could see Megan leaning over Dawn at the dining table.

Megan welcomed us back, but Dawn remained at the table, looking down at the puzzle in front of her. I kissed her on the cheek and hugged her shoulders, but she continued to stare at the puzzle, as if her face would crack if she looked at me. "I missed you," I whispered into her ear. At that, she turned, clambered off her chair and threw her arms around my legs.

"Why did you stay away so long?"

I apologized to her. "Roseville is a long way away, and we had to work all day." I'd never seen her so moody.

Megan signaled me with her eyes into the other room, but Dawn still clung to me. I told Megan I would call her later and thanked her and Jenny again.

I took Dawn for hamburgers at Jeremiah's Hut, her favorite place, and we shared a large order of fries laced with ketchup in the shape of a heart. She smiled only slightly as she watched me draw the heart with the ketchup stream. When I asked her how school went today, she said only "long." With her widest blue eyes, and still this solemn face, she asked me to take her to school and pick her up tomorrow. When I told her I could not, that this would be a long, hard week for us both, she took her fork and messed up the pile of fries, undoing the heart. She asked again at bedtime, and I gave her the same answer. For the first time ever, she turned away from me without kissing me goodnight.

I phoned Megan after Dawn was asleep. She told me that Dawn had pushed another girl at kindergarten, and the teacher had asked where I was. "I told her you had to work in Roseville this week, that Dawn was unhappy about it but there was nothing you could do about it." Megan denied that Dawn had given her a hard time, telling me only that Dawn had been quiet and a bit glum.

I went to bed in the same mood and fell into a deep, dreamless sleep, awakened by the alarm for Day Two.

I wear the second of the four dresses I had bought, this one a charcoal gray wool with sleeves to my elbows and a flared skirt. It had snowed slightly in the night, and I put on my boots.

Like robots, Dawn, Megan and Jenny all assume their roles and I arrive at court on time again.

As soon as the judge is seated, Patty's attorney announces, "I call Karen Haskins as my next witness." Analee stands next to me, helps me pull out my chair and demonstrates with her arm where I should go to testify. Her left arm brushes my back lightly, as if in encouragement.

"Ms. Haskins, who are the members of your family?" I hesitate, and Analee seems to read my mind.

"Objection: vague."

The judge tells Mr. Petrakis to rephrase his question.

"Whom do you consider as your family?"

"Well, Dawn, of course. My friends Megan and Jenny and their children are like family to me." I begin to stumble as I sense the dangerous places in this question. "My sister Patty, you know, and her husband and two children. My parents are gone." I stop.

"By 'gone,' do you mean both your parents have died?"

"My father died four years ago. My mother was in a memory care facility, and I lost track of her after I was hospitalized. I'm embarrassed to tell you I do not even know if she is still alive." I can hear a tiny hiss from Patty but dare not look at her. *How can I not even know this about my own mother?*

"How would you describe your relationship with your sister Patty?" This is intentional torture; even I recognize what he is doing.

"Estranged. We haven't really spoken since I picked up Dawn from her home last summer."

"And Dawn has not seen Patty or Ian or Sandra in all that time, is that correct?"

"Except for one visit with Patty and Ian, yes."

"Has Dawn ever asked to see Patty, Dan, Ian or Sandra in this time?"

"Objection: hearsay."

"Overruled: answer the question."

"Dawn asked to see Ian a couple times, but not the others."

"And what did you tell her when she asked?"

"That it was difficult just now, but that I'd try sometime. I didn't explain."

I push back the terrible sense of how I have lost track of my own mother, but something else takes hold of me. I know this man is set on destroying me through my own words, and I muster myself. I *deploy* myself; that word flits into my head and I grab hold. I even think he senses my shift, and he loses his own grip. His questions become more innocuous and manageable. At the morning recess,

Analee tells me I am doing well, but to keep my guard up; he will come back. He does.

"Let's go back to the day you picked up Dawn from Patty's home after the guardianship hearing."

Ah, Mr. Petrakis, I too have read my deposition, and I'm not going to handle that event the same way again.

When he asks if I'd had an altercation with Patty, I admit, "I allowed myself to be provoked by Patty, and I shouldn't have gotten angry in front of Dawn."

"You grabbed her from Patty, did you not?"

"I took her too abruptly. It was an upsetting occasion for us all."

He shifts ground again, to my hospitalization, but this time I've had my rehearsal. I can talk about it without going back into that space, and he knows it. He isn't making a dent. He lets me off the stand by noon. Analee tells the judge she will save her questions for when she calls me as her witness.

I look at Patty for the first time as she gets up for the noon recess. Her composure is apparently unruffled, but she avoids my eye. I want to ask her what she knows about Mom, but I hold back, knowing I should ask Analee first. Analee tells me in no uncertain terms not to ask Patty, that she will ask Petrakis herself, but I tell her not to; it would only enhance his sense of accomplishment. I will contact the care facility myself.

In the afternoon, Patty's counsel calls what even I would call innocuous witnesses – the director of the day care center who testifies that Patty has treated Dawn like a loving mom, a couple of friends who testify about what a wonderful, caring mom she is to Sandra, Ian and Dawn and how good the kids are together, and the pediatrician who had seen Dawn on a few occasions during the guardianship.

By the end of the day I am fed up and almost bored: I have to sit through *this* rather than be with Dawn after school and paint and teach? I think I even ask Analee whether I have to come the next day. She looks shocked.

"Our case will start tomorrow, and I need you. If you don't show up, you are likely to lose this battle; it's that important for you to be here." She glares at me.

"I'll be here." I think I have added to her worries, and I feel bad immediately. "You can count on me. I won't let you down."

"I believe you." She pronounces it as an order to appear.

On the drive home, I call the memory care facility where my mother had been, not knowing how I would ask them or whether they would even answer my question. I identify myself as one of Myrtle Haskins' daughters and ask if I can speak with her. I am told that Mrs. Haskins cannot handle telephone conversations but that I can visit her between nine and five any day. I tell Jenny I want her to take us there; it is on the way home.

Jenny is a tactful and compliant friend, but she glances at me with a look that tells me I'm crazy. She doesn't even say anything, just keeps driving.

"I guess it's more important I get home to see Dawn."

"Now you're talking."

Dawn comes running to the door this time. I lift her up and twirl her around, so relieved to see the return of her normal self. Jenny leaves without a word, and, while Dawn plays and Megan and I cook dinner, Megan tells me that Dawn had been quiet but obedient at school, not a problem like yesterday. When I tell her about my mom and asking Jenny to take me to visit her, she almost blurts something but adopts a calmer tone. She advises me to wait until the challenge of this trial is over before I tackle that problem. Megan knows I have not gone back since the Mother's Day incident when my mother handed Dawn to Patty. Megan's own mother died a few years ago with Alzheimer's. What goes unspoken between us this evening is our knowing that I will need her counseling before seeing my mother again.

I wake up before six this morning, Day Three of the trial, as full of anxiety as I had the past two mornings of trial, but this time

211

from a vivid dream. I get up in the full dark, knowing further sleep is out of reach. Of the four dresses in my closet, I choose the dark blue one I had arbitrarily designated for day three of trial. As I stand in front of the meager pickings of dresses, the dream reclaims me.

In it I hold in front of me a watercolor I had been painting of an expansive old oak with three sturdy, almost horizontal limbs. While I study it, I notice a wolverine atop one of the limbs, clambering toward the tree trunk. Transfixed, I watch in wonder as it clambers down the tree – now a real tree rather than my watercolor – and ambles toward me. I am totally frightened but frozen to the spot, and the wolverine makes steady progress toward where I stand exposed outside. When it reaches where I stand, it circles me twice, before climbing up my back. Miraculously, it causes no injury as it scrambles up my body and comes to rest on my left shoulder. Still petrified, I feel it run its claws through my tangled hair, as if combing it. Even standing in front of my closet, I still feel the imprint of its weight. That this fierce animal causes me no harm is wondrous, inexplicable.

After I dress, wash and comb my hair, and even apply lipstick (my 'stage makeup,' as I tell Megan), I wake Dawn for breakfast. As usual, she wakes with a smile at my kiss, and bounds out of bed herself, making her way to the shower. At five, she is a child of reliable habits.

Jenny herself arrives early, my steady and reassuring friend. She fluffs Dawn's orange curls when she emerges from the shower, splaying a few drops of water.

"What time tonight?" Dawn asks her, as if I would not tell her the truth.

"I'm not sure, honey, but I think it's the last day," she reassures her.

When Megan arrives to take over and drive Dawn to school, Dawn announces to her that today is the last day. They both hooray, before Megan casts me a wary look.

Today I will be cross-examined by Patty's attorney about my breakdown and hospitalization, as well as about everything else negative he can dredge up about me. I give Megan a cautious thumb's up.

In the car on the way, Jenny is quiet, waiting to take her cue from me.

"Are there wolverines in California?" I ask her.

She throws me a look that asks what planet I am on this morning.

"I have no idea," she responds after a moment. "When I think of wolverines, I think of a Michigan team."

After another pause, she asks me why I asked, and I recount the dream to her. A slow smile opens her face.

"He had your back."

I smile too, in gradual recognition. "He did." He does, I hope.

Trial Day Three begins with Patty's counsel announcing that the Petitioner rests. Analee immediately rises from her seat and announces that she calls Karen Haskins as her first witness. I walk like a zombie to the witness stand. Once there, I take hold again, remembering what we have rehearsed.

She has me describe the helpful woman at the fertility clinic, who told us over and over again that this process could not go forward unless Patty understood it was a true donation. The counselor had warned us it could be very difficult to know that a new person with one's own genetic material would not be one's own child. She'd asked Patty pointed questions about that, and Patty had told her that her own two children were all the children she'd want or need in this lifetime.

Analee asks me what I recall of the guardianship papers, and I testify that Patty had told me at the time these papers would give her the temporary authority to tend to Dawn until I got better. I recount the several times I had asked Patty to allow me to take Dawn back, and her telling me I was not ready. I explain why I had kept Dawn more than a weekend when she and the rest of the family had had strep throat, and when we had fallen in the river. On each of those times I had told Patty I would keep Dawn longer, and why. And I had returned her.

Before I know it, Stephen Petrakis looms over me again. First he tests my memory of the fertility clinic and why I remember so vividly what might have occurred six years ago.

"It was a momentous occasion for me," I explain, "and I was impressed with the counselor's thoroughness."

At some point in the afternoon he asks me whether it is true that Dawn uses an outhouse for the toilet in my home.

"Objection: beyond the scope of the direct."

"Sustained: pursue another line of questions, counsel."

He takes a different tack.

"You and Patty used to be close, were you not?"

"Yes, very close."

"You sought her advice about whom to choose as a sperm donor."

"Yes."

"And for parenting advice, you also looked to her?"

"Sometimes."

"You relied on her experience and good judgment, did you not?"

"I relied on her experience, yes, though I did not always agree with her judgment."

"And you knew she always cared about Dawn."

"Yes."

He sits down. The judge asks if Analee has any redirect. She stands, thanks the court, and slowly approaches me in the witness chair.

"What effect, if any, has this lawsuit had on your family?"

We had rehearsed this question, and I recognize it as the marker for the end of my testimony.

"Win or lose, I have lost my sister. We used to be close, and now I doubt if we can ever be close again. I feel as if she's trying to parent me, not Dawn. I will always be Dawn's mother, whether Patty is her aunt or 'another mother,' but we will never be able to be sisters again."

The judge reaches for her gavel, then seems to think it unnecessary.

"Counsel, court stands in recess. I want to see you both in chambers."

Analee does not even glance at me as she strides into chambers, with her pad in hand. Stephen Petrakis follows her, no stride in his step. I looked down at my hands, not daring to glance at Patty, but I can see her stand up and leave the room. Once she is gone, I glance at the clerk, as if to ask if I can leave the witness seat, and he indicates permission with a wave of his hand. I stumble back to my seat at counsel table, and pour myself a glass of water. I am drained of energy.

26

ANALEE

Judge Garcia zips open her robe and slings it off her shoulders, hanging it on the back of her chair.

"Sit down, counsel."

We obey, both of us meekly.

"Whatever the outcome of this trial – and I don't have any indicated decision for you – this family has been damaged."

She glares at us each in turn, her next words contradicting the indictment of her gaze.

"I don't blame either of you, but I want to see you use your skills to try to help heal this family rather than wreck it further."

She pauses and glances down, as if debating whether to say something else.

"There's a therapist in San Francisco I heard speak at a recent parenting conference, to whom I'd like you to send your clients. She works with fractured families. I'll get you her name. Or you can choose someone yourselves, but this trial is not helping this little girl, and it certainly isn't doing any good for your clients or the other children involved."

"We tried mediation before trial," Petrakis begins to explain.

"I'm not blaming you, or that mediator. These two women may

have needed to go through this ordeal before being ready to solve their problems themselves. But my decision isn't going to make their lives any better; that I can see right now. What I want to know from you two is whether you are willing to work on solving this problem rather than making your clients enemies for life. I want to recess this trial for 30 days to allow your clients the chance to mediate their own solution. Can you get them to do this?"

We each agree to ask our clients, while the judge pledges to look for the San Francisco therapist's name.

When I walk back into the courtroom, Karen sits with her hands folded and head bowed, as if in prayer. Patty is nowhere to be seen. Petrakis goes out into the hall, presumably to find her, leaving me alone with Karen.

She looks up at me wearily. "I'm so tired of this. I just want to go home to Dawn and take up our lives again. I don't know if I can do another day of this."

I describe what the judge has proposed.

"Sure. Whatever she says. I doubt it will work with whatever mission Patty is on, but sure."

I put my hand on her shoulder as paltry comfort, then go to look for Petrakis. When I leave the courtroom, I can see him hunched next to Patty on a bench down the hall, talking intently. He has the harder job. I return to the courtroom and sit next to Karen.

"You nailed that answer," I say, then immediately regret it as Karen gives me a baleful look.

"It's just true. We'll never be sisters again."

27

KAREN

Taking Dawn to school this morning is a welcome re-entry into my life. I have the day off, since it is one of the designated trial days. No one else in the home besides Dawn and me, we crunch our cereal together and grin at each other. She's dressed herself in bright red pants and a pink sweater, a tame combination for her but still festive. She hands me a folded sheet of paper, a drawing she made the night before. In it I wear a drab gray dress and a frown, and she, all in red, holds onto my leg. I thank her with a kiss atop her head, catching a gritty scent and the realization that she has not showered this morning.

"Do you have to go back?"

"I don't know, but not this week, and maybe not at all."

"Try not to," she tells me. I promise her I will try.

When we get to school, it is snowing lightly, and she holds out a mittened hand to catch flakes. I suddenly recall doing the same thing with Patty years ago, comparing the size and shape of flakes of snow before they melted, at the same school, when we were really sisters. I used to hold Patty's hand to make sure she would not fall on the ice.

On the way back to the house, I wonder when and how I had lost my role as the protective older sister. Less than two years separated us, but as a child I was much taller and the role was obvious. Probably in high school, when Patty began to shine. She became the pretty one with the boyfriends – the good boyfriends, I should say – not like the older artist I met in town, who introduced me to marijuana while Patty went to the proms with the football player. I resented her popularity and didn't try to compete in her arena, striking out with companions Patty and our parents judged inappropriate. Stereotypes, both of us, and we carried those differences with us throughout college and, for her, law school. We were both good students, but she was always the more attentive to the rules.

I think our mother despaired of me, while our father saw something in me he wanted to encourage. I decide suddenly this morning that I will visit her, whatever is left of her, without preparation from Megan. I couldn't ask Patty during the trial, but I can see for myself. I look up the location of her memory care facility and am relieved it is just outside Nevada City, not another long drive to Roseville.

The entrance is so much more welcoming than where I had stayed when I was down. The reception area is furnished like a cheerful, feminine living room, with flowered sofas and pale yellow walls. The receptionist, of course, does not recognize me but has me sign an entry register and directs me to room 137, on the ground floor. I feel a dim recollection of walking down this hallway with Patty five years ago.

The door to 137 is opened partway, and light emanates from the room. I knock and hear a faint "good morning." My mother's face is a beached seashell, retaining its fine curves but drained of all color. She sits upright in bed. Her right hand fidgets atop the covers, while the left lies dead still. "Mother," I whisper, and sit down next to her on the bed. Her eyes reflect surprise and question, but they are alive and warm. I take her right hand in both of mine and stroke it gently. The fidgeting halts. "It's Karen," I say gently. "Karen," she repeats reflectively, "Karen" again, as if to remind herself by the sound, but her face registers no recognition. Yet she smiles a welcome, stranger that I am. "I'm your first daughter, Patty's sister."

"Patty," she repeats, with the same vacant testing of the sound.

Her eyes take on a sudden radiance, as if she recognizes me. She smiles at me warmly. "You look like a younger me," she says with some small degree of wonder. I realize she is right; I am now the age she was when I graduated from college and I recall her from my graduation photographs. "Mother," I say again, and squeeze her hand. Her eyes take on a doubting cast, grow cold, and she withdraws her hand. She averts her face, as if to cast me out. Her eyes glance around the room, anywhere but at my own, ending on the small table next to her.

"My tea," she says with some authority. A glass of water sits on her table, but no tea.

"I'll try to find some for you." I get up quickly, as if welcoming the excuse, and walk down the hall toward the receptionist. An attendant in uniform comes out of a different room, tray in hand, and I ask her where I can get tea.

She gives me a knowing smile. "Is that for Mrs. Haskins in 137?"

I give her a quizzical look and tell her yes.

"I'll bring it to her, dear. Do you want some too? She always asks but never drinks it."

"No, thanks. I'm a coffee person."

"I can get you that too."

"No; I'm fine." If I had asked for coffee, I'd have to sit here and drink it with her and I am not sure I can last that long. Tea, I think, as I walk back to the room; she did always drink tea while the rest of us drank coffee. A particular kind, but I can't recall just now what it was.

When the attendant returns with tea, the ceramic cup holds a Lipton tea bag. Whatever my mother's tea was, it wasn't Lipton. I watch her take one sip and then put the cup on the table next to her.

"No good tea here," she explains. She smiles at me, one stranger to another across a public space.

"What kind do you like?" I ask stupidly, as if she can remember.

"Lemon," she pronounces definitively. Whatever her tea had been when we were all together, I am pretty sure it was not lemon.

"What else would you like?"

"Lemon," she says again, as if I had forgotten.

I excuse myself, but promise to come back.

As soon as I open the door to the outside, I feel rejuvenated, even though it is bracingly cold. The sun shines, I am outside, not in the institution, and I am free and in possession of my health and faculties. I drive directly to the eclectic tea store in Nevada City, hoping it might bring to mind whatever tea my mother drank years ago when we all lived as one family.

The front of the shop holds more exotic teapots than varieties of tea, but the back room hoards a wall full of bins of loose tea. A slender Asian man with graceful hands stands at the counter and asks how he can help me. With an apologetic shrug, I explain I am trying to recall what kind of tea my mother liked years ago, and neither she nor I can remember now.

"Can you remember what it smelled like?

"No, but it came in an English-looking tin."

"That could be anything," he tells me. "Let's try to remember what you can about its scent." He stands before me expectantly, a curiosity in his dark eyes. He likes this game, and his readiness removes my embarrassment at what I do not know.

I relax into a memory of my mother at the stove, pouring hot water from the teakettle into her lavender mug. Aromatic steam rose from the mug, a morning ritual as familiar as my childhood seat at the table, across from Patty, and to the right of my mother's chair.

"A bit of citrus, but not lemon, and not exactly orange either."

"Aah," he almost hums knowingly. "Let me try to reproduce that for you."

I glance up at the many bins while he brews a cup of loose tea and sets a timer. A timer? My mother was never that precise. He keeps the cup and his machinations in front of him, his back covering his actions, while my eyes rove over the variety of mostly

Chinese teas. I doubt my mother drank Chinese tea; it wasn't even much known, let alone available, in those days. Yunnan, Pu-erh, Oolong -- all strange words to me.

When the timer pings, he motions for me to sit at one of the tiny tables near the rear window. He places a steaming cup in front of me, and removes the saucer from the top of the cup, placing it underneath, releasing a suddenly familiar scent and a tiny cloud of steam. I lean over the cup, inhale and close my eyes, smiling with recognition. I take a sip, but don't like its taste any better now than I did as a child. Yet, the scent recreates a comfortable scene.

"That's it! How did you get it on the first try?"

"You described bergamot, which is the signal ingredient of Earl Grey tea. It's a bitter citrus fruit." He waits expectantly for me to drink some.

"I'm sorry. I don't like the flavor myself, but it's my mother's favorite. You're amazing. Can you sell me a small packet?"

"Of course." He clasps his graceful hands again and retreats to the other side of the counter, where he measures a pile of the black leaves with white flecks onto a tiny scale and then slips them into a small bag.

"Do you have a tea bell?" My puzzled look gives him the answer, and he produces from below the counter several little metal containers to hang over the edge of a cup. I thank him, pay and clasp the tiny package to my chest as if it could conjure back my mother. I want to brew her a cup right now.

Once back in the car, I realize it may take me some time to regain the courage to visit her. The imagined visit in the tea shop was far more pleasant. My cell phone rings as I drive home, and I pull over to the side to answer it.

"It's Analee. No, you can't escape me."

I laugh at her insight, and she laughs too, adding, "just when you thought you could return to your daily life." She tells me the judge has given her the name of the San Francisco psychologist she recommended as mediator.

"When is our appointment?"

"Just calling to make sure you still agree."

"Agree, yes. Hope, probably not."

"That's good enough for me," and she hangs up.

I tell myself that, if I can face Patty in mediation yet again, I am strong enough to see if my mother recognizes her tea. I drive back to the facility and sign myself in again. When I reach room 137, an attendant is just leaving, and I ask her if she can provide a mug with hot water for tea. "Of course," she says.

Inside the room, I see this pale version of my mother seated upright, with a tray of food in front of her, slices of orange and a half sandwich that looks like tuna salad. She holds a slice of orange in her left hand, peering at it as if she does not recognize it. I notice her hair, though nearly white, is still lively, buoyant and curled slightly behind her ears. She looks up at me and puts down the orange slice.

"Go ahead and eat, Mom. I just brought you some tea."

Slowly, without looking at me, she picks up the orange slice again and puts part of it into her mouth. Her jaw goes back and forth sideways as she mashes the orange, and I wonder if she still has teeth. She swallows, slowly. I watch her go through the same process with a bite of the sandwich.

When the attendant returns with a steaming mug, I place it on the bedside table, take out the tea packet and pour some of it into the tea bell. I realize my mother has started to watch me.

Almost as soon as I drop the tea bell into the mug of steaming water, I catch the scent of the tea. So, too, does my mother.

"My tea," she pronounces firmly.

I make her wait until it cools somewhat, and take the dripping bell out of the mug. She slips three fingers through the handle and grasps the mug with both hands. Slowly, and with a smile at each sip, she drinks the full cup.

"My tea." She looks at me, now fully present. At least she recalls the tea.

I sit there for as long as I can, trying to appreciate the moment, and trying with more effort not to think of where I will be at her age.

28

ANALEE

The judge's clerk e-mailed the name of the San Francisco mediator before ten the next morning: Greta Reinhardt. I google her name and check her out on LinkedIn, learn a few bits of information but not much. She has appropriate credentials as a psychologist, no bragging list of accomplishments. Her photo reveals a pale woman in her early sixties, perhaps, with thin straight gray hair, long enough to be swept to one shoulder.

I have no other names of local mediators I want to substitute for this one, and I can see the inherent benefit of complying with what the judge herself has recommended. But I doubt seriously what this new mediator could accomplish when even Matt Shipley could not resolve this. Karen has already made it clear she would never agree to any court order that grants Patty any rights over her child.

I decide to phone Petrakis and ask him what he thinks. He comes readily to the phone and acknowledges he's seen the court's e-mail reference.

"Do you know anything about this Dr. Reinhardt?" I ask.

"Not personally, but I called a colleague in San Francisco who raved about her skill, so I'm going to recommend her to Patricia." He still calls her Patricia, the only one who does.

He hesitates before speaking again. "I spoke with Patricia after our session yesterday," he begins, "and I think she misses Dawn enough to give this a good effort. But I confess I'm skeptical. What about Karen?"

"She agrees to try this mediation. She's really tired of litigation, but I don't know if these two can get past their basic impasse of who is a parent. How shall we contact Dr. Reinhardt?"

"Why don't you e-mail her and ask whether she'd be available for a conference call with the two of us?"

Dr. Reinhardt responds positively to my email within a day, and Petrakis and I speak with her a day later. She wants to know as much of the background as we will tell her, and she wants to read both Karen's and Patty's depositions, which we send her. She agrees to come to my office for the initial mediation, and asks that we reserve a whole day.

29

KAREN

On the drive to Analee's office for the new mediation, I try to recall what happened at our last session with Dr. Shipley months ago. So far as I know, the visit we arranged at Patty's home went smoothly, and I try to remember what I had offered and Patty rejected. I remember telling her that I would allow regular contact with Dawn, so long as Patty backed off on being named a parent. What I can't remember – or never learned – is whether she wouldn't trust me to allow regular contact, or whether she insisted on being named as Dawn's parent. The bottom line is that I don't know how we will ever trust each other again.

Patty and I meet Dr. Reinhardt in a small room in Analee's office that I had never seen before, with a sofa and small round table with three chairs. Dr. Reinhardt is already seated in the center chair as we come in, and she gets up to shake our hands, sweeping her pale gray hair behind her left ear with her left hand as she extends her right hand. She is taller than either of us, nearly six feet, with a warm, slim hand and penetrating pale blue-gray eyes the color of a kingfisher feather I once found beside the river. When she smiles, I am struck by the different crows' feet angles on either side of her face, the right side deep and curving upward and the left side shallower and tilting downward, creating a different mood on either side of her face. Gesturing for each of us to take a seat, she sits down again herself, with Patty and I on either side of her. Patty is to her left, where the lines tilt downward. I create an internal joke that I sit on her bright side.

Dr. Reinhardt explains that our attorneys have described our situation to her and allowed her to read some of the legal papers. She asks how our 'difficulties' started, and invites me to begin.

I describe how I fell into a deep depression almost five years earlier that led to my hospitalization and Patty's having to take care of Dawn, and to her appointment as guardian until I got better and had the guardianship terminated.

Again sweeping a limp strand of hair behind her ear, she turns to Patty.

"What was it like to see your sister in such a deep depression?"

Patty locks eyes with her and gives an answer I had never heard before.

"Deeply frightening. Not long before, I had seen our mother become vacant – as if disappearing inside while her body was present --from Alzheimer's. It's a horrific disease, hollowing someone out from inside. Our father put her into an institution before she needed to go. Then he sold the family home, took everything and moved to Sacramento. He didn't seem to want to spend time with either Karen or me after moving away. He moved in with a new woman, joined a law practice there, and then died a few years later of a heart attack.

"Karen and I were excited to create this new life in our family. Dawn was like an antidote to our parents' collapse. Then Karen fell into her depression. I didn't know what was happening to my sister, but I didn't want to lose her too, and I needed to take care of this new child."

"So it was important to you not to abandon your sister and Dawn?"

"I couldn't let that happen, no matter what."

Raising Dawn

"So what did you do for them?"

In this exchange, I hear for the first time some details of Patty's rescue. I was hospitalized in the psychiatric facility for just six days, tested, heavily medicated, and then forcibly released. Patty and Doug were shocked that I was to be ousted in less than a week, when it hadn't even been established what antidepressants would work for me. So they took me home with them. Dawn slept in the same bedroom as Ian, and I slept on a sofa bed in Doug's study. I have no memory of this time at all, but they must have been rocked. I was assigned to an outpatient program at the hospital, and Patty had to drive me there every morning and pick me up every evening. After many frantic phone calls, Patty found a group home where I could stay with other recovering mental patients, some of them drug addicts, and there I stayed for several months. They had to pay for the group home because my insurance did not cover it.

"You had to pay for me? You never told me that," I interrupted.

"What good would that have done?" Patty looked at me for the first time.

I bowed my head, unable to speak. Dr. Reinhardt encouraged Patty to continue.

"It was a hard time. The children were all scared. Doug couldn't use his study and there was tension between us. The bills mounted. And I didn't know whether Karen would get better."

"Did she?"

"Yes. She had an excellent psychiatrist, who found the right medication, referred us to an endocrinologist for her thyroid, and assured us she was improving. About a year after her hospitalization, she found her own housing, and we began to allow Dawn to go visit her."

"How did that work?"

"Pretty well, until Karen started to want to take Dawn back and end the guardianship. Then all this started."

"If you knew Karen were fully recovered, would you let go of this lawsuit?"

"No, because she won't even let us see Dawn. And Dawn is my child as much as she is Karen's. I can never abandon her."

Dr. Reinhardt leans forward momentarily to make a note, then looks up again at Patty, using both hands now to tuck her hair behind both ears. I want to give her a hairband.

"I hear you say, when you were describing your father's abandonment and your mother's illness, that you did not want to lose Karen too." Patty nods, sadly.

"Is that still important to you?"

"What can I say? We've never been further apart."

"Can you think of any way you might become sisters again?"

"I have been giving this a lot of thought, believe me. And I have a proposal."

Dr. Reinhardt nods, giving her permission to continue.

"I can make my peace with Dawn living with Karen and visiting with Doug and the children and me. Karen can have full custody of Dawn. All I ask is that I be Dawn's parent also, so that she isn't left with just one parent."

I practically leap out of my chair.

"No way! A month won't go by before you tell me that I'm making bad decisions for Dawn or endangering her or she needs to go to a different school. I can't sit here and let that happen." I see I have paced back and forth all of the three or four feet of unoccupied space in the small room, and I sink back into my seat.

Dr. Reinhardt and Patty both stare at me, expecting more. I take several deep breaths to try to sort out what I can and cannot live with in what Patty has just said. I stay quiet as long as I can. I see Dr. Reinhardt shift in her chair as if she is about to say something, but I want to go first.

"I hear Patty say that Dawn can live with me. She has not said that since filing her lawsuit. What I want to hear in that is that she trusts me to take care of my own child. I have no problem allowing her to see Dawn again. I actually want that. I want to break down the barriers to the children seeing each other again, to my seeing

Doug, to our becoming a family again. But I can't live with Patty being another parent to Dawn. That's not what we set out to do. It's not how Dawn understands our family. And I am *never* going to let Patty tell me what I can and cannot do with my own daughter."

Now Dr. Reinhardt steps in, before either of us can say anything further.

"What I just heard from each of you is a willingness to trust each other again. That's a huge step for each of you. Patty, you said you trust Karen to have Dawn live with her and make decisions for her. Karen, you said you trust Patty enough to have her spend time with Dawn again. You both know from this painful experience what it's like to lose trust. Rebuilding trust is a step-wise process. Each positive step you take with the other helps in that rebuilding." She pauses.

"I'm not ignoring the big obstacle that you each identify. But let's focus for the moment in how you can start to rebuild your family relationship. Where would you like to begin?"

I want to let Patty begin and look at her with the question in my own eyes.

"I'm not sure if this is the right first step – and I'd welcome your advice, Dr. Reinhardt. But I propose to invite Karen and Dawn to visit some weekend afternoon and stay for dinner with us."

"We'd both be happy to do that. Dawn would jump up and down at the thought of seeing Ian again. But what about Sandra? I'm not trying to ruin this from the get-go, and I'm not up-to-date with what's going on with her, but I don't want this to fail because of her."

Dr. Reinhardt looks inquiringly at Patty.

"Sandra, my older child, is having some problems we are addressing in therapy. She is jealous of attention we pay to Ian, and she was resentful of Dawn when she was with us. She struggles with making friends in general. Therapy is helping, a bit, but Karen is right; Sandra might well try to ruin the day."

"I'm sorry." I hear myself with surprise. I *am* sorry she is

Diana Richmond

struggling with a difficult problem with her child, and I'm sorry if my own troubles and Dawn being foisted on them made this worse.

Patty looks at me with what I sense is a hint of gratitude.

"It's true. Sandra would try to ruin it. I could have her stay with a friend for the day, but when she finds out what happened while she was gone, she will go bonkers."

Dr. Reinhardt suggests that Patty consult Sandra's therapist before we try a reunion of the whole family, and that we start with a small step.

I propose that Patty bring Ian to my house for an afternoon. "I promise no one will have to use the outhouse. There is now a floor in my bathroom." Patty smiles, and there is no malice in it. I almost tell her that, if I stop having to pay legal fees, I can try to find a better place for Dawn and me to live. But that can wait.

"That's great. We'd love that." I hear genuine warmth in her voice, and I see it on her face.

Dr. Reinhardt extends an arm, signaling she wants to say something.

"This is so encouraging. I sense in both of you a willingness – no, more than that – a shared wish to rebuild your family. I want to talk to you about glitches – because they will happen – and how to deal with them. If we had no time constraints, we might end our session now and re-convene after the first visit. But you're in a brief break in your trial, and the judge wants to know whether you two are going to resolve your issues or whether she has decide them for you. Shall we take a lunch break now and resume this afternoon? Or shall we break now and resume tomorrow?"

Patty asks if we can have lunch brought in and keep working. I offer to ask Analee to arrange this. Dr. Reinhardt nods. Gerta brings in menus from a local shop and by coincidence all three of us order hot chili. As soon as Gerta leaves us, Dr. Reinhardt resumes.

"I'm going to start on a different tack now. Have you each discussed with your lawyers what this judge will do if you leave the decision to her?"

232

Patty nods confidently. I haven't but interject, "she decides whether the litigation leash comes off my neck."

"That's one way of putting it. I'm going to put it a little differently, so that each of you can keep in mind what happens if you don't solve this yourselves. In a way, you've already made more headway than the court, because the judge can't decide at this time what timesharing arrangements there may or may not be with Dawn.

"If you leave the decision to this judge, all she decides in this trial is whether Dawn has one parent or two. She does not decide with whom Dawn lives or what time, if any, she spends with the other of you. One of you may decide to appeal her decision, and that process alone may take two years or more. Even without an appeal, if Patty prevails on the parentage decision, there will be a child custody evaluation by a mental health professional. That will take some months, and then there could be another trial, to decide what time Dawn spends with each of you.

"Whoever loses at law will have another few years of resentment stacked up against the other. Dawn will be older and may have different feelings toward each of you. She may lose interest in Ian and Sandra, or want to see them more than ever. Only you two can start to rebuild your family."

Patty asks how we can accomplish that.

After Gerta delivers our chili – three huge Styrofoam mugs of it – and crackers and a small plate of cheese and sliced apples, which must have been Gerta's own idea, we tackle the big issue.

I start. I tell Patty once again that I am happy to make a will that allows her to take care of Dawn if I die while Dawn is a child. I want to restart our being a family again. But our family consists of me as Dawn's mother, her and Doug as Dawn's aunt and uncle, and Sandra and Ian as her cousins. I want us to be close again if we can. But I will absolutely not allow her to tell me what to do with my own child. If we heal our family, I can see myself asking her advice, but permission – no, never again. I have said all these things before, and I fear they make no mark.

Dr. Reinhardt asks Patty what she fears most if we end this lawsuit.

"What I fear most has already happened. I've lost both my sister and Dawn. Winning this lawsuit may give me a legal connection to Dawn, but I will lose my sister and any hope of a family that works. I want to fix this, not break it."

I get up from my chair again, instinct propelling me, and put my arms around Patty. Her hair smells like Dawn's. Her body relaxes against me, and her arms fold around me. "We'll fix it together," I assure her.

Dr. Reinhardt reminds us again that there will be glitches. "They happen in every family. Someone says the wrong word or has a look on her face that another interprets badly. I bring this up because it *will* happen, and there are ways of correcting what could lead to major problems." I glance at Patty, who is as rapt as I am.

"When this happens, I suggest that the person who hears the sour note ask the other a question, like 'did you mean?' or 'what just happened?' Explore what you heard and why it sounded like a sour note. It can be as innocent as mishearing the words the other said. Or it can reveal the larger issue behind the words or the look. But ask. Try not to react in anger or hurt, just ask whether this was what you thought it was. It can help take you forward and not backward.

"Also, if you want my help in the future, I can work with you." She has us both nodding.

"Can we put the lawsuit on hold?" Patty asks. Dr. Reinhardt admits she does not know the answer but invites Patty to consult her attorney privately.

"I don't want to put it on hold. Our lives have been on hold for over a year now. We need to decide if we are going to fix it ourselves – or cling to the law. It's only going to be a club you hold over my head." I look at Patty searchingly, and she glances down a moment before coming back at me.

"How do I know you won't cut me out of Dawn's life?"

"You don't. But I won't. I don't want to. I want to have you as my sister again. You may not believe it, but I want to be able to ask you for advice again. But I'm not going to live my life under a constant threat from you. We can start over, but only if you let go of this lawsuit."

Patty sits silently for a long time. I can feel her debating the point.

"What do you need to hear from me to let this lawsuit go?"

"I don't know." She looks down and clutches each arm around the other, her fingers impressing themselves into her flesh.

I catch Dr. Reinhardt glancing at her watch.

"Is there anything Karen can say now that will reassure you?"

Patty just looks up at her plaintively. "I don't know," she repeats.

"When is our deadline from the court?" she asks Dr. Reinhardt.

"I'm supposed to report to your counsel by tomorrow noon, and they are going to communicate with the court. Do you want to think it over tonight? It's four-thirty now, and I'm sure it's been an intense day for both of you."

Patty admits she needs to talk to her attorney and think it over.

Dr. Reinhardt asks if we should meet tomorrow morning, and I wait for Patty's response. She nods, and I do too. But then I remember our prior mediations.

"We've been down this path before. We made headway in mediation and then Patty canceled it. How do I know you won't do that again?"

"I'm wasted. I can't decide. I don't know what to do." She drags her face from side to side in apparent misery.

"Patty, I want to fix this between us, for us and for our children. But I can't do this anymore, waiting for you to decide." I'm getting hot despite myself. "Come tomorrow prepared to end this lawsuit or let's turn it over to the judge."

Patty looks pleadingly at Dr. Reinhardt. "Will you work with us going forward?"

"Of course."

I leave first, and wonder afterward if I have stalked out. I walk out to Gerta's desk and ask if I can see Analee, who is on the phone. I pace while I wait, wondering if this has been yet another futile effort.

Analee keeps me waiting only a few minutes, then listens intently to my summary, asking if we have set up a definite time for a visit. I tell her no, the details dissolved into the larger discussion of whether Patty can bring herself to let the lawsuit go. I ask her what the mechanics are, and she explains Patty can either sign a written dismissal or we can appear before the judge and tell her in person that Patty dismisses the lawsuit, and it has to be 'with prejudice'.

"What does that mean?"

"That she can't bring it again based on the same facts." I roll my eyes and sink into a chair. "I will definitely need that."

She asks if I can wait outside her office while she calls Patty's attorney, and I step out.

From the waiting room, I can hear that she has connected and the murmur of her voice, but I can't hear her words. It goes on for a while, and her voice rises in pitch.

When she emerges, there is color to her face I haven't seen before.

She reports that Petrakis predicts based on his earlier discussions with Patty that she will agree tomorrow to dismiss the lawsuit, but that he insists it cannot legally be dismissed with prejudice. I ask her what it means to dismiss 'without prejudice'. She explains that a dismissal 'without prejudice' means Patty can renew the lawsuit in the future.

"The problem is that we do not know whether a parentage action can legally be dismissed with prejudice. If it cannot, then a dismissal 'with prejudice' means nothing."

"I disagree." I stand up to make my point. "If she dismisses without prejudice, it's almost an invitation for her to file again if she feels like it. If she dismisses with prejudice, she at least tells the court she intends to stick with her decision – whether it's enforceable or not."

She looks up at me with some surprise. "That's the best argument."

"Tell him it's a dismissal with prejudice – tomorrow – or we continue."

"You're that serious? Are you sure?"

"I am." I stay with her as she communicates all of this to Patty's attorney. They agree we will all meet in the judge's courtroom tomorrow at 11:30. She instructs Gerta to prepare the document, and I read it before I leave her office. It is a court form on a single page entitled Dismissal, and there are two boxes to choose from: 'with prejudice' and 'without prejudice'. The first box is checked. She e-mails it to Patty's attorney before I leave her office.

I start to shake only after I get home. I have no prediction whether Patty will sign it or not, but I have become someone I could not have predicted. Much as I fear what Patty might decide tomorrow, I love my new strength.

I drive myself to court in Roseville this Friday morning, which began with ground frost and now has warmed rapidly with the sun. The sky is uncluttered by clouds, and I can see for miles. The Sutter Buttes cast a definitive jagged skeleton on the otherwise flat horizon. But I cannot see even two hours into my future. 'Judgment Day' is today. With or without religious upbringing, these words create a kind of awe.

I see Analee pacing outside the courtroom, Patty and her lawyer hunched together on a bench in the hall. Analee informs me that the judge is finishing another matter, and that Patty and her counsel insist on a judgment 'without prejudice'.

"Just what I predicted," I tell her sarcastically. She looks at me searchingly.

"I think the question boils down to whether you can live with an uncertainty under a solution you create yourself, or turn over to the judge this fateful decision. I can't answer that for you."

The bailiff opens the courtroom doors and signals for us all to come in.

Judge Garcia looks weary. Whether it is the sight of us or

whatever she has just finished, I don't know. We take our now familiar places at the separate counsel tables.

"Well?" the judge says simply. Patty's attorney stands somberly and asks if counsel can go into chambers, and the judge nods. Analee follows him.

Patty gets up from her chair and sits down next to me.

"My attorney says that legally it's not possible to dismiss with prejudice. That's probably what they're going in to discuss with the judge.

"But I want to tell you something else he told me." She seeks my eyes with hers, and I recognize my sister in them. "He told me I have two choices: I can keep fighting or I can accept that I don't know the future and we can try to create a better future for ourselves.

"I've slept on that thought, and I've discussed it with Doug. I want you to know I'll sign this dismissal in either form. I want to rebuild our family."

"So do I," I promise her, and put my hand on hers. She grasps it firmly. My eyes flood.

———•———

Printed in the United States
By Bookmasters